VAULTS
POWER

Enjoy!

Diane

VAULTS *of* POWER

a novel

DIANE ECHER

Please visit www.DianeEcher.com

Cover and Interior Design: AuthorSupport.com

Cover Imagery: Thinkstock/iStockphoto

Author Photo: © Jason Berger 2011
www.new-york-headshots.com

ISBN: 978-0-9848171-0-8 (softcover)
ISBN: 978-0-9848171-1-5 (ebook)

For K

At the end of last summer I got caught in a nasty storm on a Florida highway. I took the first exit and pulled into a diner. The place was crowded. I squeezed at the bar. Next to me a blonde with a blues-like voice said, "You look like someone who can listen."

When she was done talking the sun was out and the place empty.

I went to the library. All the facts I could verify turned out true. So I sat at my desk and started typing.

1

ROBYN GABRIEL PUSHED the guy's arm off her bare chest. He rolled on his back. His steady breathing filled the cabin. The boat rocked and whined. Then there it was again. A scraping, maybe a faint knock. She propped herself on her elbow. Didn't hear anything. She put her toes on the floor and felt the bundle of her clothes. The guy rolled back toward her and put his hand on her thigh. She pushed the hand away and slipped from the cot into her jeans. Didn't bother with underwear. Her damp T-shirt clung to her skin. Middle of July on the Gulf of Mexico, you had to expect that.

Another, more distinct knock. The word "Captain," muffled. She felt her way to the door. The boat rocked again and an empty bottle of tequila hit her foot. She smiled.

A whole thirty-three ounces of love shots.

She cracked the door open, took in the mass of tangled, sun-drenched hair and the worried eyes. She slipped out and sighed. "Hey Parker," she whispered. "Give me a couple more hours of sleep. Tomorrow's our big day."

Parker glanced toward her cabin door. "It's Sybil."

"Oh for Chrissakes. Tell her about time zones." She turned the doorknob. "I'll call her on my time, not hers." Then she froze. If her twin needed to get in touch, she'd have called her cell. "What do you mean, Sybil? On the radio?"

"There's been an accident." Parker glanced again at her cabin door. "I just spoke with what's-his-name."

Sybil's fiancé. "Tom?"

"Right. You need to get on the first plane. He's already on his way there. Marseilles, France."

Of all places. Her throat constricted. "But she was going to Switzerland."

"He said Marseilles."

It can't be happening again.

Parker ran his hand through his hair. "Marseilles, that's where… right?"

Where their parents were killed in a car accident, thirteen years ago. She blinked tight. "Why didn't she tell me?"

He looked at her and didn't need to speak. She and Parker went way back—to detention room, thirteen years ago, when she and Sybil moved to Florida to live with their uncle and aunt. Assiduous haunting of detention room sometimes had side effects, and Parker and Robyn's friendship was one of them. Forged in rebellion, sealed in mutual understanding. Sybil hadn't been part of it. She was the straight-A twin.

Little by little, a lot of things ended up not mentioned between the two.

"I should have known," Robyn said. She steadied her hand on the doorknob, backed into the cabin and hit the light switch.

The guy's large shoulders shivered and he squinted. "Man, you're hot," he mumbled. "What's with the clothes?" he said, then smiled. "Lemme take care of that."

She found some sneakers and grabbed her tote bag. Her wallet was in there, with her passport and credit cards. She stuffed a couple T-shirts on top. "Maybe some other time. Get some rest," she said. She snapped the light off and walked out of the cabin and began forgetting his name.

* * *

Robyn didn't have a car. She had a Harley, and you didn't want to leave a Harley sitting at the airport. Parker had a Mazda RX, stick shift, electric blue, not exactly classy, not really her style of vehicle, but it did its job of taking you from A to B while providing some kind of distraction. She made sure her voice didn't slip into question-mark tone when she said, "You won't mind if I drive."

He threw her the keys in a buddy kind of fashion and looked away. Got in the passenger seat and buckled up. "Why am I here again?" he asked.

Because I need my best friend right now. "Cause someone needs to drive the car back," she said.

He didn't snap back. Parker could be annoyingly nice. When she was in the mood for a healthy fight, just to let steam out, she knew it wasn't going to happen if there was only Parker around.

They peeled off the quay. Streets were empty, traffic lights were blinking. She gunned it. She felt every pebble, every irregularity of the road through the wheel, every jump and whine of the engine through her feet and hands. She wasn't fooling herself. When life went sour, some people boozed through it. She needed to feel in control.

On the bridge spanning Tampa Bay, she turned the short-wave radio on. It crackled, then an over-excited voice came out. "*Festivities at Bohemian Grove are drawing to an end. This year we spotted …*"

Parker turned the radio down. "When was the last time you guys saw each other?"

She wanted to listen to the radio. She wanted to hear the news about Bohemian Grove. She wanted to know what Fortune 500 leaders had been seen going there, what foreign head of state had been invited. She couldn't help keeping tabs on the powerful and their connections.

And she wanted to think about something else than her own life. "Christmas, I guess."

"You guess?"

She shifted from fifth gear to fourth to third. Swerved toward the sharp exit turn. Second gear. The engine screamed. The car held the ramp curve nicely. Eased out in a comfortable acceleration. Her right hand stayed on the stick.

"Talked to her recently?" Parker asked.

"Talk to her all the time. Matter of fact, just before she left for Switzerland. About Dad's letter." She could still hear Sybil reading their father's letter on the phone, released by his lawyer on their twenty-fifth birthday.

"*My dearest daughters,*

As I write this letter I am watching you play—Robyn with your Chi-

nese chess and Sybil with your marble maze. Your mother is softly playing the keyboard and if I am lucky, you will sing along in a little while. I shall cherish this moment for the rest of my life.

If you are reading this letter I am no longer alive, and you are fully grown and assuredly fine young women. I have no doubt on your ability to live up to the responsibility I am about to hand down to you. Caution dictates that I not reveal anything in this letter. You must contact the office of Maître Durand, Attorney-at-Law in Geneva, who will deliver further instructions to you..."

An address in Switzerland followed. The letter was dated two weeks before the car accident that had killed both their parents.

That should have been enough of a warning.

But when Sybil asked her to join she said she couldn't leave the boat now. Couldn't put the diving on hold. She'd already lost time. And it wouldn't be fair to let Parker handle the whole thing on his own.

"Fair, you mean you're going to miss out on the fun?" Sybil had said.

She'd hung up on Sybil. Managed to forget the whole story. Until now, when it boomeranged with guilt.

She turned the radio back up.

"... and a senior executive of the Federal Reserve Bank of New York was seen two weeks ago entering the premises..."

The Tampa airport lights glistened in the distance.

The next flight to Europe was at 2pm. They killed time in a corner booth of a chain steakhouse in the middle of the concourse.

"What do you want me to do?" Parker said. "Send the divers home for a few days, cut the expenses?"

She thought of how she had failed Sybil. Of how, if she hadn't been so adamant in pursuing the success of her own business, things might have turned differently. And she thought about her loan at the bank and about the friends who had chipped in and how she couldn't fail them now. About the fact that late July, hurricanes could start hitting one after the other. "Keep diving," she said. "I can't afford to lose a single day."

She thought back to her father's letter. She didn't remember owning a game of Chinese chess. Never played it, for sure.

MARSEILLES, FRANCE, HÔPITAL de La Timone, fourth floor. Robyn pushed open the wide bedroom door. The smell of formalin and heat and suffering hit her stomach. She froze in the middle of the room. A life monitor beat a sick rhythm. Light seeped through a dirty window. A duffel bag with an airline tag slouched under a tired chair. A huge lump filled the bed.

Under an arch keeping the sheet off her body lay Sybil, her skull wrapped in bandages, streaks of hair matted against her shiny forehead, lips thin, cheeks hollow, nose swollen.

Under the thin, purple eyelids, the eyeballs moved wildly.

Robyn took two steps to the foot of the bed. "Billy," she whispered.

The eyeballs steadied. "Don't. Call. Me. illy."

Excellent. Hearing: *check.* Understanding: *check.* Fighting spirit: *check.* Sybil was going to pull out of this. Robyn steadied her hands on the railing. Focused on the patch of light on the sheet. "You made my day," she said, her voice as cheerful as she could. "You look like shit."

A sharp exhale. Sybil chuckling. "Lastic urgery," she mumbled.

For the first time in many years she wanted to hug her twin, sit on her bed and feel her warm, firm, live body. For the first time she wanted to say *I love you.* So she said, "What the hell happened?"

No answer.

"Sybil."

"Dunno."

The door opened brutally, and a draft lightened the air. A nurse walked in briskly, half-yelled "Bonjour" and read the vitals dangling off the foot of the bed. "How are we doing today?" She spoke French, and Robyn was grateful for the summers spent in Quebec.

"She'll be fine," Robyn said. "Where is the AC control?"

"Mademoiselle. She was beaten, branded, thrown in a dry well in the Château d'If, covered with stones. And she can't remember any of it."

Some kind of medical admin with a dash of psychological training had walked her through her sister's ordeal earlier. The memory loss was not worrisome in itself. But it probably came from a head injury, a major trauma, or both. It could be short term, or not.

"As for AC," the nurse continued, "open the window." She started pulling the sheet off the arch. "You can stay if you want, but you probably shouldn't," she said.

Robyn stayed.

Sybil was naked. Both feet were wrapped in thick bandages and the legs were a brownish red from iodine and bruises and large scrapes and cuts with stitches. A large gauze seeped pus on her thigh. Her chest bore red horizontal streaks. There was another patch of gauze under her left breast.

Bastards.

With her hands on her hips she watched the nurse's routine. "We'll get you outta here asap," she said to Sybil.

The nurse moved to the other side of the bed. Assessed Robyn top to bottom. "You identical twins?"

Yes, they were. Hard to believe, the way Sybil looked now. "I work outdoors," Robyn said. It was starting to make a difference. The last six months she'd been hauling cases and pulling ropes like any other man on the boat. Diving every single day. She didn't bother smoothing her calloused hands, fixing her broken nails, or concealing the little scars that drew white webs here and there. She didn't have time for that. And besides, from her long, tan legs to her tiny navel to her full breasts, no matter how basic she dressed, she was getting more hard, long gazes than ever. Remaining raw woman was almost a protection. Sometimes a weapon, depending on the guy. Depending on her mood.

She wore her sun-bleached hair in a haphazard chignon and heavy mascara out of a habit started too young. Pretty much, she'd discarded any exterior signs of her upbringing. She'd discarded anything that went in the way of her current business.

"Gardener?"

"Treasure hunter." Even her voice, stranded from shouting orders, had become raspy. She looked like a Gipsy and felt just as free.

The nurse seemed to think about it. "How did you become a treasure hunter?"

"Studied history. Taught middle school. Started on a Ph.D. Then just had to get out there, be my own boss."

The nurse dabbed some ointment and the smell assailed Robyn with its cohort of memories. She was eight or nine years old and she was the one in the hospital bed, surrounded by this sweet and acrid odor, pretending to be asleep. Her father was hissing, "No more hiking. No more climbing. And no more tree houses. From now on Sybil, you're keeping a close eye on your sister. Anything else happens to her, you're the one in trouble. She goes where you go, you go where she goes. You're like the two sides of the same coin. You're not Sybil and Robyn. You're Janice." And he did call them Janice from then on, only it was really Janus, but Robyn didn't understand that until much, much later.

In between, after their parents died, she outgrew Sybil. She didn't know how or why it happened. That was just the way things turned out. She became Robyn, a woman in full, not the flip side of a coin or the back of a fucked-up god or the shadow of the supposedly successful twin. She drove her life however she pleased.

Until now.

Now she was feeling every wound in Sybil's body as her own. Now she was feeling the intimate connection she had worked on ignoring. Now she was feeling the sense of responsibility that Sybil had taken too seriously, too young.

The sight and feel and notion of Sybil being attacked while she should have been with her stirred up emotions she did not care to name but she knew damn well were going to take her very far.

The nurse started removing the gauze under Sybil's left breast. She wiped her face against her shoulder. Focused back. Using long tweezers, she peeled off the last layer of gauze, heavily laden with an oily ointment, and said, "C'est joli."

Pretty? She probably meant it was healing well. "Is that where she was burned?"

"Branded."

Robyn forced herself to look over the nurse's shoulder. Felt a stab of pain in her own chest. And anger rising.

It was the size of a hand. A big hand. Brownish red. Some spots, the skin was bubbling off. Some, it was bright pink. Here and there, a yellowish fluid oozed out.

It had a distinct shape. A branding all right. Like what they did on cattle. *Sweet, soft, gentle Sybil. Branded like cattle.* Robyn couldn't keep her eyes off the branding.

It was a sign, or a symbol. Like an elaborate letter pi, with loops where the lines intersected. On each side, there was a star with rounded tips, or maybe a flower with sharp petals.

While the nurse changed the dressing, she drew the symbol on the back of her boarding pass.

The nurse pulled the sheet back on the arch, then adjusted the IV. "The police are waiting outside."

Robyn flattened the creases of the sheet, then stroked it. "Good."

"God willing," she said, patting Robyn's arm, "they will find the criminals who did this."

"God always needs a little help."

* * *

Seconds later two men were standing in front of her. "Gendarmerie Nationale," they said. They were strapped in navy blue uniforms. Spoke in voices trained for authority. There was an older guy and a younger guy. The older guy did the talking. The younger guy absorbed the technique. First, small talk. The trip, the country. Sybil's condition. Polite questions.

Robyn was no fool. There was no display of sympathy there. They had a plan, and they were rolling it out. Fair enough.

She had one too. "So what's the sign?" she asked. "Signature? Gang?"

"We ask the questions." The younger guy, arrogant.

The older guy raised a pacifying hand. "What sign?"

"The branding."

He shrugged. "Does your sister belong to a cult?"

"Of course not."

"How can you be so sure?"

"She's my twin."

"You know everything she does?"

"Yes."

"What was she doing at the Banque des Deux Rives?"

"Where?"

"Banque des Deux Rives."

"Never heard the name."

"Are you refusing to answer the question?"

"I said I don't know the bank."

"You said you know everything your sister does."

What the hell is going on? "She needed cash?"

"What was the purpose of her travel?"

"Visiting… touring," she said. "Why?"

The younger gendarme reached behind him and handed her a small suitcase she hadn't noticed yet. "Your sister's personal belongings."

She didn't even know at which hotel Sybil was staying. How could a quick trip turn into this nightmare? "What happened to her?"

The older gendarme tilted his head and sighed.

The rookie tugged at his ear. "There's some talk of a cult."

"It's only talk," the older gendarme said. "We're investigating this."

"Talk?" Robyn said.

"A tip of the crazy guide who looks after the Château d'If. We're looking into it. We're looking into a lot of things." He clapped his hands together and rubbed them, time-to-get-back-to-the-wife fashion. "There are a couple of papers we kept for analysis. We'll notify you when you can come and get them. Your phone number?"

"What papers?"

"Your phone number, please."

She gave it to him. "What papers?"

He scribbled the number on his notepad and straightened himself in a sort of salute. "We ask the questions."

3

JAMES "MACK" MCINTYRE III was the Federal Reserve Bank of New York's First Vice-President and he made sure visitors fully understood the meaning. The corner office with an angle view of Lower Manhattan, mahogany furniture and Oriental rug were standard and he didn't pay them much attention. Placing the desk against the light of the window, blinding whoever sat across from him, was a deliberate choice. But above all, it was the power wall, carefully put together around the casual sitting area in the west corner, that sent the message. From eye level up the wall was covered with artsy pictures, all black and white, all casual snapshots of Mack with anyone who counted on Wall Street or in Washington. Whoever had been moved from the blinding seat in front of the desk and the window to the comfort of a low chair around the coffee table ended dazzled by Mack's influential network.

Mack glanced at his power wall, tightened his grip around the telephone receiver, opened his desk drawer and gulped two tablets of Maalox. He shut his eyes and pictured the nuthead he was talking to, Aleister Barton, in the third underground level of his London headquarters.

He'd heard Barton say once that you needed to be deeply rooted inside the Earth when tending to matters of this world, and that it was essential to be in visual darkness when pursuing true light. "For in truth," Barton had said, "all men are in darkness, with only the bearer of light to guide them." He'd gone on to explain the meaning of Lucifer, at which point Mack stopped to pretend listening.

But Mack was quite sure that even right now, as he was talking to him, Barton, possibly swiveling in his leather armchair, was watching through his windows to the world, eyes dancing from one to the other of his several computer screens arcing his desk. Some would be displaying spreadsheets of Garden of Evil, the company he launched twenty years ago producing just one group, Sons of the Serpent, now a multinational, multi-activity business. Other screens would put him in direct eye contact with his nightclubs. From what Mack heard, Barton's favorite pastime was to take over surveillance cameras of his clubs, zoom in on healthy underage girls and watch as the magic little pills sold on premise turned them into docile yet creative sex toys.

"You're telling me this guy Toslav is commissioned by someone? As in instructed? I want to make sure we have the facts clear here," Mack said.

"Instructed. Two years ago." There was some background noise of screeching and screaming. "The mission was to track the document," Barton said. "The clients knew about the Logonikon. And they offered a bloody five million dollar fee."

Mack loosened his Ferragamo tie and rubbed his temple with his free hand. "Why would he tell you about the fee?"

"Bragging," Barton said. The background noise faded.

Mack leaned back in his chair. His cuff links projected diamond-shaped sparks on the ceiling. "You think he was lying?"

"I think he was drunk. Couldn't put a sock in it."

He swung forward in his armchair. "Tell me again how this happened." He put his elbows on his desk and his chin on his fist and locked his eyes on the framed picture of himself in Bulldog Lacrosse gear.

Barton cleared his voice. "I had someone follow the Gabriel woman ..."

"Who?"

"The Gabriel..."

"Who was following her?"

"My people." Barton sounded standoffish. "I'm handling this end of the operation, okay?" Standoffish alright.

His gaze drifted to his favorite snapshot, taken at Camp David, a spur of the moment picture of him patting the President on the back.

Barton continued, "First she went to a Swiss law firm, then straight from there to a private bank in Marseilles, France. It's got to be where the Logonikon is. Ten minutes after she had gotten there, a private investigator showed up. Shot photographs of her as she came out—"

"Did she have the Logonikon?"

"No."

"How do you know?"

"She only had a tiny purse. No document holder. Nothing."

"Keep going."

"The private was doing work for Toslav."

"How do you know?"

"He told us."

"What kind of a private is that?"

"The absurdly cheap kind. That's the bizarre part. Easy to bribe. Works with the police too. Informer. Thought you might want to know that. Anyway. I had Toslav's complete bio by midday. He's a dealer of rare books and stuff…"

"What kind of stuff?"

"Occult—talking heads, ancient tarot decks, antique Ouija boards—"

"Okay, okay, okay."

"And he's a member of a couple of clubs I also belong to."

"What clubs?"

"You don't need to know that, Mack."

"The hell I don't." He reached for another Maalox.

There was silence on the line, then Barton said, "I don't care if you're the fucking President of the…"

"First Vice-President, Barton."

"I don't care if you're the fucking President of the Fed or…"

"Federal Reserve Bank of New York, Barton. There's a difference."

The line went silent except for a ruffling noise, then Barton's voice came out syrupy. "I don't need you, Mack. I'm this close to getting the Logonikon and I don't need you."

Mack's chest pounded. "Don't even think about it."

"That's much better," Barton said. "You realize how much you need me, don't you? And you realize I'm calling you as a favor, do you?"

Mack drummed his fingers on his desk, waiting for the creep to get over his fit of power. He knew Barton from way back. From Yale, when Barton had been cherry-picked for Skull and Bones by Mack and his peers. Barton was as different from Mack as it could get in the old boys' network, and they had had minimal contact throughout the years, each climbing their respective ladders, Mack in the banking system, Barton in mind control through music, drugs and religion.

When Mack learned through his monitoring network that the Gabriel family was taking action, he could think of only one person he could maneuver to get the job done. And that was Barton. For Barton would have a vested interest too. And he had the infrastructure to get things done, which Mack did not. At least not those types of things.

At that time, two weeks ago, Barton was acting as the high priest of Bohemian Grove. So Mack packed khakis and short-sleeved shirts, made a couple of phone calls, had his name added to the ultra-selective list of guests, and travelled to the redwood forest of Monte Rio, Northern California.

Bohemian Grove is a large summer camp for a special crowd: two thousand male members of the American corporate elite and their five hundred carefully screened guests—politicians and international tycoons. As such, it provided an ideal setting for arranging deals that democracy, with its principle of separation of powers, made impossible. Legislation is discussed, vice-presidents are picked, wars decided on or ended. Bohemian Grove oils the system.

There is a religious aspect to it that Mack wasn't too crazy about. It involves sacrificing a human body to a giant owl in the deep of the night. He didn't see the point of it all, but that's how it works. Barton, being High Priest, was in charge of all this religious rigmarole. And because what Mack needed from Barton was supposed to have a religious meaning, Mack figured that showing up just before the ceremony started would put Barton in the right mood.

Barton was standing behind the forty-five foot high statue of the Owl, watching as Bohemians gathered across the lake to worship. Called by the music spilling from loudspeakers scattered throughout the redwood forest, they came in clusters of four or five and took place on the rows of folding chairs, facing him, across a small lake. Two thousand of the most powerful men on the planet. It had to boost the man's ego, Mack thought.

Barton was born in England, the only child of a fanatically Catholic mother and a Communist father. But what really screwed him up was that his godfather, the local parish priest, turned out to be his biological father. Young Barton ran away when the resemblance became too striking and the bullying too much to handle. He would have been twelve, at most. He was eventually taken in by remote cousins in the States who managed to patch up the damage, at least temporarily, and at least enough to have him accepted at Yale with full scholarship. Or so the story went.

Mack never gave the gossip much thought. To him it was more telling that the guy had managed to bring a start-up to a Fortune 500 level while maintaining total ownership, avoiding SEC control and remaining unknown to the general public. The IRS was fed clean balance sheets with handsome profits. He knew Barton's logic to be that as long as hefty taxes were paid, they wouldn't care to know where the money came from. It was Barton's strength, Mack thought. It could also be his weakness.

He stepped out of the bushes.

Barton turned around. "How's it going, McIntosh?"

"It's McIntyre."

"Is it? Terribly sorry." The British accent was cultivated, sometimes gone, and sometimes awkward. An attitude, Mack thought. "What can I do for you?" Barton said.

"I have an offer."

"Why am I not excited?" He donned a long white robe, and it made him look taller, and wider. Mightier, too.

"The Logonikon," Mack said, and felt he had an edge.

"What about it?"

"It's about to be released. I need you to intercept it."

Barton was playing with the cuffs of his robe. "Why me?"

"You have the most at stake."

"Do I?"

"It's religious."

"If it's religious, why are you informed?"

The hell with this Brit. "That's not how we work, Barton."

Barton didn't answer. A bell sounded on stage, calling the worshipers to silence. He put on a pointed hat that doubled as a mask with slits for the eyes. He looked like a Klansman, carried himself with the pride of an archbishop. Mack straightened himself, imperceptibly rolling his shoulders. Time to pull out the envelope before the freak did his show. "Everything you need to know," he said, handing him the envelope. "They're getting ready to go to France."

"Who's they?"

Mack pointed to the envelope in Barton's hand. "Get us the Logonikon."

He left Barton and walked around the small lake symbolizing the river Styx. His footsteps were muffled by the glooming recording of cellos that filled the forest. His silhouette was swallowed by the night. He sat on a folding chair on the fifth row. He was one of many Bohemians. Torn between a yearning for belonging and a sense of ridicule.

Within an hour and a half the ceremony reached its peak.

Scottish music played. Four attendants in black and brown robes brought an old-fashioned carriage to the Great Owl. On the carriage was a body tied on a gurney. Barton and two priests in black stepped forward. Torches lit the scene. The body on the gurney was naked. Barton started a prayer. Some worshipers repeated the words. Then he was presented with a dagger he called sacred.

As he raised it above the body, cries of ecstasy soared from the crowd. He lowered it with the control and precision that came from long practice. Pronouncing the last words of the ritual, repeated by the now frenzied crowd, he grabbed the heart with both hands, held it up and turned around as light flowed on him.

He presented the offering to the Owl, his bloodied hands cupped around the heart, then returned it to the body.

His hands were crimson to his wrists.

The crowd around Mack was hysterical.

A priest in a red robe lit a torch from the Eternal Flame burning at the Owl's feet. He passed it to Barton, who pronounced the ritual words, "Hail fellowship! Eternal flame! Once again, Midsummer night sets us free!" and lit the body on fire.

Now, listening to Barton on the phone, Mack could smell the stench of the burning corpse again. He still wondered about the heavy bleeding, too.

"You realize you're the one asking for the favor, not the other way around, right?" Barton repeated. On his end of the line, the screeching picked up.

"Cut that noise, will you?"

"Noise? You mean this?"

Mack had to hold the receiver away.

The screeching turned to raucous, receded, then Barton said, "It's pure music. It hardly even qualifies as metal."

"Noise to me."

Barton laughed. "Ask your daughter, what's her name again? Natalie? Ask her if that's noise."

Mack clenched his teeth. How did this lowlife, this pervert even *know* he had a daughter? He had to get him back on track. "Tell me what happened." His voice was steady enough.

"As I was saying, there is this club Toslav and I belong to but he rarely attends. I arranged to run into him and pretended to recognize him."

"Why the hell are you chasing Toslav? The Gabriels have the Logonikon."

"Let me finish with Toslav. So I meet him and turn the conversation my way and pretty soon we're talking about the Logonikon. He tells me he's almost secured the purchase from the owners and has a client calling him every day. I tell him I'd outbid his client. That's when he says he can't do that because it was the client who tipped him off to track the Logonikon down there..."

"The client told him where the Logonikon was? That's what you're saying?"

"And Toslav is all about his reputation. Thinks if he outsmarts the client he might as well start selling potatoes. When I said I'd double the price he mentioned the five million dollar figure. I suppose he thought that'd be enough to cool my feet. When I insisted, he went berserk, like he had talked too much. Then he got really pissed off when I asked if I could at least take a look at the Logonikon before he transferred it to his client." There was a silence on the line. "That's about it," he finally said. "But hey, Mack," he chuckled, "don't sweat it, huh?"

Mack rubbed his forehead. "Now tell me why you didn't get in touch with the Gabriel woman yet."

"She is out of commission. Fell during a visit. She's in the hospital."

"What?"

"Her fiancé and her sister flew in from the US. I'm working on ways to approach them."

The sister was the treasure hunter. The fiancé was the Marine. "I don't like the sound of that," Mack said.

Barton sighed. "I'm flying to New York the day after tomorrow. Let's have dinner. In the meantime I'll take care of Toslav." He gave him an address and hung up.

Mack stared at his power wall. Connections. Life was about connections.

Connect with people in the right places. Connect the dots in the right order. Someone out there knew where the Logonikon was. More than he did. Someone out there was securing its ownership. Better than he did.

Very few people knew what the Voynich manuscript was; and until now he thought no one knew where its decoder, the Logonikon, was. That he was proven wrong meant a few individuals were about to crack his country's feet of clay. He looked at his power wall again.

Barton was going to be tough to control. And dangerous. He thought again about how he had casually mentioned his daughter. *Sickening.* Nothing was casual in Barton's world. Especially not young women.

He walked down to the Starbucks on Nassau, right across the street. Asked the girl behind the counter if he could borrow her cell phone for a minute.

She gave him a blank stare. "What happened to yours?"

He didn't have one. Never did, never would. He cherished his liberty too much. "I left it at the office. It's an emergency."

"Where's that?"

He pointed across the street. "New York Fed," he said and pulled a hundred dollar bill.

She ignored the bill. "Police?"

"Bank."

She raised an eyebrow. "Can you get me a credit card?"

"We don't handle private accounts."

"What kinda bank?"

He wriggled the bill impatiently. "We make sure the economy is sound and the banks don't steal your money," he said. "May I use your phone now? This is a national emergency and I am compensating you tax free."

She snapped his bill and handed him her phone. "You're just calling your mistress."

He went toward the restrooms and heard her say something about pictures. He locked himself up and dialed a number in Virginia. The old familiar voice picked up. Good. "How's it going," Mack said.

The guy was quick. Mack hadn't pronounced a name, so he didn't answer and waited.

"You still have your contacts in French Domestic Affairs?" Mack asked.

"Depends."

He told him his idea.

"Guess that could be done," the answer came.

"Just a scare, okay? I'll take care of the consul."

"You bet."

Mack hung up and brought the phone back to the girl.

She took it with two disgusted fingers and gave him a nasty look. "Anything else?"

* * *

"Tell me I didn't miss the police." The hospital floor squeaked under Tom's polished shoes. He closed the door neatly. The back of his shirt was soaked with sweat.

"You didn't miss anything. They're as useless as tits on a nun."

"How would you know?" He gave Robyn a quick hug. He was holding a can of Coke. Warm. No condensation on it, and it had to be in the upper eighties in the room. He sat on the only chair. Snapped the can open. Took a long sip. "What did they say?"

She told him.

He let it sink in. "So goddamn typical." Took another long sip.

"What was she doing here?" She still couldn't believe Sybil would go to Marseilles without telling her.

"Did she tell you about the appointment with Durand?" Tom asked.

"The Swiss lawyer? Last time we spoke was before Switzerland." She looked at Sybil. No eyeball movement. Imperceptible breathing.

He ran a hand over his cropped hair. "Long time ago."

"What did she tell you?"

His answer snapped. "I didn't have network." Meaning, he'd been away, not in touch with Sybil.

She thought about it for a beat. "So you don't know shit either."

He cleared his throat. "Did you ever discuss that letter?"

"No."

"Anything strike you as strange?"

"About the letter?"

He nodded.

"Everything strange." First their father's lawyer released a letter written two weeks before his death in Marseilles. Next, Sybil was almost killed in the same God-forsaken place. It was more than just the letter.

"What were your parents doing here when they had that car accident?"

"Visiting."

"Marseilles?"

"The French Riviera."

"Okay. Where exactly were they killed?"

"Some small road. Car fell off a cliff." She looked at Sybil, grey and thinning, and the bitter taste of loss filled her mouth. "We were just kids."

"You were sure it was an accident?"

"I didn't think like that back then. It never came up later."

He nodded and stayed silent, maybe on his own trail of thoughts.

She was trying to think things through. What was it that their father needed to "hand down" to them? Was he aware of any danger? "Any idea what this is?" she finally asked, and handed Tom her boarding pass.

Tom took his time, then said, "Where d'you see that?"

"Her branding."

He glanced toward the bed.

"Nurse changed the dressing while I was here," she said.

"Police mention anything?"

"Course not."

"Let's leave it that way," he said.

There was a long silence. He looked at the drawing. She looked at the drawing, upside down. Then he said, "Was your father interested in old manuscripts?"

Her father had been in genetic research. "Are you?"

"Usually not." He stood and patted his back pocket, where his wallet made a bump. "I'll be back in an hour or two."

* * *

After Tom left, Robyn paced, looking through the dirty window, then to Sybil, then back to the window. Thinking things through. Thinking about the letter and the odd symbol. Thinking to avoid feeling. Thinking while the room filled with stillness and she couldn't stand it anymore.

She noticed Sybil's lips were cracked. Dehydration. The IV was still trickling. Must be the heat. She wasn't much of a caretaker, but she figured an atomizer or lotion would feel good. She went down the hall in search of a nurse. Found a long office with a half-eaten snack on a desk full of paperwork, next to a plastic tray holding meds and syringes. No nurse. Went down a hiccupy elevator to the main entrance, a large glass affair that must have been sleek in the seventies but hadn't received maintenance since then. No one in the hallway. She located a vending machine behind a dusty plastic plant. Fumbled through her pockets for change. Didn't have the required euro coins.

Back in the room she pulled a T-shirt from her bag. Let the water run in the bathroom, long enough to get cooler water and wash down the most of whatever accumulated in the pipes. Then she soaked a corner of the T-shirt and moistened Sybil's lips in light dabs. Pressed the fabric to let just a few drops slide inside the mouth. "We'll make those bastards pay," she said. When she figured she'd done enough dabbing, she stretched the T-shirt on the back of the chair. Then she opened the suitcase.

The clothes were folded neatly, the contents shifted to one side. The style was typical Sybil. Silk tops, designer jeans, Italian shoes, chiffon dresses, lace things. Hard to tell what they were without un-folding them, and Robyn didn't want to unfold anything. She took each piece of clothing and stacked it on the other, shallower side, in unsteady piles. She kept sifting, hoping for some answer, stifling the bundle of tears forming in her throat.

When all the clothes were on the other side of the suitcase, there was only Sybil's handbag left, crushed along the edge, probably stuffed in there by the police. She opened it and pulled out a purple Filofax organizer. Thumbed through it. The appointment with Du-rand had been last Thursday at 10 AM. Nothing written down for the rest of last week and this one.

She fumbled some more and felt the sleekness of a cell phone. No password. The battery was running low. The last calls were US numbers, not foreign. One call to Tom on Wednesday, aborted. That would have been the day she landed. Nothing on Thursday. Nothing after, incoming or placed.

Emails. Junk emails and work emails. One sms, unknown number. She clicked on it. No message, just a blank space.

Tissues, a small wallet, a passport, a bunch of keys, lipstick, a pen and a small box of Advil.

And a thick, brown envelope.

The names "Sybil Gabriel & Robyn Gabriel" were printed in an old typewriter font. She flipped it over. The back flap, tightly glued, was embossed with an elaborate seal. The envelope was cut open. She slid her hand inside and retrieved two things. A small, flat key. No tag.

The other thing was the statue of an animal, no more than four inches long, its tail outstretched, flat and with cut-outs. It was off-white, lightly shiny and soft. She put it on the floor. It rolled to the side. Its odd shape prevented it from standing. She nestled it in her palm. It looked like a lioness, with large paws, a gaping mouth and piercing red eyes. Or an Asian dragon.

4

LI MEI LOOKED at the incoming number on his cell phone's screen. He let it ring out. The phone rang again, once. Then a third time, just once again. He felt a rush of adrenaline and controlled it with deep breaths. He stood from his black laminated desk and stretched and walked to the window. Paris had been stuffy and dirty and waiting for the storm since morning but suddenly the wind was picking up. He watched the clouds scatter over the slate roofs.

It was happening just the way it was supposed to, and that in itself was a good omen. It meant he had planned things right. Found the right man to do the job. Chen Guang would say he was thinking like a Westerner. Maybe he was. Maybe that was the trick, too. Become your enemy to defeat him.

The doorbell rang. It was an old-fashioned doorbell, with a long high shrill that resonated through the three rooms of the apartment. No video or fancy thing. Nothing that could be recorded. That was the main feature of the apartment. That and the layout of the building. With one entrance along a busy street and one in a quiet backstreet. His apartment spanned the width of the building. One window on each street. And it was on the floor before last, high enough for a good view. There was also a main staircase around an elevator. And a service staircase. So two exit routes from the apartment, and two from the building. And an extra floor on top just in case.

The bell rang again. He looked through the peephole. Toslav was not much taller than he, dark hair combed back, straight nose, olive skin. Slanted eyes the way he remembered them from the only time he had met him in person, years ago.

They shook hands, Western fashion, after the door was closed and locked. Toslav walked with a cane and it clicked on the hardwood floor. Li showed him to his study and they sat on low chairs on either part of a black, Ming style coffee table. Toslav propped his cane against the table.

Li asked to see Toslav's cell phone. Snatched the battery out of it and slid the pieces in his pocket.

He reached inside the drawer of the lacquered coffee table and pulled a dull grey metallic box, five inches long, with a small screen. Activated a switch. The box made a rattling sound. He checked the screen. No eavesdropping device in the room. He put the box back into the drawer and nodded.

Toslav got the message. He pulled out a thin file from his briefcase and started talking. "There was an attempt to access the vault Friday."

Li pinched his nose. Four days lost.

"Title to the safe-deposit was presented by a lady. American," Toslav continued. "Sybil Gabriel."

So it was still in the family.

Toslav pulled out an envelope from his briefcase and with two fingers retrieved a four by five glossy shot. Pushed it toward Li on the lacquered coffee table.

Li picked up the picture. It was a close-up, taken with a powerful camera, of a very American-looking young woman. Straight blonde hair, perfect teeth, full lips, blue eyes, pink cheeks. She looked innocent enough. And healthy, and wealthy. He thought of the Chinese women her age in the villages in the province of Henan. The absence of schools. The illnesses due to sheer poverty. The lack of hospitals. The deaths in childbirth.

He put the snapshot back on the table. He knew the face.

Toslav went on. "Access was denied on pretense of the need for an appointment. Appointment was taken for yesterday morning."

Li flexed his fists and forced a steady breathing.

Toslav looked at him. "No one showed up." He sat back in his chair. "Miss Gabriel was half-beaten to death. Her sister and fiancé both arrived from the United States. She is being treated in Marseilles, Hôpital de la Timone. The gendarmes have no idea what happened to her."

Half-beaten to death. Against the gaping dragons painted on the table, Sybil Gabriel was smiling back. *I have more than a clue what happened to you,* Li thought.

Toslav slid a spreadsheet across the table. He put it right next to the picture. "This is a summary of my expenses so far."

"Where did she go after the bank on Friday?"

"Straight to her hotel."

"Weekend?"

"The private detective applies surcharge for weekends."

Li rubbed his constricting temples. "Meaning?"

"He resumed his work Monday morning." He looked at Li straight in the eyes and pushed the spreadsheet closer to him. "My expenses," he said. "With an advance I could have arranged for round-the-clock surveillance."

Li did not look at the paper. He nodded, a short nod with a faint smile that meant he was annoyed, but that most people interpreted as approval. He knew about the frequent misunderstanding and counted on it. He stayed firmly in his chair and said, "All expenses will be covered when your work is done. And a hefty fee. We have been through that."

Toslav stroked the silver handle of his cane. "I am an antiquarian, Mr. Li. Not a private detective. I buy and sell rare objects. I don't follow people around. I had to hire someone for this job. I had expenses."

Li nodded. "Are you reconsidering the terms of our agreement?"

Toslav twitched in his chair. "No, of course not."

Li stood. He reached for a sleek cell phone on his desk with a sticker note on the back. Handed it to Toslav. "This is your new cell phone. Safer. Paid for. The calling number is on the back."

Toslav pulled himself out of the low chair. His hands trembled a little when he reached for the phone. He took it without a word. He put his briefcase on the lacquered table and buckled it.

"Don't forget your documents," Li said.

Toslav did not look up. "They're yours."

"Not yet." And I won't need them when they are, he thought. "I asked for the Logonikon, and that is what I expect from you."

* * *

Robyn was still sitting on the floor, turning the statuette in her hands when Tom walked in, a coffee-table book tucked under his arm. He took a long look at the open suitcase, didn't say anything, squeaked to the head of the bed and lightly kissed Sybil's forehead. He dropped the book on the chair.

"Found what you were looking for?" Robyn asked.

He took three slow steps and crouched in front of the suitcase. "How did this get here?" he said and started stacking the clothes neatly back in.

"Police brought it earlier. Thought you saw it." She held Sybil's handbag open. Put the tissues, keys, lipstick, pen, Advil and Filofax back in. Gave the passport and phone to Tom. "Nothing on the phone, nothing on the organizer."

He pointed his chin toward the statuette in her hand. "Was that in her suitcase?"

"With a small flat key. In there," she said, showing the brown envelope.

"Swiss lawyer."

"I guess."

She handed the statuette to him. His time to turn it around, set it on the floor, watch it roll.

"It's probably white jade. Rare. Old."

He tilted his head and clapped his tongue. "Something you had at home?"

She shook her head slowly. "Don't remember."

"Is it a lion?"

"Could be. Or a dragon."

His gaze wandered over Sybil's clothes and he handed the statuette back to her. "Do you remember Sybil playing marble maze?"

"At twelve years old? No." She looked from the statuette to Tom. "Do you think the date on the letter is wrong?"

"Do you remember her playing it at all? Or you?"

"No. Don't really know what it looks like, and pretty sure I never played a game of Chinese chess either."

"Chest."

"Chess."

"Chinese chest. The letter said Chinese chest," he said.

"Typo."

"In a handwritten letter?"

"Misspelling, is what I mean." God the guy was anal.

He stayed silent for a while. Just re-packed the suitcase.

She thought back to the letter. It just didn't compute. According to the date, when their father drafted it they were in seventh grade. Still kids in a sense, no boys in the picture yet, but feeling very serious about themselves. Outdoors most of the time, or at least out of the house. Cheerleading for Sybil, karate for Robyn. Softball for both.

Indoors felt almost like a punishment. And there was something else.

"My mom didn't play the keyboard," she said. "She played the violin."

He turned around, his shoes squeaking horribly on the linoleum. "No keyboard?"

"Definitely not."

"How can you be so sure?"

"What do you mean?"

"You don't really remember your toys, but you're positive about the keyboard."

"Always wanted one. Never got it. I'd remember if there had been one around." She put the statuette and the flat key in the envelope and the envelope in her tote bag. Glanced at him. Their eyes connected a fraction of a second.

He stood. "I should have known," he said. "There was more to the letter. Now it's too late."

She felt the burden of guilt settle somewhere right above her stomach and radiate in waves of shame through her whole body. She was the one who should have known. "He died thirteen years ago. You can't just sit up from the grave and order people around," she said.

"You want to travel military or civilian?" he said.

"Travel?"

"I'm taking Sybil home. You coming with us?"

"Today?"

He snapped the suitcase shut. "Helicopter transfer to Italy, then a US Air Force plane will fly her home." He put the suitcase next to his bag, against the wall, then pulled out his cell phone again. "Hey Chuck. We're all set. You got clearance?" The cell phone sputtered.

"Roger." He put his phone on the windowsill and turned to her.

"Last time I saw a hospital in such a bad shape, was in Iraq. And they were repairing it," he said. "You'll need to go downstairs and sign the discharge. As next-of-kin."

Sure, he could have asked for her opinion. But there wasn't much to debate.

When she reached the door, he said, "Don't get into details. Frogs'll freak out if you say the M word."

M for Marines.

It took close to an hour to get through the lines and the paper work. When she came back, Tom said the chopper was on its way and they just had to wait now.

He was back in the chair, thumbing through the book. His cell phone was still on the windowsill. It was one of those large items with a screen that flipped open length-wise and a comfortable, full keyboard. Serious stuff.

"Can I use it?" she asked.

He hesitated for a beat, but didn't ask any questions. Just, "Let me unlock it."

"Want to run Chinese chests images, see if I remember anything," she said. "It's been bugging me."

She sat on the edge of the armchair. The page was already on Google. She typed *Chinese chest*, then clicked on the image tab.

The screen was big enough to make out the vignettes. She zoomed, just to be sure. Nothing familiar. No souvenir popping to the surface.

She did the same with *marble maze*. Same non-result.

She surfed a little, tried combinations.

Chinese marbles.

Chinese keyboard.

Chinese chest keyboard. Results for unlocking games came up.

Chinese marble. Kitchen countertops lined up.

Chinese keys. Several recipes. A website selling stuff Parker would have loved, and displaying pictures of keys that looked more like locks to Robyn. An article on ancient Chinese keys. She clicked on it.

During the nineteenth century, elaborate keys had the shape of animals. They were usually made of bronze, and their flattened tails were the opening device. She enlarged the illustrations. Zoomed in. Pulled the statuette out of her bag and compared it to the picture on the small screen. Everything fit. Everything, except the material. Her key, if that was what it was, was made of jade. White jade, the most precious kind.

She looked again at the red eyes, the clutched paws. Went back to the animals on the screen. They were similar. The legend said dragons.

She looked at her key. *And now what?* she thought.

She continued flicking through websites.

There was an article on Chinese locks. Chinese locks operated like puzzles, not like regular locks. She scanned through the page absent-mindedly until she was ripe with frustration. "So I guess you didn't find what you were looking for? That errand you ran?" she said.

"Of course I did." He looked at her as if she'd said some profanity and handed her the coffee-table book he'd been looking through.

Her fingers made moist marks on the cover. It was black and gold and glitzy, with a title in French, "Le Code Voynich". *The Voynich Code*. Sub-title, *The Most Mysterious Manuscript in the World*.

The cover art was a picture of an ancient manuscript, three folios wide with the right-side looking like it was meant to be folded. Something she might have heard about on the Discovery Channel but never made it into the curriculum of her all too serious History studies.

She flipped the book open. A long introduction in French, then it was page after page of reproduction of the ancient manuscript. She was holding the only published fac-simile edition of the so-called Voynich manuscript. "Where did you get this?"

"Doesn't matter," he said.

The inside was glossy paper with picture after picture of eerie drawings and writing that bore a vague resemblance to Latin script, but was nothing close to any existing alphabet. Here and there, o's and a's, and maybe m's. And sometimes digits—9,4,8. The rest of the characters looked like letters and were grouped in neat clusters looking like words—but they weren't. Beyond studying ancient Greek and Latin, she'd come across enough foreign or ancient languages to know this wasn't written in any known tongue. Many lines started with the same letter or a variation of it.

Something like the letter pi, with loops where the lines intersected.

A letter she had taken for a symbol just hours ago, when she saw it burnt into Sybil's flesh. She looked up at Tom.

"How d'you know?" she said.

"Cipher courses," he said. "It's a classic. The ultimate unbroken code."

What struck her first as a historian was how unique the manuscript looked. It wasn't the orderly affair of a copyist monk, where line after line of perfectly formed letters aligned in neat rectangles on the page. Here, the penmanship flowed regularly enough—the produce of a stable hand—but without any aesthetic effort.

The looped symbol pi, as she had thought about it, repeated itself often and sometimes appeared with more elaborate forms of looping. The letter stood taller than the others and usually at the beginning of the words, although in its inflected forms it could appear in the middle.

She pointed to it. "That's the letter on Sybil. It's like the trademark of the manuscript. That's what put you on track?"

He didn't say anything.

She turned to another page. "The drawings seem the most important part. See how the writing is ordered around them? It's not text and illustration: it's representation and text around it." She ran a finger on the page. "Strange plants… they look more like sea weeds, don't they? See anything familiar?"

"No," Tom said, "but I'm not much of a plant person." He grabbed Robyn's T-shirt from the back of the chair and stepped into the bathroom. Water gurgled.

She kept turning the pages slowly. The drawings were more fascinating than the strange writing. On almost each page, a plant was sketched out in fading ink, its leaves in washes of green, the roots brown. Sometimes, flowers in shades of blue or red. Rarely, yellow and purple.

The overall effect was lively and artful. How could this be related to Sybil's agony?

Tom came back and started patting Sybil's forehead with the T-shirt. "Anybody who studies cipher tackles the Voynich manuscript at one point or another. I know I did. Wasted my time." He folded the T-shirt in a neat rectangle. "Now I'm having second thoughts about it being a scam."

"Scam?"

He shrugged. "That's what people are saying now. Makes them feel comfortable for not being able to break it."

She pored back over the book. Past the middle of the manuscript, the contents changed. Over twenty astral diagrams followed, one on each page, and all different. Some had concentric circles filled with the cryptic writing, others had radiating segments with stars or more writing, and some had strings of naked women merry-go-rounding or standing in buckets around a central zodiacal symbol. All conveyed this sense of efficacy, of precise information and all were utterly elegant and decorative. Whoever had drawn this had a beautifully balanced mind, both scientific and artistic.

She flipped to another page.

Weird.

Stark-naked women, either plump or pregnant, were thigh-high in basins filled with green water, often holding hands. Some were alone in buckets, holding tubes from which water spurted. All the buckets and basins seemed to be linked together by a flow of water running continuously through the pages, thin currents either streaming freely around the text or channeled by hoses in varying degrees of design and complexity.

On one of the pages there was only text, about forty lines arranged in three paragraphs each marked by a star.

Stars with slightly rounded tips, or flowers with pointed petals. Just like the branding on Sybil, on either side of the letter pi.

"You coming with us or you traveling civilian?" he said.

"I'm not going anywhere," she said, and kept turning the pages.

Then she got to the last page and said, "Oh-oh."

5

"OH-OH WHAT?" TOM asked.

Robyn couldn't keep her eyes off the last page of the coffee-table book. "The colophon," she said. "It could be my imagination, but this looks like the name Marseilles here."

"Hold it," Tom said. "What's a colophon?"

"An addition to a manuscript, with the name of the author and the circumstances of the writing, pretty much anything that can enlighten the text." She handed him the book. "You would remember that. That would have been the place to start the deciphering."

On the last page, four lines were scribbled. Different. Same handwriting, but different. The first line was only four words long: *quo lebee simon nutzer*. All in Latin script. The next three lines mixed Latin script and the unknown alphabet. On the second and third lines, words were separated by plus signs.

"Where d'you see Marseilles?"

She showed her the word. "It's a stretch," she admitted.

"That there doesn't say Marseilles."

"Could be Phocea, no?"

He made a face. "Maybe. That mean Marseilles?"

"Ancient name. Greek."

"How'd you know that?"

"How'd you know where to book a helicopter and an Air Force flight?"

"Okay." He was still looking at the last page.

"You recognize anything?"

He looked closely. "Yeah, that long line maybe," he said, pointing to the second line. "But not the other ones." He looked some more and shook his head. "Nope."

"Not even the name Simon?"

"No." His phone chimed. He glanced at it and handed the book back to her. "Time to go."

"It's an indication, some kind of key," she said. "Has to be."

He rubbed his forehead with two fingers. "You can read French, right? Concentrate on the introduction. You may find something that could relate to your father. But forget about the manuscript. It's undecipherable."

Something was not right. He remembered the manuscript enough to make the connection when he saw the symbol on Sybil, but he hadn't committed the colophon to memory? Any deciphering work would have started right here, yet all he had was a vague memory of the second line.

"What did you work on? The whole manuscript? Excerpts?"

"Copies of random pages was all that was available. Never had the whole thing."

"That last page?"

"Don't think so."

"Then how do you remember that line?"

"There was a theory about it being the key."

She tried to read the line. It started with something like *anchicon oladaba8*. The rest was not readable as such.

"Mind showing it to one of your buddies?" she said. "That last page?"

He shrugged. "Sure." He pulled his cell phone again, played with the touch-screen, shot a picture and then another one from a different angle. Played with the screen again and took two more pictures with the flash. Thumbed on the keypad. His large fingers barely moved over the small keys. "Done," he said, snapping the cell phone.

* * *

It was nearing dawn when the chopper landed on the parking lot. Tom wheeled Sybil out on a stretcher. Robyn carried the luggage. The elevator hiccupped its way down, the doors opened painfully, and they walked out without any questions. Apparently once you were signed out from a French hospital, you no longer existed. Worked fine for them.

"I can't imagine there's a way to talk you out of this," he said.

"Out of?"

"Staying here."

"Damn right."

"Why don't you keep her suitcase," Tom said. "You'll need a change of clothes. And I could do without the burden."

She stayed silent. Tightened her grip around the piece of luggage.

He seemed to want to say something.

"What?" she said.

"It's not your fault."

"Damn right. Not yours either."

He didn't pick up on her sarcastic tone. "Then let the police take care of it," he said. "It won't change anything for Sybil. She'll need you at her bedside."

"I'm not the bedside type of person."

6

HOTEL LA BASTIDE was above Marseilles' old harbor, across the industrial port. It had a view of the sea and a view of the city. Waxed furniture, heavy armchairs. A park with lavender and a swimming pool. Terraces and air conditioning.

"This is the middle of August," the receptionist apologized to Robyn. "All our rooms are sold out. The suite with Jacuzzi and dining room is gone. I can offer you our villa." He clicked through his computer. "Unless you want the suite with a fully equipped office?" he grimaced.

The office turned out to be the only room in which she didn't feel like a fraud.

The bed was four poster and flowery canopy and lace and Louis XVI chairs and pale rose carpeting. Robyn slept until dawn with the window open, against claustrophobia.

The bathroom was twice the size of her boat cabin. The faucets seemed gold-plated. The toilet was separate and the end of the tissue folded in the shape of an exotic bird. She showered quickly and escaped to the harbor for breakfast. Sat in the sun at an outdoor café and ordered espresso and buttered baguette.

Looked at the big blue sky and started feeling better.

She fired up her Blackberry, called Tom and got his voice mail. Left a brief message.

The waiter brought the baguette and espresso—half a tiny cup of thick brown coffee. She downed it in one shot. It burned her stomach and cleared her mind. She ordered another one. Double, in a large cup. Dunked the buttered baguette in it. Eating slowly, she thought things through.

She thumbed through her phone and looked up the address of the bank. Mapped it. It was within walking distance of the café. She'd go there right after breakfast. She also wanted to see where Sybil had been found. Château d'If, the nurse and the Gendarmes said.

Before she left for the bank she called Parker and gave him a toned-down description of Sybil's wounds. Didn't mention the branding. "Tom brought her back home," she said as if that settled it. "I just need to take care of a couple things before heading back." She didn't want him to ask questions. "How's the diving going?"

Right where she predicted, he said, they had come up with a bucket of gold coins. Sybil's words echoed in Robyn's memory like a blame. *You mean you're going to miss on the fun.* She wondered how things would have turned out had she gone to Switzerland with Sybil. Maybe not that different. She wanted to believe there was a reason she stayed behind. "I got something else for you," she said to Parker. "I need a file on the Voynich manuscript." She spelled it out.

"Got it," he said.

"Anything you can get your hands on, ASAP."

The line filled with static, then his voice came out somewhat staccato. "What else?"

Despite the distance and the static the bitterness came across. She hadn't told him why she needed the research on the Voynich.

"Get me that stuff—"

"—I know. ASAP," he said.

* * *

Every now and then, after work, Mack would stop for a beer in the city to get the pressure off before heading home. When he needed to take some kind of pulse of the markets he'd stick to the downtown bars. But elbowing Wall Street guys wasn't his idea of relaxing. So when he just needed to unwind, he'd head mid-town. Mingle with strangers around Grand Central. Or walk a few blocks north and hook up with some old boys. Swap war stories. Help out a friend. Hear them say, "I owe you."

Mack never asked for help. He was born into money, was smart and hard working. He'd never needed a favor. That was about to change.

Barton had screwed up in France, and the job was the easiest it would get. All he had to do was steal the Logonikon from the girl. She was alone, the perfect prey. Mack didn't know if he bought the accident story, but he sure didn't like the other two coming to the rescue. The sister would be taken care of by the French police and the US consul. That left the fiancé.

The man he was looking for was predictably sitting at the far end of the bar, sideways so he could see who was coming in and out and still talk to the barman and check out the women's bare legs when weather allowed. He wore a brownish blazer over dark grey pants, a light blue shirt and a dark blue tie. Crew cut hair, thick strong arms and a recent beer belly. His name was Butch. His grandmother and Mack's grandmother had been life-long best friends, their offspring like family. In Mack's opinion, better than family.

After graduation Butch got irritated with comfort. He disappeared. When he showed up a quarter of a century later he had a young body and a hard face and an office waiting for him at the Pentagon.

For some reason he didn't care to explain and Mack would have loved to know, he was now based in New York.

Mack picked up the tab.

"What can I do for you?" Butch said. No bullshit.

"Care to do something for your country?"

"I serve my country every damn day. Shit or get off the pot."

Mack slid him a paper with the fiancé's name on it. "Can you keep this Marine out of my way for a couple weeks?"

Butch glanced at the paper. Didn't touch it. Nodded.

* * *

Robyn climbed under the scorching sun. The bank was on top a steep hill. Cars wormed along a one-way street with no sidewalk. Pedestrians could cut straight up on stairs carved in the rock. The harbor gradually turned into a slit in the ochre city, deep blue with the white speckles of boats.

She verified the address on her cell phone and looked up. Private house. A glass, bullet-proof round door system was the only clue that the building might be a bank. No flashy neon sign, no classy brass slab. She pressed a button and the first door revolved. She stepped on a round rubber mat. The revolving door clicked shut behind her, a recorded voice said something, the cubicle chimed and the door scooped around to let her in.

Plush carpeting. Dim lighting, restful. Roses stacked tight in a crystal vase.

"Miss Gabriel." A male receptionist stood from his antique desk and picked up a phone. "Monsieur César, Miss Gabriel is here," he said in French.

She hadn't said a word yet. *Welcome back to twinhood.*

Monsieur César tornadoed in, tall and thin, waves of silver hair around his patrician face. A studied three-day stubble roughened the superior air of the hawk nose. Except for the grey slacks and navy blazer, he looked more like a trendy art gallery owner than a banker. "Miss Gabriel, this way please," he said in English, opening a door. A staircase winded down. "We expected you yesterday." The tone going up as in a question, but out of politeness.

"You said today." The staircase kept going down. "I thought." She let her hand glide on a thick burgundy rope along the wall. Sleek aluminum spotlights distilled a soft glow. "I'm sorry," she added.

She was mistaken for Sybil and had not done anything to clarify the situation. This meant two things, one good and one bad: she was going to know what business Sybil had here. No power-of-attorney needed, or however the heck they did things in this country. That was the good thing.

The bad thing was she had started lying and she better watch carefully what she was going to do or say.

"Not to worry," César said. "But we do have a larger problem." His voice was clipped, as if he was in a hurry or upset. His accent was French applied to British. "Something came up since we met."

She kept quiet.

"A judge is about to authorize a search warrant into our vault. Because of your safe-deposit. The contents thereof."

The winding staircase butted against a round metallic door operated by a wheel.

He turned around to face her. "We cannot allow that to happen. I did not get into details when you visited us unexpectedly last

week, but you need to know that this bank was built for a *purpose.*"
He said it as if there were some kind of spiritual mission involved.
"The whole hill is ours. We own all the buildings and rent them out
to tenants we control. The city farmed out the utility maintenance
to our subsidiaries." He knocked on the wall. It made a dull sound.
"This vault was carved in the limestone of the hill." His eyes did not
leave hers. "In other words, this is a fortress. No one enters without
our permission." He pushed his hair back. "Using the force of law to
break us is unacceptable."

He turned toward the submarine-like door. Slid a hand in an
opening inside the wall. A reddish glow blinked. The door clicked.
"We need you to empty your vault and close your account. For your
protection, ours and our clients'."

So far, so good, Robyn thought. *Nothing I can't handle. A fake signature here, a handshake there and I'm off.*

The thirty-inch thick iron door glided seamlessly into the depth
of the rock, revealing the vault room.

Semi-circular arches were carved off the roof of the cave in a
Romanesque church style. The back and side walls were lined with
rows of black deposit boxes with brass numbers, interrupted only by
a small door off the right wall. In the center of the room, a glass cubicle held larger deposit boxes. One of its panels had a double set of
walls, with a double-door system. "Your safe is in the air-controlled
area," César said, pointing to the glass encasement. "Twenty degrees
Celsius, twenty five percent humidity, year round, rain or shine,
backed by a power generator with six months of self-sufficiency." He
made a proud pause. Punched buttons on a control panel on the first
door. "I will need your key," he said.

First roadblock.

"Miss," César said. "The key please."

She processed the little she knew one last time. Their father's
letter. Sybil's meeting with the Swiss lawyer, still a mystery. But in
Sybil's handbag, an envelope with both their names on it and two
keys inside.

She slowly reached in the back pocket of her jeans. Looked César
straight in the eye when she handed him the flat key. *That better be it.*

"That's it?" he said.

She shrugged. Could mean, *Sure, that's it.* Or, *I don't know.* Or,

Let's see. Could mean pretty much anything and at this point she needed options.

He looked at the key in the palm of his hand. Looked back at her. Shook his head.

A bead a sweat started forming on her forehead.

"Your problem." His time to shrug.

Then he turned around, taking his time. Slid the key in the lock. The lock opened.

He pulled out a thirty- by forty-inch box, mumbling, "Who carries that key in their pocket?"

He came out of the glass encasement and told her to follow him to a small room carved inside the rock. He put the box on the table, pointed to a button next to the door and said, "Ring when you're done." His footsteps resonated through the vault. The round door glided and shut with a thick click. Then silence. Just Robyn and the box.

There was a strong earthy smell in the small room. Neon tubes cast a cold light. The furniture was efficient. Two steel chairs, a steel and glass table on which the box lay. It was the standard bank box, with no lock, just a sliding top. Robyn slid the cover off. Two large, red ribbons were folded on top a wooden chest that fit snugly in its encasing. She pulled the ribbons and the chest lifted out. It was solid cedar, soft and warm, with brass corners and a peppery smell.

And a lock. A small rectangular slot managed in an intricate design of brass on the small side of the box. She took a closer look at the designs. Flames coming out a dragon's mouth. This time there was no question. She pulled out the jade key from the padded envelope.

It entered the lock smoothly, its whole length disappearing inside, and stopped with a soft click once the tail was entirely in. She tried to turn it to the right, but it wouldn't move. To the left. Blocked. She pulled on it slightly, in case she had pushed too far. It didn't nudge. She tried to wriggle it. Nothing. Wriggled a little harder. The box moved with it. *Shit.*

Jade was sturdy, but the key was thin. Eventually, it could break. *I'm missing something.*

Her finger played on the engravings around the lock. Her nail clicked when the level of brass changed. She looked closer. At that particular place right above the lock, the top flame was on a much higher level than the rest of the engraving.

Chinese locks operated like puzzles. That's what she had read on some website she accessed from Tom's cell phone just yesterday, when she had found out that the statuette was not just a statuette, but a key. What else did she read in there? She tried to remember. Turning a key just didn't do it. The person opening the lock had to know how to operate it. It worked like a combination lock. If you didn't know the digits that formed the combination, there was no point trying.

She looked inside the envelope again. There was nothing else in there. How could their father give them the key without instructions as to how to open the lock? She dropped the envelope on the table. It glided on the glass surface and flew to the floor, hovered mid-way like a faulty paper plane, then landed with a soft swoosh, the only outside sound she'd heard in a while. Glided and hit the wall and lay there upside down, the writing hid, the embossed seal showing.

Robyn picked it up and sat on a chair. Her finger went over the seal in a mechanical gesture, her eyes looked without seeing, her mind wandered in search of an answer, the only link to the outside world the feeling of the bumps under her forefinger. *Just like…* Her gaze focused. *Just like the brass plaque, with its flame sticking out with no particular reason.* She took a closer look at the embossing and its intricate designs. *Waves?* She pulled her cell phone. The network logo flashed on and off. But the battery was full. She took a picture. Zoomed on its display on the screen. The flash had flattened everything. She tilted the envelope, turned the lights off and took another picture. The flashlight snapped in the darkened room, and this time, when she checked her screen, she could see the trick had worked. Shade enhanced the design. She zoomed again until the picture was much larger than reality.

Not waves. Flames. Just like the ones on the cedar chest. She took a closer look at the lock, then at the picture.

Same designs, but something was different.

In the middle of the seal there were only straight angles. Like a labyrinth, simplified. She looked back at the chest, leaning over. It had only the flames.

Could the labyrinth be a representation of the inside lock? She'd give it a try.

She scrolled through the picture on the screen, then lay the camera on the table and put two fingers on the key. *Forget about the key for now. It clicked when you entered it, so something's happened in there already.*

Usually these locks had exterior devices that had to be moved in a certain order. She looked around the chest. Nothing. The front part had different levels of brass flames. That had to be it. The top flame, right above the lock, was made of a different sheet of brass, cut out and affixed on top of the rest. It stuck out. It wasn't there for effect. It was only useful.

It was meant to be moved, activating an inside process.

She pushed it to the right with her nail and it tilted easily. Something clicked inside the box, and the flame came automatically back to its initial, upright position. *So far, so good.*

She looked back at the picture of the labyrinth on the camera. The next move would be a right.

It wouldn't make sense to move the flame again. Robyn tried the key. It moved right into place, one quarter of a circle to the right.

The angle on the embossed seal was to the left.

She tried the key again. It yielded, half a circle left.

Then left, and that was it.

She wiped her hands on her jeans, and turned the flame left. There was some clicking inside the chest, the flame jumped back in position, and the lock popped open.

Inside the lid, dozens of sharp blades were folded. Had she entered the wrong combination, or attempted to force the box open, the blades, activated by complex clockwork, would have shredded the contents.

She reached inside and picked up a strange book. The smell of cedar yielded to that of leather. Its back and cover were made of calfskin, free of inscription. Two leather straps ran through coarse holes and tied the pages together. She opened the book. The inside was thick, creamy paper. The first page was blank and had small holes. She turned to the next page. It, too, had small holes, at different places. She leafed through the whole volume, and it was pierced vellum page after pierced vellum page. No writing at all. Nothing but holes.

Looking closer, each hole appeared to have been punched with cutting-edge preciseness. The holes were randomly arranged, sometimes spread over the whole page, or grouped in one area.

César wanted her to empty the vault. She could probably take the chest with her and fly it home. She glanced at it. There was something on the bottom that she had not noticed, in her haste to open the book. A folded sheet of paper.

She opened it.

Her heart missed a beat. It was her father's handwriting. Just one short line on a plain piece of paper, in black ink. There was a small smudge where the writing started. He'd used a ball point to write a name—*Monastère Sainte-Thérèse, La Sainte Baume*. A monastery. She slid the paper in her bag.

She needed to go to the monastery and she needed to go to the Château d'If. She needed to think things through. The chest and the book were stored in the controlled-atmosphere portion of a very private vault for a reason.

César would have to wait.

But there was the looming search warrant, and the police's questions. Both probably linked, both equally puzzling. *All this for a bunch of holes?* She picked up her cell phone and started shooting pictures of the book. The memory filled. There was on and off network. She started emailing them to herself. Less than thirty seconds later they were uploaded to her email account. She repeated the process until she had captured over two hundred pages, then pulled out her passport and pictured it next to the book, for measurement.

She put the book in the chest and the chest in the box and rang for César.

He was down in a minute, glanced at the metal box on the table and put it back in the air-controlled glass encasement, handed her the key and walked out of the vault without a word. Under the careful stubble, his jaws bulged rhythmically.

As they reached the top of the staircase he cleared his throat and said, "Monsieur Toslav is here to see you, Miss Gabriel. Perhaps he can solve both our problems."

In the hallway, a bony man was killing time admiring the bouquet. Swinging a cane in his left hand, he turned toward them. "Doryan Toslav," he said.

She extended her hand. "Sybil Gabriel."

Toslav looked amused, took her fingers and tilted her hand, then bowed above it.

A proper baisemain. That doesn't happen every day. His hand was cold and dry, his skin brittle. She stroked her arm.

"I hope my car won't be in the way," he said to César and waved toward a deep red Silver Cloud, stopped right in front of the glass door, blocking the whole street, a young man behind the wheel.

"Not at all. We are not expecting anyone this afternoon."

Not expecting anyone. And it sounded like good news.

César walked them to a small lounge with floor-to-ceiling windows offering views of the sea and the nearby islands. One of them the Island of If, where Sybil had been found nearly dead. César pointed to low armchairs arranged around a coffee table and busied himself behind a small bar. "Coffee?"

Toslav set his cane against the table, pulled on the creases of his pants, and dropped in his seat. "Champagne." His long legs angled upward. "Uncomfortable seats, but a beautiful view. Is this your first visit to Marseilles?" he asked Robyn. His skin was taut against the bony features of his face, parchment-like, with liver marks. A modern mummy in a silk bow-tie. His accent didn't place him as a native from any English-speaking country, but wasn't distinctly foreign either.

"Where are you from?" she asked.

He waved his hand around. "I'm from many places."

César set three glasses of champagne on the table and sat with them.

The mummy smiled, uncovering small, yellow teeth, the creases around his mouth rippling to his ears. He lifted his glass. "Welcome!"

To Sybil, Robyn thought as she sipped her champagne. *Somewhere in transit, or in a hospital bed.* They thought she was her, and it made her feel uncomfortable and strong at the same time.

The mummy was looking around and seemed to just want to enjoy his drink. His neck was too thin to fill his collar, and it pleated when he turned his head. "I always combine business and pleasure." He smiled and winked. "I'm one of those lucky few." He brought his glass down and rested it on the edge of his armchair. "You're young," he said. "Follow the advice of an old man who's seen it all. Turn whatever your pleasure is into business. It's the only way to get gracefully through this vale of tears."

That's exactly what I'm trying to do, she thought, *but I'm not going to discuss it with you.*

"Let's talk," he said, and pulled a card.

César set his empty glass on the table and excused himself. The door shut softly behind him.

She picked up the card. The name was Doryan Toslav. The occupation, Acquisitions Department, Fondation Blaise Pascal. The printed phone number was crossed out and replaced by a scribble. "And… what does this foundation concern itself with?" she asked.

"Lost treasures of the French culture."

She wondered whether he was one of those treasures. "I'm afraid you'll have to do without a business card." She smiled. "I doubt you would have any business with me, though."

"On the contrary, Ms Gabriel, I'd be delighted to. It was a pleasure dealing with your father."

"My father?"

He raised his thin eyebrows. "Why of course! We've met once, here in Marseilles. Quite a while ago. Fifteen years, perhaps a little less. Great man. We had friends in common and went golfing. They had this one golf course outside the city. Lousy. Still is, I believe." His gaze became a little hazy, and he shook his head, as if trying to clear his memories. "Your father was an excellent golfer, I remember. And quite a gentleman. Pleasure dealing with him." He leaned over to reach for his drink. "A terrible thing, that accident. Your mother too, I heard?"

"Dealing with him?" Robyn asked.

"We had some unfinished business. I'm assuming that's what you're here for?"

Robyn slugged the rest of her champagne.

"It's a small world, Miss Gabriel. Word gets around very quickly." He cleared his throat. "Your father got in touch with me concerning a manuscript he had. A rare… edition, of no market value per se but of great interest to the foundation I represent. He stored it at the Banque des Deux-Rives at the time. It's probably still here?"

"What kind of manuscript are we talking about?"

"The Logonikon."

"Never heard the name."

Toslav went on. "It's rubbish if you ask me—no offense—but some people regard it highly as one of the greatest artifacts in occultism. The next-to-ultimate manuscript. Your father didn't know what to do with the Logonikon. The market wasn't ripe for it at the time." He put the cigarette holder back between his lips and Robyn thought she saw him draw on it. "I wasn't with the Fondation Blaise Pascal at the time. I was dealing curiosa back then, and having a hard time educating my clients to appreciate the occult. I told your father to hold on to the Logonikon until I sensed a genuine interest leading to solid market value." He paused and clearly mimicked pulling on the cigarette. "When I finally tried to get in touch I learned he had been... killed."

"So someone eventually wanted to buy it?" Robyn asked.

"If you're willing to part from it, we can look at different options." He tried to cross his legs, but the coffee table didn't give him enough room. He just sat there, his knees poking up. A vein beat in his temple. "I have a few international clients who would be serious bidders for the Logonikon. The Fondation Blaise Pascal, on the other hand, has more limited means but offers recognition to its donors. Some people like to believe their name on a brass plaque in a museum is more valuable than a few million dollars in a bank account." He waived the cigarette holder as if a seven-digit figure were a puff of smoke in his world. "It's entirely up to you."

A few million dollars. "Can you tell me a little about these buyers?"

"Definitely not," he coughed up. "The thing is," he said, waving his cigarette-holder, "now is the time to either sell or donate, and in your position you should be glad to even have the choice."

"In my position?"

"The ownership is challenged," he said. He finally managed to stick his right foot on top of his left knee. "Surely you are aware of that."

"Why would you buy or receive an artifact of tainted origin?" she asked.

He barely looked at her, and turned to the window. "Because my clients don't care. And neither does the foundation. Right now there is interest for the Logonikon. There might still be two years from now, and there might not be in three months. There's no way to know."

"You're saying the ownership is questionable," Robyn said, "yet you represent people who are ready to acquire, or receive the Logonikon or whatever you call it. Shouldn't they be concerned too—about the possibility that their ownership would ultimately be challenged?"

Toslav straightened in his chair and looked at Robyn. "Quite frankly, I doubt the foundation will offer any money for it. You could donate it to them as a philanthropic gesture, and if they have to relinquish it to someone else, there will not be any damage. The serious clients I have are abroad and private. No one will ever know where the Logonikon is once the transaction is completed. The fund transfer would be invisible, as well." He waived his hand in a regal gesture. "You see, only if you decided to put it on the market through an antiquarian or at an auction might trouble occur." He finished his glass of champagne.

"You seem to know a lot more than you're willing to say, Mr Toslav," she said.

"The less *you'll* know, the better off." He folded his cigarette holder. His hands trembled a little.

"That'll be a problem," she said.

He turned his question-mark eyebrows to her.

"I was born nosy."

7

THE CADILLAC KNEW the road back home. Mack only needed one finger on the bottom of the wheel to control it all the way to Sunken Heights. After twenty-eight years of marriage he could tell it still irked Elaine but he had long taught her to keep silent. She would never understand him, but at least she showed respect.

The car was heavy and soft and glided above the road. Street noises were dulled, road bumps swallowed. He knew exactly where the potholes were and avoided them by a swing of the finger.

He liked that, avoiding obstacles by a swing of the finger.

It didn't happen overnight. First you had to foresee the obstacles, by careful study of the terrain. Then you had to be driving an obedient machine.

Barton was not obedient. He had, by necessity, become part of the machine Mack was driving, but he was not obedient. He was a malfunctioning accessory that needed to be fixed. *Just like this garage opener*, Mack thought as he pulled into his driveway and the garage door stayed closed. He pressed repeatedly on the small box, through the car's open window. Nothing. He should have taken care of it when it stopped responding from the street. *I can't let Barton become a larger problem*, Mack thought, grabbing his briefcase with the garage opener and walking to the front door. *I have a darn good plan for Barton and I'm gonna start working on it right this minute.*

That was another thing he liked about his Cadillac DTS. The great ideas he got in there.

The hallway smelled of home-cooked food. He'd told Elaine to fix Bolognese this morning. She needed that kind of guidance. He thought there was a whiff of burn, too, but that couldn't be. She wouldn't risk it.

"What's the stink?" he shouted. Always keep them on edge, always. Staff, partners, wife, same thing. Keep the upper hand. He dropped the garage opener and his briefcase in his office and stomped to the kitchen. No one in there, but on the range a large pot was bubbling. His mouth watered. "Elaine." The burn smell was there all right. And there was broken glass in the sink. And a puddle on the floor. Maybe broken glass there, too.

"Dammit, Elaine." He stormed out of the kitchen and froze in the living room. The coffee table was pushed sideways, a small change that brought chaos to the room. He aligned it back with the sofas.

He turned around and saw a black leather jacket thrown on his easy chair and a woman's handbag he'd seen before, right in the middle of the seat as a statement. Natalie. His daughter was here. That explained the chaos.

Half-hiding under the jacket, Austin, her bunny, was rolled in a ball of trembling fur. Mack picked it up and held it against his chest. "Come to Daddy," he whispered, and the warm fuzz trembled a little less.

His shoulders slumped. He scratched Austin's head and the bunny dug its paws into his shirt. He went to the front door and checked that it was closed tight. The bunny loved to wander outside. Then he pulled himself upstairs. His footsteps were muffled by the pale green carpeting. He stopped on the landing, taking in Elaine's sobbing. He hovered between anger and despair. Veered himself toward cold-blooded decision-making. As always. Because he had no choice.

He walked into the bedroom, still clutching Austin. Ignored the shrunken shape wrapped in soft pink, shaking on the bed with her head in her hands. Set Austin on the bed, took his clothes off, folded them and changed into khaki shorts, a white polo shirt and tan docksides. He left the bunny on the bed and went back into the hallway.

He considered the shut door across the landing. There used to be a sweet little girl in there, who not so long ago would run out singing "Daddy Daddy" when he came home. She'd show a good enough report card, washed her hands before sitting at the table and went to bed when she was told to.

And she would never close her door.

Now, he could not risk the humiliation of finding it locked so he shouted, "Natalie, I have something for you."

He went downstairs and poured himself a tall bourbon and sat behind his desk. Natalie would spend the next couple hours, maybe more, brooding over his bait. But she would take it. She always had. She'd come downstairs and he would not tell her to sit down and he'd put the deal out on the table for her, take it or leave it. She'd take it, as always, and life would be simplified for the next six months or so. Only thing was, he had to raise the stakes each time.

Maybe today, if he hit really high, if he went beyond her wildest expectations, he'd tackle the problem at its core and make it go, once and for all.

He went to the door of his office and shouted, "Y'all better do som'thin' about dinner 'fore it's completely ruined." He heard Elaine's footsteps. She knew it when she went too far. And if she didn't, she got the message when he started talking nice to her as he just did.

He slammed his door.

Family under control. Time for the serious stuff now.

He paused at the entrance of his office. The window was to the left, with etched glass and pewter like in the old days, and it overlooked the driveway. The desk was straight across the door. It was a solid oak affair with a banker's light on it and a green leather swivel chair behind it. A small angle table held the computer. Cabinets ran along the wall, holding books and trophies and pictures. Smack behind the desk was the rifle cabinet, with Mack's collection of firearms. They were the only genuinely old objects in the office, and they were the only objects that weren't there for style. They had all been fired by McIntyres, back in Texas. And they were now maintained in working condition by Mack, starting with his first rifle, a Winchester 67 youth he got for his tenth birthday. Its wood was soft and warm and darkened where his hands had held it, afternoon after afternoon at his grandpa's ranch. There were several Colt rifles, an M1911 and a Heirloom Commander. He kept his Smith and Wesson 638 Airweight in the glove compartment of his car, and the 60-15, a .357 Magnum, at the office, so he could practice at the firing range the Fed had on location.

None of the guys at the bank went to the firing range. It was only him and the FRBNY police. And that was where he made his only friends from work. They were all police. Not bankers. Once in a while, he went for a beer after work with Diego, the chief of security. Diego had a solid sense of humor. That was all Mack needed after work. The guys at the bank were all East Coast stuck up, and once in a while it was good to let go.

He looked to the far right of his cabinets, where years ago he had locked a file now crying for his attention. He had put off studying it because it didn't seem like something he'd ever have to worry about, and because it consisted of several old notebooks, handwritten, barely legible and most of all, because they weren't even written in English. Keeping the file safe at home was part of the job, his predecessor at the New York Fed had told him. He also said he could read it, if he was curious about it and if he could read French. Or he could wait for the shit to hit the fan, if it ever did, to bother about the notebooks.

Shit was hitting the fan, full speed. He had wanted to read them.

So he had placed an ad for translators, had set up different appointment times. Had locked each of the applicants in a separate room with one notebook each. Had given them a stack of paper and a pen, and asked them to translate these old, insignificant notebooks as fast as they could, as a trial for future missions. Told them not to worry about style but focus on content.

As each of them finished at different times, he had thanked them and said they'd get a call within twenty-four hours if they had the job. They left ignoring the others' presence, unaware the notebooks were anything else than historic research. At the end of the day Mack had all his notebooks translated. There never were any phone calls of course. Just polite letters.

Mack fished a key from the top drawer of his shelf, unlocked the cabinets and pulled out a stack of yellow letter-size notebooks, each of them bound with a rubber band to the stapled, handwritten translations. He sat down at his desk, fired up his computer and while the screen flicked, flipped the first notebook open and set the translation aside for now.

The notebooks smelled like mushrooms and dust. The stiff pages cracked a little as if they'd dried out after being soaked. There was a newspaper clipping neatly wedged between the cover page and the first page. Mack set it aside with the translation. The diary started on the top line of the top page, aligned on the left with just a slight indentation on the first line.

The handwriting appeared regular on the page, with only a flourish here and there, but close-up the words were crammed and barely decipherable. It was a strange handwriting too, not like anything he'd seen before. He heard someone explain once that handwritings were different in each country. He didn't quite get it then. Now he saw what they meant. It had this air of foreignness that flashed a red light in his mind.

He turned to the translation. The handwriting was legible, but he'd rather type it. He was going to need solid material, a decent file. Something that could be emailed and printed if need be.

The computer screen settled on the desktop. He opened a blank document and began typing with two fingers.

NOTES BY HENRY SIMON

He stopped and compared the translation to the notebook. That was an addition to the document. A note added by whoever had found the diary, apparently, scribbled in pencil on the inside of the cover page. Maybe the name of the author was somewhere in there, but that remained to be proven. It was not on the first page, and not on the last. He checked again. *I'll just add brackets.* He stopped and gave it some more thought. *I'll add a question mark too. Just to be on the safe side. And also, CLASSIFIED.*

He typed slowly, one finger at a time, right, left, right, left. He was not used to typing. He had always had people do that for him. He was not that old, but the computer frenzy had hit in the nineties, when he was senior enough to have a full staff of secretaries. Administrative assistants, they called them now. He never needed to learn how to type. So he didn't.

Before he got really started, he hit *Save.* He decided to create a folder, labeled 00, on his desktop. That much he had learned to do—saving a document to the desktop, to find it right away. Something he did not worry about was naming the doc. It got saved under the first words, or title, and that was always perfect anyway. Told you immediately what the paper was about. This one was Notes.

He would scan all the notebooks and the translations and save them under that folder too, for added security. Pritchard, the boss at the bank, was a stickler for electronic communications. When the time came, it would be good to have everything digitalized, like Pritchard said. And the time may come very soon.

After some typing he was staring at something neat and legible, not the scribble of the translation. He printed out the page, saved the document, Notes, under Folder 00, and started reading.

July 27, 1914
N.Y.
I am getting accustomed to wearing civilian clothes, but still have trouble knotting my tie.

I brought the chest and its precious content to Langlois this morning. The man is much to my liking. Taciturn and devout, a faithful member of the Society of Jesus although I doubt if many of his friends even know this. Given the atmosphere in France, I would not be surprised if he kept his allegiance a secret. This best serves the Society's interests in this matter.

I have endowed him with monies amounting to a small fortune to ensure the safekeeping of the chest and its content. I recommended building a small fort in the countryside but Langlois hinted that this may attract attention. He said he would think over an idea during the crossing of the Atlantic. His ship, the Deux-Rives, is a small steamer, light and sturdy. She should reach Marseille within two to three weeks. I expect to hear from him before Autumn. As much as I hate parting with the document, this was the best decision. They are getting too close now.

The harbor was bustling with a frenzy of shipments this morning. The cab driver nearly ran over a dockhand as he drove to the Deux-Rives and swore that he had never seen any such thing. Hundreds, thousands of kegs were being hauled, most, if not all, accompanied by armed guards. Tens of ships were lined along the docks.

The timing of these events is a sign of God's will for us to act. It is one thing to witness History in the making; yet our duty is to make History. I shall pay a visit to Mr. William McAdoo, Secretary of the Treasury, tomorrow. T. provided me with an introduction.

It was the end of the page. The next page bore the next day's date. Mack would get to that after dinner.

He rubbed his eyes. He wondered who T. was. He thought about the Society of Jesus, aka Jesuits. He wondered what an obscure Catholic priest had to say to the US Secretary of the Treasury.

He took the newspaper clipping he'd set aside earlier and unfolded it carefully. It was an article from the New York Times dated July 28, 1914.

Mack smoothed its creases open before him. The ink smeared. His forefinger was blackened. The print was blurred by time. The headlines were a little tilted, as if some clumsy kid had cut and taped them. The paper was yellowish and thin. He lit his desk lamp and started reading the article, headlined *Gold Shipments Set Record with $10,600,000 for Today.*

The story boiled down to European countries dumping US stocks and shipping US gold to finance their war. In the summer of 1914 Europe was bracing for conflict. The European countries, in need of money, started selling their holdings in American securities, redeeming the dollars they received for American gold, and having the gold shipped to them.

In doing so, they threw the United States in two crises: a financial market crisis because of the massive selling; and a banking crisis in exercising their right to redeem the dollars obtained from the sale of stock for gold and having this gold shipped to them.

The ships Simon had seen on the harbor were being loaded with bullions taken from US vaults to finance World War One. The paper mentioned over ten million dollars shipped on the Kronprinzessin Cecilie, and went on to explain it would have been more save for the insurer's refusal to assume a greater risk. Still according to the article, eight million dollars worth of gold were going to be shipped on Cunard Line's *Carmania* the next day.

Mack glanced at the diary's translation again. *"The timing of these events is a sign of God's will for us to act. It is one thing to witness History in the making; yet our duty is to make History. I shall pay a visit to Mr. William McAdoo, Secretary of the Treasury, tomorrow."* No doubt the diary would mention that encounter. He would read about it after dinner.

There was a note in English in the margin of the article, by the same handwriting that filled the diary: *From what I saw, much more than that. They are trying to avoid a panic.*

So according to Simon, a lot more gold was being shipped over-seas. *But how did that affect the then non-existent Federal Reserve Bank of New York?* Mack wondered.

It had to, or the diary would not have been transmitted to him along with the embarrassing secret passed from First Vice-President to First Vice-President.

He'd have to continue reading. For now, he needed action. Results. Blood on the walls. He thought how Barton was failing him. That made him think about Natalie. To have his daughter and that pervert in the same trail of thoughts was nauseating. That made him think of someone else, and he knew what to do. The nausea went away. He picked up his phone.

The New York State Banking Department operated on institution-al hours, a mass of paper pushers who accounted for the budget and a few workaholics who ran the place. Mack had the four digit extension number of one of these workaholics on his rolodex. The paper push-ers were long gone home but the automatic answering service let him through. The phone rang twice and a deep voice said, "Listening."

No more than twenty seconds were wasted on catching up with the last ten or so years—or was it twenty? Then Mack dropped his bomb.

"Remember Barton?"

Silence on the line. Barton had slept with the guy's girlfriend, and that was putting it very, very nicely. Of course he remembered.

"Wanna help me nail him?" Mack said.

The sound on the line was maybe the ruffling of fabric, or the thoughtful rubbing of stubble. The guy was thinking, or shaking off the day, grabbing a pen, holding a vengeance. Careful not to say anything compromising.

Mack gave the workaholic the specifics of Barton's holding com-pany, Garden of Evil, and of its subsidiaries, and hung up. Fifteen minutes later the scenario was wrapped. The workaholic's examiners received a high priority note on their blackberries to scrutinize the books of the bank each was currently auditing. Find if the bank held accounts for these companies. In which case, be prepared for money laundering patterns.

The workaholic was back on the phone. "My guys are going to smell blood."

"In his line of business, they'll get lucky," Mack said.

"Here's what's going to happen. I'll be receiving Suspicious Activity Reports." He paused to let it sink in.

Mack was getting exactly what he wanted. Suspicious Activity Reports, or SARs, meant that the workaholic was going to get a bunch of papers saying Barton was into very illegal stuff. Stuff that could send him right to jail. Before that happened, stuff that would make his bank accounts close overnight. No court decision, nothing. The words *drugs* or *terrorism* could make wonders.

"All I need to file them, is one phone call from you."

Meaning, the SARs would be sitting on the workaholic's desk, but unless Mack called, they would not be filed. It was simple, perfect blackmail.

Mack would show a copy of the SARs to Barton and make sure he understood that he, Mack, was just one phone call away from the guy who made the executive decisions after SARs were filed. One phone call and his bank accounts would be frozen worldwide. And that was before the actual trouble started with law enforcement and such. Mack had friends in DC, just as he had friends in the City.

Unless Barton handed the Logonikon, in which case Mack would never phone his buddy the workaholic who would forget about the SAR's. Or not, depending how he felt about the whole girlfriend story. At this point, Mack wouldn't care.

"How long to get started?" Mack asked.

"Twelve to thirty-six hours," the workaholic said, then hung up.

Barton would have his head on the block, with Mack holding the ax. He'd hand the Logonikon. Three days max.

He stretched in his chair and heard a faint knock on the door.

Natalie.

Last problem of the day.

She stood in the doorway, leaning against the open door, her gaze arrogant, her shoulders slumped, Austin the bunny clutched against her as her sole source of affection.

There was something different about her again, and again he couldn't tell what. Something about the eyes. Or was it the hair? He'd given up keeping track of her physical changes a long time ago.

She was perched on wobbly heels, her skinny legs wrapped in tight gold pants, her waist caught in some pinkish fabric that seemed to cover her marble-white bosom only by chance. It hurt him to think that she looked more like a hooker than anything else. He saw her gaze turn from arrogant to hateful. He tried to look at her kindly, for she must have read his thoughts. But it was too late. She was the stranger, the enemy, the shame again.

But she was still his daughter.

"Sweet-heart, I've been thinking lately." He tried a smile.

She stared back.

"We never got around to getting you a proper car, did we?"

She pursed her lips. The car, like many other things, had been hanging there between them on the long list of her irrational requests and his steadfast refusals. "Any kind you like in particular?"

She shook her head slowly. "Like that's gonna happen."

"Well, it's going to." He rapped a pencil on his desk. "If that doesn't help you get back on track, nothing will." He thought he saw her eyes get shiny, as if she were about to cry, but her lower lip didn't quiver and the shine withdrew. Good. Last thing he needed was a display of emotion.

She stayed there and looked at him stack the notebooks together. She started petting Austin frantically. He didn't expect a thank you, but some kind of talk would have eased the moment.

He locked the notebooks back into the cabinet and put the key in the desk drawer. "Why don't you go help Mother with dinner," he finally said. "I don't know what happened between the two of you, but the whole kitchen needs cleaning up."

She turned around. Her shoulders seemed straighter. She hadn't talked back the way she usually did, hadn't argued. It was understood the car was conditional to her behavior. In accepting it she had subscribed to his rules.

"Natalie," he snapped. "Call Columbia first thing in the morning. I want you to get that degree."

8

ROBYN DECLINED TOSLAV'S offer for a ride to her hotel in his chauffeured Rolls Royce Silver Cloud. She let the oversized car squeeze through the narrow streets, and took the pedestrian shortcut down to the harbor. There, she tried to get a boat ride to the Island of If. It was late afternoon, the sun still high in the sky, but a weariness falling on the city, traffic worked up to a stall, blaring horns covering the clinking of sailboats, crying kids dragged by worn-out mothers, outdoor cafés filling up. The tour boats were wrapping up the day. Too late for work.

She called the monastery. No one answered.

Back at the hotel, she ordered room service and called Tom. Got his voice mail and left a message, "How's Sybil?" *You think the guy would keep me posted,* she thought. *She's my twin. And what about that research from his buddy?* She picked up the phone again and hit redial.

Voice mail, direct. "And when you get a chance, lemme know what your guy said about the four last lines." Hung up. No ifs, no please. *She's his fiancée. He should start getting involved, and not only as a nurse.*

A cold shower took care of the wear and the frustration. She called Parker, stepped on the balcony's soft, red tile while the call went through and leaned on the wrought iron railing. Her room overlooked the hotel's park and the sounds of the city were distant. The air was sweet with whiffs of rosemary and lavender. The small valet parking lot was to her left, silent and dark. To her right was the park, filled with the trills of hundreds of crickets.

"I was going to email you that Voynich stuff," he said.

"Tell me what you got."

"Now? Aren't you supposed to be taking care of Sybil?"

It was time to tell him. "I am," she said. She took a deep breath. "Tom is flying Sybil back to the States."

"And?"

"And I have to check a couple things here."

"So what's with the Voynich?" Because of the treasure hunting, she and Parker were often looking into old documents and maps, and the story surrounding them. Parker thought that was what she was doing. Research for a new venture.

"I wanted to be sure before I told you," she said and stepped into her room. "Sybil was branded. With a sign like typical Voynich graphic. Voynichese, they call it. That hooped letter pi?"

"Shit."

There was silence on the line, filled with static, then Robyn went back on the balcony and said, "What are your sources?"

More static, then paper shuffling. "Internet websites. Online libraries. Hard copy books." His voice got firmer as he spoke. He was getting over the first shock. "Lots of stuff."

"Where do we start?"

"Let's get rid of the BS first," he said. "There's a bunch of theories on what the manuscript is. The religious book of the Cathari—"

"Someone mentioned a cult," Robyn said.

"Crap if you ask me, but let me see what I have." The sound of pages being flipped came through. "There. This Leo Levitov started with the assumption that Voynichese was a language, not a code. He assigned a phonetic value to each symbol, translated the Voynichese into Latin and the Latin into English. Said the outcome was an oral language, a mixture of the Northern European languages spoken by the Cathari. In the case of this manuscript, the text he came up with had to do with death. Ergo, said Levitov, the Voynich manuscript is the liturgical manual for the Endura rite of the Cathari. A ritual of purification before death. You buy that?"

"I'll keep it in mind," Robyn said.

"For the record, Levitov is considered a lunatic in Voynich circles. His translation is supposed to be gibberish."

"Then maybe he's right."

"You have a point."

"What else?"

"World War II. High caliber cryptanalysts tried their hand on it."

"Why should we care?"

"Because they would have spotted a hoax."

"Good enough."

"First, Hitler. His Ahnenerbe, the occult bureau, had a sub-group to decode the Voynich. He was also known to be looking actively for the decoder to the manuscript. Second, the guys at Station X, outside London, who cracked the German Enigma machine during World War II? Cryptanalysts, cryptographers, linguists, you name it. They'd get together for fun after work and try to the crack the Voynich. Never got anywhere."

"These guys cracked the Enigma but couldn't figure out the Voynich?"

"Makes you think, right? But listen to this. Here in the US, the guy who broke the Japanese Purple code before World War II, and who'd become Special Assistant to the Director of the National Security Agency, guy named William Friedman. He and his wife are legends. They spent their whole life in cryptography and basically without them, who knows what goddamn language we'd be speaking now. Japanese or German. Remember, these people are paid government wages, right. Their inventions and discoveries belong to the government. Now their idea of fun when they're done with their World War II daytime job of deciphering enemy messages is to try and crack the Voynich. But years go by and they don't make significant progress. So in the 60s they ask for permission to use a huge RCA computer to help them. Permission granted. They start designing the programs and stuff on the weekends and evenings. And when they're about to launch their program—Boom. Access denied."

"Did Friedman publish a memoir or something?"

"Nada."

Robyn stayed silent. Parker stayed silent.

Finally Parker said, "Some of his colleagues, Voynich freaks. One of them got hit by a tram. Another died of the flu at the hospital. Another one committed suicide. People started talking about a curse."

People loved euphemisms. "I guess that means a couple interesting things," Robyn recapped. "One, the Voynich manuscript is *not* a bunch of crap."

"I agree," Parker said. "Cryptographers as good as Friedman or the guys at Station X would be able to tell right off the bat if it's a hoax."

"Two, assuming the people who cut the Friedmans' access to the RCA computer were government-"

"Which they had to be-"

"This means the US government doesn't want the Voynich to be decoded." *What could be on that manuscript that still mattered in the twentieth century?* Robyn thought. "And that's leaving the deaths out of the equation."

"Which we're not."

She was not going to have that conversation. "What else did you find out?" she said.

"The real stuff now." He cleared his throat. "Here's the big picture. First mention of the Voynich manuscript is in 1915—

"I thought 1912."

"You want the story or the facts?"

"Facts."

"Okay then. Nineteen-fifteen. The Chicago Art Institute exhibits a collection belonging to Wilfried Voynich, a dealer of rare books. The exhibition includes the whole collection of manuscripts belonging to the Hapsburg family, straight from their Vienna castle, and '*a work by Roger Bacon in cipher to which the key has never been discovered*'. That's a description from the Chicago Daily Tribune. It's the first mention of the Voynich manuscript."

"1915. Ok." The crickets fell silent. Someone must be taking a walk in the park. She stepped back into the room and looked outside through the closed French doors. "Tell me about Voynich. The guy."

While Parker searched his notes, her thoughts drifted to her father. *Why did you bring us here? What did you want from us?* She strained to conjure his features. She remembered his build, his hands, his voice, but couldn't command his face to her memory. Her mother's, she could. The tilt of the head, her eyes. Her smell made of perfume and makeup and love. But it was her father's face that she needed now, and it kept eluding her. *Why do I always feel let down?*

"Wilfried Voynich," Parker said. "Polish. Born 1865. Poor. Studied Chemistry in Moscow. Got involved with the Polish nationalist movement. Spent two years in prison for that, was moved to Siberia, escaped and made it to London. In little time had a huge catalogue of rare books and a respected position in London."

"From poor Polish chemist to political activist to prisoner in Siberia to fugitive to top of the food chain on the London art market. In how long?"

"The time it would take to get a Masters'. Or a Ph.D., max."

"Takes sense of opportunity."

"And guts."

"And creativity."

"Contacts."

"Imagination."

"I don't believe a word he says," Parker dropped.

"'Course not."

In the park, an incandescent dot dangled in the dark. She kept her eyes on it while she talked. A cigarette butt, with brighter phases as someone drew from it. Below the cigarette butt something was sending long bright flickers. Something metallic and long, reflecting the lights of the hotel. The red dot and the silver band stopped moving. A cigarette and a cane. Toslav?

"What's his story about the manuscript?" she asked.

"He said he found it in 1912, in a castle outside Rome, called Villa Mondragone. The castle belonged to Jesuits. They were hurting for money. He bought a case of old books from them so they could pay for new ones."

"The Jesuits? Hurting for money?"

"Made me wonder too."

"They did get in trouble with the Vatican," she thought out loud. "That might explain. Not sure when exactly."

"I can check."

"What else?"

"Supposedly there was a letter inside the Voynich manuscript." The sound of ruffled pages, then Parker said, "From a Jesuit, Joannes Marcus Marci of Cronland, to another Jesuit, Athanasius Kircher. Dated 1666. In the letter Marci asks Kircher, the polymath, for his help in deciphering a manuscript he received from a friend. Basically, the letter states some hearsay about the provenance of the book and names the author as Roger Bacon, the Englishman."

"Roger Bacon," Robyn said then started thinking. *A Franciscan monk, most brilliant mind of the thirteenth century. Pioneer of scientific reasoning. Author of works on mathematics, alchemy and optics. Anticipated flying machines and steam boats, among other things. Was accused of sorcery. Had to write chained to his desk or something like that. Why would the US government prevent the decoding of anything he would have written? It simply doesn't make sense.*

"Voynich waited until 1921 to mention the Marci letter," Parker dropped.

She couldn't believe it. "You mean it was not displayed at the Chicago Exhibition in 1915?"

"No."

"Not even mentioned?"

"Uh-uh."

"Oh boy." It was standard procedure to display or publish any document that came with a manuscript at the time of its discovery or acquisition. Especially in the case of a letter from one scholar to another and relating to the provenance and possible authors of the manuscript. A basic rule broken again. "The same type of thing happened with the colophon," she said, referring to the four lines added at the end of the manuscript. "It was not made public until 2005."

"How do you know that?"

"Tom. He took code-breaking classes. Long story. But it's a different pattern here. I can't nail what's going on."

"Hiding the colophon prevents deciphering," Parker observed.

"And fabricating a letter to influence dating and authorship amounts to pretty much the same result," she said. "Having people come up with a pre-formatted interpretation."

"That colophon thing means Voynich is not the author of the manuscript," Parker reflected.

"But the Marci letter could be a Wilfried Voynich fabrication. Two things are going on: keeping people from decoding the Voynich; and giving false clues," Robyn said.

In the park, the red dot went from right to left to right to left. Waving. Then its flicker hopped back to the right, the bright streak following it in diagonal strides. Back toward the hotel's front door, then out of sight. "Any other facts?" Robyn asked.

"The Voynich manuscript had several owners since 1912, and some of its pages, eight or so I think, are missing. It's currently owned by Yale's Rare Book and Manuscript Library, Beinecke. The Beinecke library refused to let the document be scientifically dated for decades."

"Come on."

"They finally let two teams date the vellum through carbon 14 and the ink."

"And…?"

"And the results have not been properly published."

"How about that."

"I know."

"Back to square one," she said.

"There's only one thing that cryptanalysts, linguists, and computer wizards agree on: it was written by two people, who were not insane, in a human language."

"Good enough for me", Robyn said.

"The conclusion of the last serious book on the topic is *Better left unsolved*," Parker added. "Be careful Robyn".

Too late, Robyn thought as she hung up and sat behind the computer in her suite's office. She accessed the Beinecke library's website and sent the curator a request to access ms 408 for purposes of her current research to support her Ph.D. thesis, *Historic Ventures for the Contemporary Scholar: when Greed meets Creed*. Threw in references, jargon and salutations.

Then she logged into Skype and sent a message to Parker, explaining briefly about her visit to the bank, and asking for his take on the strange book. She attached a few of the pictures she had taken in the vault.

As she hit *Send*, a loud chirp startled her. A brown cricket, perched on the bedroom's doorframe, was rubbing its forewings. She grabbed it in a swift motion. It tickled her palm and had a harsh feel. She cracked the windows open and unfolded her palm. The cricket stayed there. She blew softly on it. It jumped on the balcony railing and resumed its song.

No red light or bright streak in view. But the thump of a car door, headlights inundating the valet parking and a powerful purr filling the night. The car heading for the gate had a long hood, short trunk. Old fashioned style, oversize body. Deep red. Toslav's Silver Cloud.

She looked down. Three stories. Thirty feet. She climbed over the railing.

9

TWENTY-FOUR HOURS AFTER Toslav's frustrating visit to his Paris apartment, Li Mei was in Hanoi, reporting to the Elders.

He sat on the only remaining chair. It was smaller than the others, forcing him to sit lower than the four other men in the circle. He had been initiated just like them. Years ago they sent him to the best universities in the Western world—in France and then in the United States. He studied mathematics and information technology. Made contacts he called friends. That was part of the mission. Since then he had always lived in the West, carrying his duties, coming back for short trips, feeling he was treated more and more like a stranger. But looking at his peers now, he felt it again, as he did each time. They were his family. He belonged to the cause.

Kwong Yul burned grass in a bushel on a small table serving as an altar. Next to the bushel he lit three sticks of incense in a tripod underneath a lantern representing the King of Heaven, the Jade Emperor.

The smell soothed Li Mei. The memory of his initiation rite flowed. It was held in China, their homeland, over twenty years ago, next to the river, and he still remembered the sacred words by which he pledged loyalty to his brothers, he remembered passing through the gate of swords, he remembered the iron taste of chicken blood mixed with liquor to strengthen his words and strengthen the bond between the members of the Society.

He held as true the legend of the foundation of the first Society of Heaven and Earth. In the eighteenth century, during the Qing dynasty, when the unworthy Manchu minority ruled the country, Shaolin monks successfully answered the Emperor's call for help in defeating the barbarians in Northwest China. As a token of gratitude, the Emperor bestowed the monastery with a triangular seal, which conferred great power upon the monks. Some court officials could not contain their jealousy. An army was sent and the monastery set on fire. Thirteen monks fled. Of the thirteen, only five survived the long escape trek. And when all seemed lost and they were about to be captured, their pursuers drowned in the river the monks had just crossed.

A white incense burner appeared in the river, bearing four characters that meant "Restore the Ming and Extirpate the Qing." The monks concluded a blood covenant and pledged to carry out this mission; the first Society of Heaven and Earth was born, later dubbed Triad by foreigners because of the symbolism of the number three it so often used. They were joined by Zhu, a descendant of the imperial family of the Ming dynasty, then parted and founded triads throughout China.

Li was given passwords like "The Zhu will rule all under Heaven" or "Never forget three". He was taught to use three fingers when drinking, smoking, or passing an object in a social setting, so that his peers would recognize him.

And above all, he was intent on finishing the job.

Under the Qing dynasty the Manchu minority ruled over the large Han majority who had been in power for the nearly three centuries of the flourishing Ming dynasty. Manchu were considered barbaric by the Han, and under their governance the country went down the drain, sold to foreigners. The 1911 revolution in effect restored Han rule, accomplishing the aim of all triads.

In doing so, it deprived its members of any purpose. With no more income, until then provided by the people to support their cause, and an anger for most of them over not having taken part in any combat during the four-month revolution, triad members quickly turned their skills to criminal activities. From then on, triad meant organized crime.

There was one group, however, who knew all wrongs had not been righted by the revolution, and that was Li's group. One of their members had witnessed a perfidy the Manchus committed against China in the last days of 1911. He had paid with his life his proofless accusations, but his brothers had taken his word and gathered clues.

For nearly one century now they had steadily pursued their goal of righting the treachery orchestrated by Yehenara, the Empress dowager known under the name Long Yu. Theirs was the only triad that remained pure and faithful to its oath.

Li's heart filled with pride and his shoulders felt heavy.

He had never failed his duties, and a sense of orderly purpose invaded him. He looked at the other men, all barefoot and in bright silk attire like him. One family.

The five men went through the lengthy verbal preliminaries, then Zhu Fai said to Li Mei, "We are listening to you."

"I believe we are approaching our goal," Li Mei said, looking at each of the four men in turn. "Our middleman is conducting his task in an appropriate manner."

Chen Guang, who had worked for years for the CIA, leaned forward in his chair. "Can't you do the job yourself?"

"I believe we've been through this before," Li Mei answered, looking at each one except Chen Guang. "We agreed last time it was best not to act directly. I did as was agreed."

"How much is this going to cost?" Chen Guang asked.

"Nothing," Li Mei answered, looking at Kwong Yul, who was their natural leader. "I believe I already explained the middleman will be paid after we successfully exploit the document. Money won't be a problem then."

"And how do you believe you can trust this foreigner?" Chen Guang spat.

"I offered him a cell phone," Li Mei said, finally looking at Guang. "He doesn't use it much, but he keeps it with him at all times. I record everything he says, on the phone or not."

"And what does he say?"

"He is a person of strange mores, but I believe he is a trustworthy merchant, if a stupid one." Li Mei cracked a thin smile. "He declined an offer for double our price, just yesterday."

"Double our price?" Wang Shaiming said.

Zhu Fai's eyebrows lifted. "Who made the offer?" Zhu Fai was a man of few words and deep wisdom.

Li Mei's heart sank at his question. "I don't know," he had to admit. "Collectors are interested." He could see the disappointment on the Elder's face.

Wang Shaiming nailed his gaze on Li Mei's. "Bullshit," he said in English. "You know what that means, you've been to America. You believed that?" He looked at Chen Guang and they both stared at Li Mei.

Kwong Yul extended his hand in a peaceful gesture. "Who do you think offered twice the price?" he asked Li Mei.

"We know who," Chen Guang burst. "The likes of Matteo Ricci. Their hand is in every shadow."

Kwong Yul asked again, "Do you know who, Li Mei?"

"He said his name was Barton," Li Mei said.

"If he offered twice the price", Kwong Yul said, "he knows what it is. He is not a collector."

Li Mei nodded. It was a race now. They had had a century to gather clues, and now, suddenly, because somehow, somewhere, someone else knew, time was running out.

"You know the rule, Li Mei," Chen Guang said. "He who leaks the occasion ..."

...*Perishes by the sword*, Li Mei finished. He didn't believe he would betray the occasion—the restoration of the Ming dynasty—but he would accept his brothers' judgment nonetheless.

"Enough," Kwong Yul said, raising his hand. "Li Mei has fought for the occasion. And he will again, soon. Let us share the jiahexing."

Jiahexing meant *the family is strong and flourishing* and it was the triad word for liquor. The men drank, strengthening their mouths to empower their words.

* * *

Robyn pushed herself off the railing. Thirty feet. She rolled on the ground to absorb the impact. It used to be her favorite part of martial arts as a kid. Rolling with the chin tucked in, shoulder first, and standing right back up. Until she realized she could also send a *boy* twice her size flat on the tatami.

She went toward the entrance of the hotel. Passed a low building with a small door and windows cracked open on chatter, neon lights and cigarette whiffs. A service entrance. Squeaking and cracking came from a gravel trail cutting through the park. She crouched behind a fat topiary. A young guy dressed in white was pushing a bicycle. He put the bike against the wall and pushed the small door open. A crude rectangle of light spilled on the gravel, throwing the park in deep darkness. The chatter built up and faded with the closing door.

Robyn waited a few seconds then continued to the front of the hotel. Glanced right toward the driveway. The Silver Cloud was purring, Toslav talking to a tall, athletic man. Handsome forties. Savile-Row dressed. The Gentleman's Quarterly type. *What's a GQ doing with the mummy?*

Toslav took his time fitting his legs and his cane and his ego in the back seat. Leaning out the window, he called to the GQ. "I can't help you with the Gabriels," he said, "but I can drop you off."

What the hell did that mean? The GQ had asked for something concerning her sister and her and Toslav could not or would not deliver? Who was the guy anyway?

GQ had a nervous chin movement, as if easing from the tie he wasn't wearing. Pulled a cell phone. Looked right and left. Texted. Took a step toward the car.

Robyn ducked back and thought about the bike guy being stuck at the hotel for the time of his shift.

GQ was putting the phone in his pants' back pocket. Now he was climbing in the car.

Robyn could only think of one thing to do. Keep following them. She ran to the service building and lifted the bike toward the entrance. It was a light item, the racing kind, with ultra-thin wheels and low handlebars. When she got to the asphalt she straddled it and kicked it in motion. The size was about right for her.

She could easily catch up with Toslav. The hotel was on top of a hill served only by a narrow one-way street that wormed up one side and winded down the other. Toslav's chauffeur couldn't speed to the bottom. Not with a Silver Cloud.

She fit her feet in the pedal straps. Hunched over the bike, she passed the incoming lane marked with a large wrong-way sign and darted into the exiting lane. Streetlights cast warm puddles of yellow light. The air whistled as she gained speed. She straightened herself. The saddle was a thin, hard, uncomfortable thing. Three hundred yards and she saw the lights of the Silver Cloud. She squeezed the brakes and settled in the middle, away from the puddles of light. Followed from a distance.

At the bottom he'd make either a left toward the Old Harbor, or a right toward the Corniche. Depending on how fast the driver was, she'd be able to follow or not.

But when the car came to a stop, no blinker went on. The visibility was hindered by high walls on both sides, and then the road slumped into a deep gutter running alongside the main street. The car inched into it, brake, inch, brake, inch, the chauffeur cautious not to scrape the car's body. Still no blinker. When it cut across the four-lane street Robyn thought it was going left merging into the farthest lane, but the Silver Cloud continued right across and climbed up a ramp so narrow and dark she hadn't noticed it. Then it made a tricky left turn into another narrow street. She waited for the rear lights to disappear and followed. Traffic was light. The bike jumped across the four lanes. She switched gears and crept up the ramp. Made the left turn. Stopped.

The Silver Cloud was idling a hundred yards ahead, in the middle of a plaza with the harbor below and to the left, and thick walls towering on the right. GQ got out. He left the door open and stood there looking at something he held in front of his eyes. The thing glowed. A cell phone. He tucked it inside his jacket.

A man limped up to the car. Dark suit and silent shoes. Crew cut. Close to two hundred pounds, but athletic. Like a baseball player, but with a limp. GQ patted his shoulder. The guy with a limp got in the car. The two didn't talk. The car took off.

GQ stepped to the right and disappeared behind a fold in the walls.

Robyn kicked the pedals and looked up. There was a tall, sturdy crenellated tower. Another tower a little way down. In between, crenellated walls. No windows. A sturdy, fortified castle, overlooking the harbor.

Except it wasn't a castle.

* * *

After the meeting with the Elders, Li Mei went out, through the small garden and into the street. He hailed a cab and went to the railway station. He'd do everything the conventional way. He couldn't risk being traced here. His electronic gizmos had done marvels so far, but now they could be dangerous.

He bought an international calling card and picked up a public phone and placed a call to France. Toslav's phone rang then disconnected. He tried again and this time it picked up. "Monsieur Toslav?"

There was a short silence and then a British accent. "Are you his five-million dollar client?" Definitely not Toslav.

"Who is this?"

"Call this number back in a couple of days."

Li could have panicked, seeing the occasion escape him as his only link to the Logonikon had snapped. But success was all about planning, and Li had planned for Toslav's failure. Not anticipated it, not expected it. But planned in case of it.

The plan involved a triad based in New York City, with extended family links to his triad and extended expertise in organized crime. Li and his contact had been over the scenario in detail about a month ago, face to face in Chinatown.

Li placed the call to the United States. "I need the job done. Now."

He had never used the help of another triad before. But he knew this man and he trusted him. The man understood he would only get paid after the job was completed, and only if it was done right.

"Give us two hours," the man said.

Li felt in control. Felt he had never lost control.

An hour later the man was on the line. "Done."

Li's pulse went back to normal.

* * *

Towers, crenellated walls, no windows. Not a medieval castle, but Saint Victor's Abbey, or what was left of it. Robyn had read about it in a glossy art and history booklet in her hotel room. Founded in the fifth century over the burial site of a martyr, rebuilt in the eleventh and twelfth centuries with Moorish attacks and massacres in mind, only its church remained now, two sturdy towers and a thick wall flooded with pastel lighting for urban décor.

Robyn kicked the bike to the fold in the walls where GQ had disappeared. On the side of the first tower, there was a door.

She tried to turn the knob. It didn't budge. Pulled, shook. The door didn't move. Felt for a latch. Nothing. Not even a damn lock.

GQ had gotten inside somehow and bolted the door. He was expected, or he was a regular.

She went to the corner and pushed the bike up a dark side ramp. Heavy tarps attached to metal scaffolding lined the church. The ramp opened onto a back street with low buildings. Laundry drying off the window sills. Garbage bags scattered on the sidewalk. Piss-colored street light. No opening.

She set the bike against a stack of barriers in the dark ramp and gave this some thinking.

The outside shape of this church wasn't helping. No apparent transepts, no majestic exit that, from the outside, would have indicated the narthex. But medieval churches in Western Europe were built pointing toward the East, their altar toward Jerusalem, the Orient. The word *orientation* was cornered when maps showed the Orient on top.

Marseilles' Old Harbor marked the limit between the city's North and South. This side was south. The harbor was to her left. That made her facing the West side. Where the main door would be.

She lifted the tarp. Stepped inside the scaffolding. Reached a wall. Her eyes not yet accustomed to darkness, she felt with her fingers until there was a recess. She stepped in, climbed up some stairs, and got to a landing and a small side door that opened without a creak.

She took in the coolness, the whiffs of incense, the flickering candles. The church was small. She padded up the aisle. Shadows kept still, and her steps were the only sound. Then the silence around her thickened as chanting seeped from beyond walls.

It permeated the whole Church, not really coming from any definite place. Something deep, Gregorian. Like an incantation. She wondered where GQ had vanished.

She passed alcoves that were too small for chapels, but large enough to hold glittering reliquaries. There would be small bones on crimson velvet cushions. She sure could picture Toslav helping himself in there. Was GQ in this line of business as well?

The alcoves stayed dead silent. The altar shimmered. The nave was still.

She turned away, back toward the rear of the Church. A bunch of red votive lights on the left of the door, a green emergency exit sign with a silhouette fleeing a fire on top of the door, a bulging dark construction supporting the great organ. Below the organ, a pair of large wooden doors with a sign, *Crypte*. She pushed the doors and the chanting was more audible.

Inside, darkness was nearly complete. Smell was heavy, earthen, old stones, primitive church, ossuary. She tiptoed toward the sound, toward a dark gray void. Stairs. One careful step down. She held on to a metal railing. The staircase curved and the darkness turned reddish. Here and there, thick dark shapes suggested pillars. A few steps down and she had a better idea.

The red glow engulfed all other source of light. Black shapes moved against it.

Then the chanting stopped and all Robyn could hear was her own heartbeat.

No footsteps, no voices, no sign of any activity. She waited seconds that felt like minutes. The shapes were still. The silence, thick.

She took another step down. She barely dared to breathe, and then even that was loud. Another step. Still total silence. Her eyes must have invented the moving shapes, an effect of sheer light; no one was down there, the chanting was a recording, played as a tribute to the dead or to the founders of the abbey or whoever else's bones were in here. She was wasting her time.

She turned around. Her footsteps would thump on the cold stone. Didn't matter.

Then a loud voice burst and she startled so hard she tripped and hit her shin and gasped. Caught herself and sat on the stairs. Took a few deep breaths and tried to sort the baritone harangue echo from the blood pounding her ears. She leaned against the cool stone. The voice continued. She tried to understand what it said and detected approximate Latin mixed with French. "*In nomine domine nostri...*" *In the name of our father...* Close to the liturgy of the Roman Catholic Mass. Not quite, though. "*...ad eum qui laedificat meum..*" The echo scrambled the words. "*...adjutorium nostrum in...*" More echo. Then, definitely not catholic.

"*Domini Inferni, qui regit terram...*" "*Lord of Hell, who reigns on Earth...*"

She didn't know this existed outside of second rate movies or urban legends.

A Black Mass.

She went back down. Her leg jerked awkwardly when there was no more step and the railing ended. She looked up and there was the red glow. And the black shapes. And the voice, down a notch, now a routine oration with occasional audience replies.

How was she going to find GQ? It was so dark she couldn't see her own self. And what would she make of it, if she spotted him? She kept her left hand alongside the wall, for direction and security, and probed with each of her feet before taking a step. You never knew what crypts had in store. Randomly placed sarcophagi, stairs. Poor maintenance and its load of open ossuaries, uncovered wells and other pitfalls. She circled around what seemed to be a large central room, until she reached the farther part to her right, where the ritual was going on. To her left was another opening. She backed into it and watched.

Candlelight isolated the ceremony from the rest of the crypt, too feeble to reach her, strong enough for her to see what was going on.

Rows of wooden benches with about fifteen people seated, their backs to her, faced a small stone altar. Behind the altar, an inverted cross topped by a pentagram hung from the bulky scaffolding supporting the Church's stone structure. Two black torches flanked the altar, doubled by two black candelabra on the table.

Holding the candelabra, lying across the altar, her lush black hair spilled on a crimson cushion, a woman lay naked, her knees spread open toward the inverted cross, her breathing lifting her chest.

The priest was busying himself around the altar, muttering. His long black robe was topped with a pointed hood that continued as a mask, with slits for the eyes. He pulled a board from behind the altar and unfolded it, revealing three panels.

The assembly mumbled, and the priest walked back to the altar. He set the triptych on it, in the curve of the woman's arm, and with his back to the audience, raised both hands and began to speak. He had the tone of a reader, and Robyn assumed he read from the triptych, but she didn't understand a word. The speech was foreign but nothing she had ever heard. There were lots of o's and a's, and syllables were sometimes repeated two or three times… *Like the strange writing of the Voynich manuscript*, she thought. She wished she could see the triptych up close.

He switched to French. "*Frères et soeurs, je vous félicite du mag-*

nifique travail réalisé par votre communauté dans ce pays... Brothers and sisters, I commend you for the beautiful work your community has achieved in this country. The signs of the Roman whore are no longer visible, and her treacherous teachings, despised at last." Against the backdrop of the torches, his uncertain silhouette paced between the first row and the altar. The woman's amber body glowed like a pulse in the shadows.

Oblivious to her, he ranted, "Everywhere, the reign of Our Lord is at work, and His signs are visible." He played with the audience, wheezing and waiting for the sarcastic laughs to die down, continuing with, "I no longer wonder why Our Lord has chosen this nation to reveal his word," silencing the murmurs with an extended hand. "In tribute to your accomplishments, I brought the Black Gospel for you to worship." He pointed to the triptych. "Behold the Word of Our Lord!" he thundered, then grabbed a torch, lighting the triptych, and paced through the audience.

From her dark vantage point, Robyn got a good view of it when he stopped less than thirty feet from her.

The three sheets displayed were yellowish, with green shapes and grayish areas that looked like text around a drawing. She couldn't see much, and she might be biased, but these faded drawings... with text around... And the text he'd been reading, with o's and a's and repetitions... *Voynichese. Definitely. Could it be a copy of the Voynich manuscript? Or some of the missing pages Parker had mentioned?*

"I have a surprise for you," the priest was saying in French. "But first, let us celebrate."

Back behind the altar he raised a crystal glass filled with dark liquid above the naked woman, and lifted his mask just enough to drink from it. Recorded music hummed from somewhere. Classical music, solemn and gloomy. Cello, a low rhythm. Communion, Satanist style. The worshipers were now at the foot of the altar, taking turns drinking from the chalice.

They weren't exactly frightening, Robyn thought. Frighteningly gullible or stupid, maybe. They followed the basics of turning the Catholic ritual upside down. They said their mass close to the dead, in the lower Church. *Suit yourself,* she thought. *But what's with the pages from the Voynich manuscript? Could these people have hurt Sybil?*

She felt anger and frustration rising. "I can't help you with the

Gabriels," Toslav had said to the GQ guy. *Where was GQ, anyway? In the audience? Could he be the priest?*

She'd seen enough. Time to get out of here before they found her. She'd hide somewhere in the street. See if she could spot GQ coming out. Follow him some more.

She took two steps forward, out of the back room. The music would cover the little rustle she might make. To her left, everyone was busy walking to and from the altar. She glanced ahead and her mouth dried up.

Two lights flickered where it should have been pitch dark, and they lit two pointed hoods, slowly moving toward her.

She backed up, her gaze fixed on the lights. She wondered if they'd known from the beginning that she was there, if this was a trap she'd stupidly fallen into. *I have a surprise for you,* the priest had said. It couldn't be. They couldn't be coming for her. They hadn't seen her. She needed to stay still and wait.

She thought of Sybil and her branded body. Of Toslav and his Logonikon. Of GQ and the weirdoes out there and the triptych and the Voynich. She got angry enough to take them all if they jumped on her now.

But she'd hide.

The music was still going on, and louder, it seemed. Screeching violins. Once in the back room, she retreated farther then she had before, until she felt steps, and waited. The two silhouettes carrying the lights materialized ten seconds after her.

Oh. No.

Instead of turning right, toward the priest and the assembly and the horrible music, they turned left. Toward her.

She scrambled back, then felt an alcove, long and low and large enough for a body. A niche holding a sarcophagus. She sat in its middle and eased her shoulders down and inside and stretched her legs on the stone. Flattened herself against the wall. All in one swift, silent motion. She pushed herself as far as she could from the room. Sideways so she would use up less space. So she could better see what was going on. So she could give a nasty kick, too.

The two pointed hoods came up the steps, in a slow, controlled pace. They stopped level with her alcove and put their candles down on the floor. The music stopped for a beat and changed to cellos, more harmonic but gloomier. She prepared her feet for the vicious kicking. And stopped breathing.

The stone was cold and wet and smelled of mushrooms. She squeezed herself against it as much as she could. Then there was a clicking and a rattling. The faint flicker of the candles lit iron rods opposite her alcove. A gate. One of the pointed hoods opened it, and the other one pulled something from his robe.

The beam of a flashlight danced on the gate and beyond. Lit a hole in the wall the size of a cell. Random rocks and earth on the floor. A sarcophagus. The two pulled a metal bar from somewhere. They slid the bar in the sarcophagus and lifted its lid, reached inside and pulled out a heavy plastic bundle four feet long, two feet large.

A third pointed hood joined them and the three marched off, carrying the bundle down the steps, toward the altar.

Robyn breathed. Waited. Gave it some time. Then eased out of her hiding place. She was stiff and wobbly and her T-shirt clung to her back. There were "Oho's and Aah's" coming from the assistance gathered around the altar, hunched over the *surprise*. She took three long strides, her eyes focused on her steps. The cries of awe hushed, and a loud shriek echoed. Robyn kept moving. When she was past the steps, she looked ahead to make sure everyone was busy.

Oh. Fuck.

No more amber woman with lush black hair on the altar. Instead, a young body, naked. Short pale hair. Ashen and stiff.

Maybe fake. Or dead. For as the participants took turns stabbing it in slow, powerful blows, no blood spurted.

When the next hysterical shriek echoed, she ran through the middle room.

Before she could reach the stairs, a strong grip closed on her elbow, a hand pinned her mouth, she was lifted off the floor and pulled into a corner. She kicked back and the grasp winced for a split second.

Then the claw tightened and straight into her ear a whisper said, "Bad timing, love." Two silhouettes, lit by the candles they were holding, were coming down the stairs she was about to take.

Once the silhouettes passed them, the whisper said, "Now." The clasp around her unfastened. Her vision was completely accustomed to darkness. The noise level was high in the crypt. She sped to the stairs.

Three steps up was an acid-reeking mass thumping and rattling down. She had time to see two long legs clad with more chains than fabric, and military style boots. She also made out huge hands, long arms, and longish hair. She crouched and lunged toward the groin and up, and the mass tripped on her hunched back, backflipped as she stood and landed flat with an awful crack and a, "Putain."

She sprang up to the crypt door, flew to the exit and jumped through the scaffolding to where the bike was. Another muffled shriek behind the door. Then came calm footsteps. She got out of the tarped scaffolding and back to the bike.

Her head spun and she felt weak and she threw up in violent jerks, turning away to avoid the bike. She puked again when the image of the body imposed itself on her. She wanted to believe it had been a dummy, but there was something about its appearance, the details of its bony legs, its color, grayish, and its sickly thinness.

A soft laughter filled the night. Against the tarp, GQ was standing with his hands in his pockets, saying, "They're exquisitely eccentric, aren't they?" He threw his head back in a harder laughter. "Were you in there all the time?" He walked toward Robyn, a big smile on his face. He was as Robyn had figured him, in his forties, lean and elegant. He spoke with a British accent. "What did you make of it?" He stopped at a comfortable distance.

"I was looking for answers," Robyn said, wiping her mouth with the back of her hand. "Not sure I got them."

GQ was going to talk when he patted his pocket. Pulled a cell phone. Waited for a beat. Gestured an apology. Listened. "Are you his five million dollar client?" he said.

Robyn straddled the bike. Waited, rocking back and forth on it. What had Toslav meant when he said, "I can't help you with the Gabriels?" Toslav wanted something from her. What did GQ want?

Still on the phone, GQ said, "Call this number back in a couple days," and hung up. He looked around. "Care to have a drink somewhere?"

She did need answers. "I'm staying at hotel La Bastide."

"Blimey," he said without looking the least surprised. "I was there this evening. I'll pick you up in an hour."

10

SHE PEDALED AWAY from the Church, onto the plaza. Now that she was outside, she felt comfortable waiting to see what kind of creeps attended the ceremony. The taste of puke lingered, but everything else was back to normal. Pulse, breathing, relaxed limbs, anger. Below her, along the harbor, traffic was scarce. Across the dark sliver of water, on the north shore, the baroque City Hall was illuminated, as was Fort Saint Jean lining the entrance of the harbor, St Laurent's church above it, and the Vieille Charité. A nice little postcard.

Hushed voices and shadows trickled out from St Victor's abbey.

Her stare still across the harbor, Robyn stood on one pedal to get the bike started and close up on the worshipers. But her foot fell straight down, the chain rattled smoothly, and the bike did the trickling sound of loose clockwork. She looked down. *Shit.*

A bony white hand held the rear wheel off the ground. Up the thin black sleeve a pale girl with heavy makeup was smirking. "Hi there," the girl said in French. Her grip on the wheel was so tight her knuckles were yellow against the white skin and the tremor of her muscles ran through the bike right up to the handlebars.

Robyn answered, "Hi." Looked around.

"There's no one here," the girl said. "It's just you and me." Her smirk hung there for a few seconds then vanished. "I saw you there. Tonight."

"Where?"

The girl jerked the wheel. "Don't even try this." The air was hot. The girl's gaze, two lifeless pools. Robyn shivered.

The girl was saying, "You're almost one of us now, whether you want it or not. Whether *we* want it or not. You were there, you breathed the stifling air, your soul is filled with its energy." Her mouth tensed around the words, her pale lips barely moving as she spat them. "You should be thankful *I* saw you and found you here."

"How 'bout that," Robyn squeezed in. She could probably knock the girl down in five seconds. But then maybe not. There was no telling what brainwashing could do to people.

"Soon you'll feel terribly lonely and desperate," the girl continued. "Because you've been part of things you don't understand. Tonight, tremendous energies have been unleashed, and only those worthy to receive and understand them will be able to channel them." Her gaze wandered up and down Robyn as if to assess her life expectancy.

Robyn was still twisted on the bike, toward the girl, right foot on the ground, left on the pedal, ready to take off.

"There's a part of you that knows." The girl dropped the wheel. "When you're ready, come to me."

Robyn stayed there, wondering how to turn the conversation around to the triptych.

The girl was fumbling in a velvet pouch she wore across her deep purple dress. She scribbled. "When you feel you can't handle it anymore, come to me," she said again, handing the note to Robyn. "My name is Rebecca. I'll be your mentor."

Robyn glanced at the paper, several lines. She tucked it in her pocket. Leaned harder on the handlebars. The bike inched away. She looked at the girl. At her hands that must have stabbed just minutes ago. She was ready to gun the bike or use it as a shield.

The girl looked hurt. "You can thank me later."

Back in her room, Robyn's phone blinked with two new text messages.

The first one made her freeze: *How is your twin?* None of their friends called them twins.

She thought of half a dozen answers. Waste of anger. The number was *unknown*. No one she knew called her with blocked identity. *Tom had good instincts*, she thought. *Sybil needed to be out of here.* Was Toslav the kind of person who'd do that? For the Logonikon? Was

GQ connected to this?

There was also a message from Parker: *Skype?*

She launched a session. Parker's face was bluish but the sound was good. Barely any lag.

He skipped the preliminary niceties. "It could be music sheets, an alternative form of writing, the first computer sheets. But I think you've got yourself a Cardan grille, and I think considering Sybil, you should shoot immediately for Voynich."

"One sec." She kicked her shoes off. "We're talking about that document with holes?"

"You in slow motion?"

She turned the laptop away and took her jeans off. "Shoot."

"'time is it in your part of the world?"

Late. "Refresh my memory. Cardan grille?"

"A sheet with holes owned in duplicate by the author of a coded message and its recipient."

"Right." She grabbed a long, black lace, sleeveless tunic from Sybil's suitcase.

"The author of the message sets the grille on a sheet of paper and writes his message through the holes. Then he removes the grille and fills the sheet with text so as to conceal his message."

"Gotcha. All the recipient needs to do is apply his own grille to hide the filler and reveal the message. Classic." With the laptop safely turned away, she took off her T-shirt and bra. Stretched a little. Brushed her hair. The AC on high felt good. She caressed the goose bumps on her body.

A scratch came from the laptop and Robyn could picture Parker rubbing his three-day stubble. "Problem with that," he said, "is the pattern. Two people use the same grille all the time, their enemy gets some of the messages, they'll see imperfections in the text. Spaces, letters above or below the rest. A pattern is established, and the enemy can build their own Cardan grille and read the next messages."

Robyn saw what he was getting at. "Only way around that is to have a disposable set of grilles. One per message." She unzipped the tunic and slipped it on. It reached the middle of her thighs. "Or one per page, in case of a long document." She fumbled with both hands in her back for the zipper.

"Not quite."

"What do you mean?"

"Lower."

"What?" Her fingers found the zipper.

"There. Wish I could help."

She whipped around. "What the…"

"Bathroom door mirror."

"Why didn't you say something!"

"Don't tell me you didn't know, honey."

"Don't call me honey." She turned the laptop and faced Parker with both hands on her hips.

He had a stupid smile. "Is that legal?"

"No. I should report you."

"The thing you're wearing. That legal?"

"It's called a dress."

"No way."

She turned around and looked for shoes. "There was an old guy at the bank, an antiquarian named Toslav. He wanted to buy the artifact from me. He called it the Logonikon. As in…"

"*Logos* and *nike*. Victory of words…"

"Or victory over words…" She found medium black heels. The strap was a little tight. She bent over.

"Doesn't makes sense," Parker said.

"Course it does. The Logonikon is a decoder…"

"Leopard undies and black lace."

"…and the Voynich is a cryptic manuscript." She tugged on the tunic. "Both are over two hundred pages long, both have some pages folded. On the Logonikon, the holes are sometimes concentrated on one area of the page. On the Voynich, many pages are part drawing, part text.

"Could match, I guess."

"If the Logonikon is the decoding device of the Voynich, and if Sybil's branding is a letter from the Voynich, it could be a threat."

"Or a signature."

"But who and why?"

"Get your leopard ass here and start working on the Voynich, honey."

Rebecca might have some answers. She looked at her note. There was an address, and a time—3am tonight. She thought her options through. Either she went with Rebecca and tried to learn a couple things on a cult that could be responsible for her sister's attack, at the risk of being killed herself. Or she didn't, and she'd never know.

It wasn't Robyn's idea of a choice. She'd go.

But first, GQ. He might have some answers too, and he was one hell of an attractive guy. You had to look at the bright side of things.

"I still have work to do here."

"In that costume?"

"In that dress, you bet."

"Dresses are for ladies, honey."

* * *

Robyn found out GQ's name was Aleister and Aleister didn't think much of the hotel bar. His idea of a drink was behind the old harbor, a cobblestone street, a thick wood door, and a bouncer in a double-breasted suit holding three hundred pounds of fat together.

Inside, there was a sweet smell that could be illegal and drumming seeping through double doors. Black floor, black ceiling, black walls, silver candles and gilded mirrors. Aleister stayed back to talk to the bouncer. A mirror gave out his stare glued to Robyn as she fluffed her hair, the tunic inching up her stretched legs, her back arched, the lace molding her breasts. She gave her hair extra attention.

After two sets of soundproof doors, metal rock screamed. Robyn walked in with Aleister's hand on the small of her back and the music tearing through her solar plexus.

The black room had touches of red—horns on top of the bar, triangles on the floor. The screeching came from a small scene, where a singer-guitarist was sandwiched between a bald drummer with a Rasputin beard and a bass player spurting sweat and spit.

Three women Sybil would have called lethal blonde, stilettos hooked under the barstools and shoulders hunched, threw mean stares at Robyn. A group of flabby guys nipping small glasses in deep armchairs dangled their heads. No one else. Middle of the week crowd.

Through another double set of soundproof doors, a short hallway was guarded by another dark suit with a crew cut who looked vaguely familiar. He limped toward a door to the side. He was maybe two hundred pounds, but athletic. *Like a baseball player, but with a limp.* The guy who'd stepped into Toslav's car when Aleister stepped out, in front of the church. It was him.

He nodded quickly at Aleister and ignored her. Aleister patted his shoulder.

The backroom was a soothing contrast of jazz and old rock, purple and golds, faux fur couches, and a barman in a burgundy tux.

On the right, a cluster of guys in black shirts and serious looks. No other customers.

Aleister led her to the far left, where the seats were really low and the tables small little nothings and all Robyn could do with her long legs was to let them be right there under Aleister's eyes. He took the seat next to hers. Their knees almost touched.

Robyn asked the barman what kind of tequila they served.

"Tezon. Maestro Dobel. Herencia. Trago. Agavero Liqueur. Mezcal."

"Herencia. Reposado?"

"Reposado, yes."

"No salt, no lime."

"Of course not."

Aleister asked about their whiskeys and settled for Brora. "Dry."

The trumpet tried a lazy tune. The bass player had to look at his strings.

Aleister pulled a sleek metal box from his jacket and waved it toward the bartender. Nodded a thank you and asked Robyn if he could smoke. Yes, he could. If she would like a cigarette. She considered the offer for a beat. The brand was Camel Rare. It looked precious. She declined.

He inhaled as if his life depended on it, his charcoal eyes half-closed, lost in the distance.

She let her gaze wander on his profile. High cheekbones, Greek nose, a thin scar that cut through the eyebrow, spared the eye and continued on the cheek. The guy was a walking cliché, part fake, part complicated. She could have looked at him for a long, long time. She said, "So what's with you and Toslav?"

He took another, quick drab and rushed the smoke through his nose. "I'd stay away from the old chap if I were you."

"You guys been to the same business school?"

He chuckled.

"The threat thing," she said. "That a trade mark?"

He shrugged. "Hang around him all you want."

"He said I should visit that church tonight."

"Quite fascinating, isn't it? Did you not say you were looking for answers?"

"I might have said that."

"And what triggered this sudden curiosity?"

"Does it matter?" The answer came out too quickly, so she tilted her head and smiled.

Aleister flicked his cigarette over the ashtray. "Why, yes. I believe it does." He was looking at her as if she were the most important thing to him right now.

Robyn played with her shot, giving the liquor a small twirl, but all she could see were Sybil's hands in the hospital, white and frail, with the forearms blued from the repeat IVs.

"What were you doing there?" she asked.

"Research," he said. "I'll tell you later. You go first."

"It's about getting in control of one's life. Cutting through the BS of the official churches."

"But there's always a triggering event."

"I suppose what happened to my sister a few days ago." Her eyes welled up a little. *Good.* "I don't want to be a victim, and I understand their teaching is about revealing the God within us. Learning to navigate this life and the afterlife."

He nodded slowly and pulled on his cigarette. "What happened to your sister?"

She looked away. Weighed the risk she was taking, one last time. Either he knew, or he didn't. In any case, there was no going back. She looked at him straight in the eye. "She was abducted and nearly killed. Found in a dry well, covered in stones."

"When did that happen?"

"Few days ago"

"Where?"

"Château d'If."

"Who did this?"

"They don't know yet."

He blinked too slightly to tell if it was sympathy or recognition, sat deeper in his chair and said, "And how is she doing?"

"She'll be fine," Robyn said. "If she makes it out of the coma," she lied. She could do with less questions.

He shifted. "And how are you doing?" He finally gave his single malt some attention, playing with the glass under his nose, breathing the vapors in, drinking it straight.

"Oh, me... I just need to cope with this feeling of guilt."

"Guilt? Over what?"

She downed her shot of Tequila, her eyes on Aleister's. "Let's dance."

His hand around hers was cold and strong. He pulled her tight against him and his breath fell in her neck in chilling waves. She was too close to look him in the eye. The band seemed to wake up, or maybe they just needed a purpose. Aleister turned out to be a good enough dancer.

They went without talking for a while. Whatever the music was, Aleister held her tight against him. If she tried to pull back, he pulled her closer, gentle and firm as if to protect her. She finally settled on closing her eyes and trying to just get a feel for the guy.

Behind the musky cologne he smelled of soap and clean laundry. There was also a faint whiff of camp-fire, and that kind of felt good. His left hand was warming up and his breath caressed her neck. His right hand was almost disappointingly steady, only firming on her when need be. He didn't seem to be after anything else than a relaxing evening. Nice change from the diver-types. Nice challenge, too.

He started humming to the music.

She tilted her head toward him. "What was that?"

"Carmina Burana."

"What?"

"They're playing a jazzed version of Carmina Burana."

"I meant, the ceremony..."

"It's absurd..."

"They seemed into it..."

"Jazzing Karl Orff..."

"That stabbing?"

"A crime."

She stiffened. "You mean... the person was alive?"

He looked down at her. "In the church? What a ridiculous idea. Of course not. The stabbing of Care, a scapegoat function. As in primitive societies. The scapegoat is loaded with the troubles of the community. They kill the scapegoat, troubles are gone. Same here."

"But this... Care. It's a human body."

He chuckled. "Oh dear no. It's a well-done imitation. The human shape lets the worshipers identify with the scapegoat. Killing him, they kill what they abhor in themselves. They purify themselves. Am I making sense?"

Bullshit. "Lots of sense."

Robyn eyed the barman. "Mezcal," she told him. "With the worm." Then to Aleister, "How can I join this group? Do I need an introduction? An application form? Any prerequisites?"

He smiled and said, "You have to demonstrate worthiness. Add something to them. Or have a connection with spirits."

When the barman brought her order to the dance floor, she looked at Aleister inches from her through the gold liquid. The worm floated mid-way. She downed the shot. When the worm reached her tongue, she closed her teeth slightly around it, enough to control it, not enough to bite through it. She pursed her lips and with her tongue moved the worm in circles, feeling between her lips its stiffened curb wiggle outside her mouth. She gave Aleister an eye smile, made a sucking sound as she swallowed the worm, and said, "Is raising worms from the dead worthy enough for them?"

His eyelids closed slightly and his gaze went down from her mouth to her neckline as he answered, "I don't know about them but I could show you a couple things. Take you to the next level."

She could sure go to the next level with him, but she was running out of time. She needed answers. She needed to know who wanted the Logonikon bad enough to nearly kill her sister. Toslav didn't want to say. Aleister seemed clueless.

That left Rebecca.

11

AN HOUR LATER Robyn was following Rebecca down steep Metro stairs. A train came in. No one got out. Footsteps hurried behind them, a couple holding hands running down the stairs. They jumped inside the car between the closing doors. In the deep of the night, traffic would get scarce. Robyn wished they had rushed it too. Now they'd have to wait.

The stairs led to the very end of the platform. Rebecca stopped at the bottom of the steps, tilted her head as if listening for something, looked left, looked right. Darted away from the platform, toward the tunnel and ducked under the *No Trespassing* sign. "Move it," she said, as she hurried on the small sidewalk that lined the tunnel.

Before darkness closed in on her Robyn followed. Faint lights at regular intervals gave some kind of bearing. Robyn kept her right hand on the wall and followed the sound of Rebecca's quick footsteps. After a while Rebecca stopped and used her cell phone as a flashlight. She walked a little more, then said, "This way," and seemed to disappear in the wall. Robyn followed inside a corridor. Then Rebecca pulled a metal door, and flicked a switch. Under a pale light bulb, steep stairs ran straight down. Rebecca plunged. Robyn followed. Her pumps slipped and the tight dress didn't make it easier. She kept her eyes on her feet and on the yellow glow of light beneath her, then jumped off the last steps.

The ground had the silent, bouncy feel of earth. The air felt scarce and cold. Water dripped somewhere. She turned around. Then jumped back.

Hundreds of skulls were staring at her, neatly lined, forming walls of empty grins.

Rebecca vanished across the small room and down a corridor, still not talking, still acting as if she was trying to lose her. Robyn caught up with her and glanced right and left. The walls were made of rows of skulls tight against each other. The three-foot space between each row was artfully filled with bones—little round protrusions that looked like stones. Every inch of wall was covered. And the brownish color mingled with that of the floor and ceiling. Robyn's hair tingled a little and her shoulders tightened as she followed Rebecca again. *Stupid,* she thought. *They're dead and harmless. I'm just worn out.*

Rebecca led her under a skull-lined lintel into a larger room. There, a few privileged skulls had earned the distinction of space around them and epigraphs. Music seeped from further ahead, where Rebecca was rushing. Another room, another corridor. Then a large room filled with people in plainclothes. And some in black gowns and pointed hats.

Everyone was standing in small groups, movement was limited to social mingling. Speech level was cocktail party loud, with the occasional burst of laughter. Then the lights went on and off several times, and silence fell. The black gowns, three in all, assembled in the back of the room. The plainclothes distanced themselves and withdrew toward where Robyn and Rebecca were standing, lining the walls in a tight row, a foot from the skulls.

Now that there was some kind of order Robyn had a better view of the room. It was circular, about forty feet in diameter, its walls entirely lined with skulls up to about seven feet, where they curved inwards enough to become the ceiling.

The door behind Robyn's back was the only one in the room. Someone shut it. The lights went off for good.

A flicker in the back of the room, then another and more. Candles, on a small marble table Robyn hadn't noticed in the crowd. A gong sounded and the three priests lined the table. The one in the middle held a triptych and presented it to the assembly.

Same triptych, or an exact copy, of the one she'd seen earlier in the crypt. She was closer to it now than she had been in the crypt, and what she saw displayed was either a very good copy of excerpts of the Voynich manuscript, or simply some of its missing pages.

She craned her neck to get a better view. Rebecca shot her a dirty look, then smiled, tight-lipped.

Robyn ignored her. She wondered how these pages got there. She wondered if she had locked herself with the group who had attacked Sybil. If this was the cult the gendarme had alluded to.

The priest spoke English. "Oh mighty and terrible Lord of Darkness, we present you with this sacrifice. May you accept it on behalf of this assembly, upon whom you have set your mark."

The research put together by Parker mentioned a theory according to which the Voynich would be a liturgical ritual for the Cathari. If she remembered correctly, the Cathari, persecuted in France in the Middle Ages, had practiced a dualistic religion. They believed in God and Satan as antagonistic gods. And they believed in rejecting the material realm to free oneself from Satan.

She didn't know what the cult here was about, but it certainly was not Cathari.

What did the Voynich mean to them?

Suddenly a strong hand pinned a thick tissue on her mouth and nose. The smell brought her instantly to Sybil's hospital room.

"May we prosper under your protection, for the fulfillment of our desires," the priest was saying.

Her limbs were limp and she felt nauseous. Top and bottom scrambled.

"We praise and honor Thee, Lucifer, and thee, Beelzebub…"

Someone pulled her dress off. She wanted to scream and kick but her will stayed trapped. She felt lifted and saw the keystone and knew they were putting her on the table. A priest materialized before her. Their eyes locked. Then his gaze went down her body, slow and intense. There was chanting of some sort. Faces around her, people moving in a circle that encompassed her and the priest. She was too weak to think but lucid enough to realize what was happening. The priest held a small knife and made a circling movement toward her solar plexus. The knife came back up and she was still alive. He was grinning at her, wetting his lips. Her eyelids were getting heavier. She fought against oblivion.

Before she passed out, the priest was pulled away and Aleister appeared above her, a crease of genuine worry between his eyebrows.

He made angry movements with his hands and covered Robyn with her dress. He picked her up in his arms. She allowed her eyes to close.

* * *

The caress of a finger along her naked leg pulled her slowly from her dreams. She felt the tingling start at her toes, then make its way up her calf. The finger stretched the leopard undies up to the hip, then let go. As she felt the fabric slide down she observed herself thinking, *Ladies don't wear leopard thongs*, then she thought, *Go to hell, Parker, I'm busy*, all the while knowing that Parker was part of her dream, and that the hands now playing with her body were real. And good at what they were doing. They settled on her hips, paused for a moment, cupped the bones and pulled her slightly off the bed. She was light and flexible, and her waist curved steeply up. Eyes closed, she pictured her perfectly shaped navel, round and tight. She imagined the lust in her lover's eyes, whoever he was that night, and just the thought of it doubled her rising pleasure. She felt him lean over and lick her. She shivered. He growled and ran his tongue up her body, slowly. She moved a little.

"You slutty little bitch," he mumbled. "I know you're awake."

She tried to open her eyes but couldn't. He pulled off and grabbed her full and firm breasts, almost hurting her. She sensed the heat of his body over hers, then his hard kiss on her neck. He pinched her hardened nipples, and still she couldn't open her eyes. She still couldn't picture his face, still couldn't remember where she had picked him up. She didn't even know where she was—all she could tell was that she wasn't on her boat. When he reached between her thighs and stroked her, breathing hard, her pleasure augmented and she became more alert. When his tongue ran back down she was able to peak through her eyelids. A pale green canopy closed her bed, a gilded mirror topped a small console, pink ribbons fluffed around a small window. *Where the hell am I? Keep going, keep going. Keep going!*

"Don't you hate this decoration?" The guy was sitting up, but she couldn't open her eyes enough to see him. Then he said, "I was planning on doing that wild little thing, Rebecca, in here."

She blinked and looked around.

"This is everything I hate, delicacy, preciousness, classical culture. Which is why I booked this suite. Fuck it."

She focused on him and felt a bolt of fear in her body before she realized who she was looking at.

"Told you you were awake," Aleister said. "Now get dressed, if you please." He pointed to her lace dress on a Louis XVI armchair. "I'll prepare tea."

She was dizzy and battling a headache, on top of frustrated and angry with herself. The dress had a short tear below her breast. The previous night's events came back to memory.

When she entered the living room he smiled. "You are a very brave woman." He showed her the couch. He was busy behind a kitchen counter. Dawn was breaking.

"What business did you have following me last night?" she said.

"I saved you twice."

"That's once too many."

"I shall keep that in mind."

"There won't be a next time."

"Let's hope not."

She felt her cheeks flare with anger. "Who are you, Mister…"

"…Barton. But do keep calling me Aleister. Please."

"What were you doing with Toslav?"

"I'm helping him out. Temporarily."

"In what quality?"

"He and I go way back. He asked me to use my connections. He needed information on a potential client I am doing business with right now."

"You're in business with that cult."

"I'm a music producer and event organizer. Whoever wants the best death metal concert calls me. And I work for whoever will pay me. Business."

"What info did Toslav want?"

"He has a client for the Logonikon. After what happened to your sister, he asked me to look into that cult."

"He knew about Sybil?"

"Of course."

"Why didn't he go to the police?"

"And tell them what?"

She stared into space. His confidence was unnerving.

"What did they do to me?" she asked after a while.

"I admire your courage. Others are usually hysterical or prostrate when they come back. If they come back." He looked up at her. "They did not have time to do anything to you. Although I must say, you looked positively magnificent on the altar, your skin glowing under the candle lights. The perfect sacrificial object." He sighed. "You were under just a few minutes. It was just a little prank."

He moved a heavy candelabrum from the coffee table to the dining table to make room for the tray. "Milk? Sugar?" He sat next to her on the couch.

She straightened herself and the dress inched higher on her thighs. "A little prank? Not sure the police would think so."

He laughed. "The police would love to know what business you had participating in an array of unlawful activities." He poured the tea and pushed a cup in front of her. "After what happened to your sister."

"Are they Cathari?"

"The Cathari were massacred centuries ago."

"They worship the missing pages of the Voynich manuscript. They would want the Logonikon."

"Or not," he said.

"I see…What if it turned out to be some medieval cookbook, right? That would be embarrassing."

A nervous tick took hold of his eyebrow.

I'm on to something, Robyn thought. *The Logonikon could mean the end of the cult.* She drowned her tea in milk and sugar and forced herself to drink it. "If I sell, it won't be through Toslav."

"No?"

"I have a firm offer from a serious buyer."

The eyebrow tick again. "I hope you don't play poker, Robyn. You don't handle bluff very well."

"Beinecke Library," she said. "You'd be surprised at the amount they offered."

The tick vanished completely. He cracked a wide grin and stared at the tear in her dress. "You're a very brave girl, Robyn." He pushed a strand of hair behind her ear.

She jerked back a little but didn't resist him. She felt her lips part but no answer came.

He leaned towards her. "Look at you, all mellowing, like clay ready to be worked." He ran his finger from her hairline to her neck. "I thought we had something going, last night at the club."

She glanced up at him. "We did."

"Any chance to salvage that?"

She tilted her head. "Slight."

"I never apologize, but I'll make an exception."

"I didn't ask for an apology."

He inched closer. "I should have told you I worked with Doryan Toslav. I would be honored to help you."

"I guess that will do."

Robyn savored his warm hand on her nape and his kisses down her neck.

She unbuttoned his shirt and ran her hand down. He lifted her off the couch in one easy motion, and she felt his muscles harden. He carried her to the bed. A thick vein beat between his eyes. She let her gaze slide down his unbuttoned shirt to his charcoal slacks hanging low on his hips, and his black leather belt with a tiny silver skull on it. He leaned over her. His breath was accelerating. He took her chin and forced her gaze back up. Closed his eyes and kissed her. His mouth was soft and his tongue strong. This is good, she thought, and there's nothing like pillow talk.

She ran a hand down his back and felt him shiver. She unbuttoned his pants, caught a glimpse of black underwear, slid her hand inside soft fabric and began stroking him. He stopped kissing her, growled and stayed there above her, his gaze on her mouth, the vein between his eyes turning purple. She played with him for a while, savoring her power, until he forced her hand away by pulling the dress off, over her head. His eyes were bulging. He grabbed her by the waist and carried her to the dining table and took one step away from her. She grabbed his wrist to pull him back on her, but he shook her grasp off and lit the candelabrum. Then he pulled her to the edge of the table and took her standing up, fast and urgent. She tried to hold his hips but he threw her hands over her head and said, "Grab the edge of the table and stay like that." She did. It made her arch and feel him better. Flickers of wax soiled the table with every one of his movements. Even overwhelmed by his own needs, he was good, very good. She moaned as he became more powerful, then saw him stand transfixed, still, frozen in pleasure, his eyes shut tight. "More," she whispered, frustrated. He stood still then opened his eyes suddenly and shook his head as if he had passed out. "More," she said again.

He carried her to the bedroom and sat on the easy chair. She slid to the floor and took him in her mouth. Moments later he was ready, and took her standing up again, her waist curved around his arm, her back on the bed. He knew exactly what he was doing and she abandoned herself to him, and when she climaxed he did too, transfixed again in pleasure, his eyes shut, his body a hardened mass.

After a few moments of stillness he opened his eyes, threw himself next to her and fell asleep. She pulled away from him. He had the innocent look of any sleeper. The body of a regular exerciser. And a snake tattooed under his left nipple.

So much for pillow talk.

She stared at the ceiling. Her inner thighs were softly sore.

She was anything but sleepy. And she was not making any progress. She sat up and turned her back to him. His clothes were scattered on the floor, his cell phone within her reach. She glanced over her shoulder. He was breathing regularly, his mouth part open. She leaned over and pressed the call button. A long number, starting with 011844. Foreign. Incoming. She memorized the first digits and put the phone back on the floor.

There was the sound of rumpled sheets and his breathing changed.

She lay back down and rolled against him, awakening him. "Maybe you could help me?" she said.

His time to sit up. "Help you?"

"With what happened to my sister."

He didn't answer, just stood and turned around and looked at her. No cigarette lighting, no tender after moment. He was focused on her breasts, gliding down her waist, stopping on her open legs. He was hard again.

She tried to keep her eyes straight on his. She pulled the sheet up her legs. "Someone mentioned the Cathari," she tried again. He hadn't picked up on that earlier, just said that was centuries ago.

"I was wondering… if you'd know anything?"

He squatted to the bundle of clothes. "The Cathari?" He was limp by the time he stood, holding a shirt.

"Yes. Heretics, back in the twelfth century..."

"You said that earlier," he said. He put his shirt on slowly, one sleeve after the other. "You believe in ghosts?"

"Someone did mention some kind of cult involvement."

"Who?"

"Not sure. The police?"

He stopped buttoning his shirt. "Anything else?"

"No." She pushed the sheet off and sat up next to him. He still had only his shirt on. She slid a hand between his legs.

He hardened a little and shot her a half smile. "Leave some for the others," he said and pulled a pair of black silk briefs from his pants. "And what did the police say?"

Leave some for the others? She grabbed her dress and pulled it on. "They're still going through things."

"About the Cathari. What did they say about the Cathari?"

"I probably got this wrong."

"Why would the Cathari choose your sister for payback?"

I never said payback, she thought. "Never mind."

He stayed silent for a while, then walked toward her. "Are you cross?"

"Not at all."

He laughed silently then grabbed her and fumbled between her legs. "You're always hungry, aren't you?" he said.

The verbal brush had aroused her. She could certainly go for another round with him. "If you're going to have to use your fingers, forget it."

He turned her around, pushed her against the wall and took her from behind, in long strokes. "Never try me, Robyn. Never," he said and accelerated. He pulled her hair back and breathed hard in her ear, then pressed his mouth against her neck, his tongue and teeth competing with his loins for her pleasure, sending shrills through her spine in crescendo waves until she culminated, caught in the maelstrom of sheer physical pleasure, his brutal force and her power over him. When he climaxed she was pinned against the wall and could hardly breathe. His heart, out of control, resonated through her chest, and the rest of his body was hard as stone, still for long seconds.

Then he buttoned up his pants and said, "The Cathari believed in the dual nature of God. Everything material was created by Satan, including the world." As if there had not been any interruption in their conversation. He put his shoes on and started playing with his keys.

She smoothed her dress. Her legs felt weak. "So they're still around," she said.

"From what I've heard, could be."

"That's not what you said earlier."

"A name means nothing. I don't know what the groups who call themselves Cathari now believe in. I just know they're violent. If they did this to your sister, she's lucky to be alive." He put his keys in his pocket and stroked her shoulder. "These people are crazy." Then he said, "They're having a massive get-together next week in the South of France. Les Baux de Provence. There's a valley there that was Dante's inspiration for the Inferno." He ran a finger under her chin. "My company is in charge of the entertainment—the opening concert. Why don't you bring the Logonikon over? Maybe we can figure something out. The document for the name of whoever did this. One week from now. Next Tuesday, in the village of Les Baux."

12

AFTER DINNER, MACK locked himself back in his study. The evening had gone smoothly. The women rattled on and on about the car. Mini Cooper seemed to be Natalie's final choice. European car. Exasperating, but he was not going to argue over that. He suspected she had chosen that car just to test him. No one in their right mind could really want to squeeze in there. And the price…

If peace has a price, expect it to be expensive, he thought.

Back to his number one problem.

His problem had a name and that name was Pritchard.

Pritchard was his boss at the bank, the president of the Federal Reserve Bank of New York, but oddly enough, Pritchard had but a vague idea of what the nuts and bolts of the business were. He was political, he had the right connections in Washington, he was a great speaker, the public loved him, and that justified he held the job. The daily stuff, the dirty work, what kept the machine going—that was the duty of the Macks of the bank.

Mack held a piece of information he had once thought he should merely keep secret and transmit to his successor. But it looked that no, he was going to have to deal with the problem and at some point, share it with his boss and let him make the final decision. After all, politics was his turf, and this problem was political. If the story became public, the consequences would be devastating. Forget the bank. The whole financial system, the nation's credibility were at stake.

Mack didn't even want to begin thinking about the international implications.

But before he brought up the problem to Pritchard, he had to know and understand what had happened at the very beginning. How they had gotten themselves into this mess.

He picked up the translation of Simon's diary and typed the next entry.

July 28, 1914.

Met with Secretary of Treasury McAdoo this evening in the Vander-bilt hotel. He was getting ready to meet with New York bankers to ad-dress the shortage in gold reserves. Despite closing the New York Stock Exchange, the situation is desperate. Frank Vanderlip, Edward Shelton, J.P. Morgan Jr. and the likes were waiting for him but he did grant me a five minute interview, considering I came recommended by T.

Mack paused. When World War I dawned, the European coun-tries funded their military effort by selling their stock in American companies, obtaining dollars in exchange, and redeeming these dol-lars for gold as was their right. The dollar was backed by the gold standard, which meant that anyone with a greenback could demand the equivalent of its value in gold from the American Government. The issue was not that the Europeans, with their massive selling of stocks, would bring the stock exchange down. There were many investors willing to buy and stock values would remain reasonable. The issue was that the European countries would redeem their dol-lars for gold, and the gold reserves of the country at the time were insufficient to meet the demand. If no one did anything about it, the United States would go bankrupt because the Europeans were going to war. The Secretary of Treasury had decided to close the Stock Exchange, but judging from the diary, too late. Mack did not remember the specifics. He just remembered the story from when the US abandoned the gold standard, under Nixon. And from the newspaper clipping he had read earlier.

He continued reading.

The man is thin, with a prominent nose that accentuates the will-power that emanates from him. He has a pragmatic approach to problems, and though he craves preparedness, he is proving he can deal with a crisis. He comes to New York with a favorable a priori; no one here forgot the man who created an underground passenger railroad under the Hudson River, between Manhattan and New Jersey.

He was impressed by my proposition—how could he not?—and our meeting lasted for a quarter of an hour.

He told me how J.P. Morgan Jr. had opposed his decision to close the New York Stock Exchange.

"There is no risk of the stocks losing value," J.P. Morgan Jr. had said. "Shorts are like hungry dogs, waiting for the stocks to be on the market. Let the European markets close. We'll be open. Business as usual."

"How much gold in the vaults of our banks?" McAdoo had finally asked. "About a billion dollars' worth."

McAdoo told me he knew the answer, of course, but needed to tame the young banker. "And the Europeans own four billion dollars worth of American stocks," he had answered. "Let them sell one quarter of that. Then let them take full advantage of the gold standard. Unlike them, we are not at war. We have no reason to suspend it. What happens next?" He paused. Morgan knew exactly what he was getting at, but McAdoo needed to word it nonetheless. "They walk to our bank tellers, redeem their greenbacks for gold bars. We're wiped clean of all our gold, and our banks can no longer honor their obligations."

Morgan had stayed quiet.

"I have been appointed to organize the Federal Reserve System," McAdoo had said. "I need time, and in that time I will not sit and watch our banking system fail." That was what he had told Morgan, and he was repeating it to me. "We are too big to fail," he said several times.

Clearly, my proposition did not meet his ideals, but it solved his problems.

Mack closed his eyes. How did his grandfather use to put it? *Great men are principled but pragmatic.* The first time he heard that was just after he'd seen his father drown a litter of kittens, holding the burlap bag under water until it stopped wiggling. He must have been five or six. He cried. These were his grandpa's words of comfort, and they came handy more than once.

His father had also used the words when, terminally ill, he'd written to his son. Mack found the letter waiting for him in his college mailbox when he returned from the funeral. Only then did he understand why his mother had asked him, when he left, to *Please take this rifle out of my sight*. No one told him about his father's last moments. He figured it out for himself, and never spoke a word about it to anyone. The rifle was in his office now, and Mack still felt proud of his father for not putting an unnecessary burden on his mother. He didn't care that suicide was morally wrong. He just understood. *Great men are principled but pragmatic*. Maybe if his daughter didn't have such an easy life, she'd turn out alright. Or maybe if he'd had a son instead of a girl, the tradition of hard work ethic would have been passed along naturally. Or maybe it was the East Coast that was to blame. That made him think of the last time he saw his father, just before leaving for college. The old man shook his hand with some sort of awkward emotion and said, "Study hard, but remember you don't build anything on books." Mack buried the memory.

A feeling of kinship with McAdoo lingered. More than ever, Mack felt the Fed was his responsibility.

The page of the translation was blank after that, as was the page of the diary. In the diary, another newspaper clipping was stuck between the pages.

Mack lowered his desk lamp again and read a clipping from the New York Times dated July 29, 1914. The article developed two pieces of information.

One, the US government was able to meet any demand of gold. Yes, the shipments of gold abroad were still closely monitored, but they no longer affected the Treasury's capacity to face its obligations. *Well well*, Mack thought. *July 28, 1914, we're close to bankruptcy if the European countries keep selling their US stocks and redeeming the proceeds for gold. The next day, the problem's gone.*

The Treasurer cited several reasons. *Rather, one huge undisclosable reason*, Mack thought. A reason that even Simon thought better than to put clearly in writing in his diary. But that Mack had been told about when he was appointed at the New York Fed. He was just seeing the other aspect of the story, and the puzzle was falling into place.

The second piece of information Mack got out of the article was the Treasurer's adamant refusal to give any details about government gold movements and the resorting to coins versus gold bars. He didn't care to discuss that, the article stated.

Of course you don't, Mack thought. In just hours the gold situation in the United States had gone from worrisome to perfectly under control. Thanks to the mysterious Henri Simon. The economy would go back to normal, as long as everything was kept quiet. It seemed the press got the message.

Now, one century later, someone else would have to get the message.

13

ROBYN CAUGHT A taxi from Aleister's hotel to hers. Another bright day starting. Another day through hell, the way things were going. She walked through the hallway in her torn black lace dress, ignored the receptionist, ignored the stares of the crowd in the hallway. Straight to the elevator, then straight to the shower.

She was wrapping herself in a robe when her phone rang.

Unknown number. She took a deep breath and picked up.

A guy, saying he was Tom's friend, calling about some code. The four last lines.

"What time is it for you?" Robyn asked.

"I can't disclose that." The voice was somewhat pissed, somewhat embarrassed. "Here's the message. It's Latin letters really translating into Ancient Greek, then arranged in a Vigenère code. Piece of cake." He read out loud and slowly, signaling the change in lines.

"Drafted by Simon and Nutzer, s.j.
For the power of the twelve American cities
And the glory of the Dragon
To be sheltered in Marseilles, April 1912."

Robyn finished scribbling and had him repeat.

"Don't know what s.j. stands for," the guy said. "Sorry."

"Society of Jesus. Jesuits."

"If you say so," the guy said.

"Any key in there to decipher a document?"

"Nada," the guy said. Then, before hanging up, "Tell Tom I said hi."

Where the hell is Tom? Robyn thought.

"What do you say," she asked Parker. She'd just skyped him. She needed him to bounce ideas around.

He was in bed, holding his laptop too close, his webcamed face distorted. Eight a.m. in France, 2 a.m. his time. He mumbled.

"First off," she said, "the date. 1912. Forget Bacon. Forget everything. It's the year Voynich bought it from–guess who? Some Jesuits in Italy. I can't figure out why the American cities. But here's where it gets better." She began pacing the room. "All the stuff ever written on the Voynich mentions one line on the back of the manuscript. One single line that was supposed to hide the code. The guy said there was no such thing as a key to deciphering the Voynich in those lines, by the way. It's as if all these people out there, arguing about the meaning of the Voynich, wanted to make sure no one outside their circle knew about the four lines. So they hid them. Didn't print them out. Didn't even report their existence."

"Well," Parker said, scratching his scalp. "You have what looks like a Cardan grille. You have the Voynich. Come back and let's figure this out." He yawned.

"I have a facsimile of the Voynich."

"And?"

"And none of the pages are in scale."

"Shit. Can't use the Cardan Grille."

"That's right. I need the real thing."

"What are you waiting for?"

"An answer from Beinecke. I'm waiting to hear back from the curator."

"How long's it gonna be?"

"I don't know."

"What excuse you come up with?"

"My thesis. I'm still officially working on it."

"The greed versus creed thing?"

When Greed meets Creed. She didn't think he would have cared enough to remember. She smiled and logged off. She needed to press César, at the bank, for answers.

She slipped into one of Sybil's dresses again, this time a button-down, and gave her make-up extra care. Slipped on some sandals, stuffed ID and cash in a tote bag and left the room.

The bank opened in half-an-hour.

She'd walk it.

What did not make sense was timing. If the Voynich was a Cathari document, it had to be close to a thousand years old. Yet the last four lines had the date 1912. And the mention of America. Could it be a late addition to the manuscript? Two Jesuit priests scribbling something on the back of an old manuscript? It didn't work. The graphic style of the last four lines was different from the rest of the manuscript, but not radically. It was the same hand, making an annotation.

And then there was the content of the four lines. The twelve American cities, the Empire of the Dragon. The Jesuits. What did that have to do with the Cathari?

There were some links, however.

The Jesuits had had a strong missionary presence in China, the Empire of the Dragon. In general and throughout history, they had been persecuted because of their immense knowledge and concentration of brilliant minds. When it came to their action in China, the Roman Catholic Church reproached them the liberties they took with the official dogma and liturgy.

They had proven to be independent minds.

They could have deliberately decided to salvage a heretic text they had come upon, just for the beauty of it. Supposing they had discovered a decaying liturgical manual for the Endura Rite of the Cathari, they could have copied it.

But then, why no mention of the Cathari on the back page?

Why the twelve American cities?

And what was the link with China?

* * *

César's office was small but its sleek furniture and absence of clutter gave it an air of quiet efficiency. A black bookcase displayed decorative items and the picture of a sturdy woman smiling feebly to the camera, two toddlers at her side. The wife and kids, Robyn assumed.

César twirled a pencil. "As the beneficiary of the deposit, and not its direct owner, you are not allowed access to any information," he said. He focused on the pencil for a while, then looked up. "Our rules are very strict. For your own protection."

There we go again. "Monsieur César, I am not the person you saw last Friday."

He raised his eyebrows. Twirled the pencil back and forth on the table where it made a rattling sound. Scrutinized her, top to bottom.

She crossed her legs. The button-down linen dress was on the tight side and it parted high on her thigh. "My name is Robyn Gabriel. Sybil is my twin."

César cleared his throat. "Well, you did catch a breach in security. Congratulations. But you are on file too. The two of you have access to the vault. There was no wrongdoing on our part. Although I admit we should have asked for identity —"

"That's not my point. Sybil was attacked. Brutally attacked. She was thrown alive in a well and the well was then filled with stones." Tears built up in Robyn's throat. She clipped her lips and shut her eyes a few seconds. "Shortly after she came here," she said. "It has everything to do with the account. What's in the vault makes no sense to me. I need more."

César ran a hand through his hair, his eyes locked on his pencil.

She fired. "Monsieur César, believe me, I understand the privacy rules. I treasure your craftsmanship. It's wonderful to have our most prized possessions in the hands of a man like you."

César's eyes lifted slowly, not yet on hers.

"Please," she sighed. "I only need to know who opened the vault account and when. We could do this very swiftly, just a quick glance at your archives, no one would ever know." She slipped a finger under her neckline, right where his gaze had finally settled.

His eyes shut briefly and he shook his head. He pulled a sheet of paper, slid it to her and rolled the pencil across the table. "Gaston Fabre," he said. "He's the bank's living memory. If there's anything worth knowing he will tell you." He spelled out an address and while she wrote, stood and walked behind her chair.

She took her time writing, then leaned against the back of the chair. "You're sure there's nothing you can tell me?"

"No. And you'll need to empty the vault by tonight. They'll be here first thing in the morning with the search warrant."

She stood and turned around to face him. Very close. "One last thing," she said.

"Yes?"

"What was Toslav doing at the bank?"

"Toslav?"

"The mummy."

"Right," he chuckled. "He said you had an appointment."

"Here?"

He shrugged. "Yes. Is something wrong?"

"Is this customary—having appointments on your premises?"

"We are a private bank. We accommodate our clients as best we can."

"Toslav must be a big client."

"He's not our client. You are."

"But you seemed to know him."

"I do. He's a local character. But he can't afford our keeping fees."

Keeping fees? "I see," she said.

14

THE STAIRCASE SMELLED of dirt and sweat. Robyn felt for the light switch. A bare bulb cast a feeble glow. She took a look at the elevator and went for the stairs. On the third floor she stopped and wiped her brow, then pressed an old doorbell under a small brass plaque labeled FABRE in bold letters.

There was scuffling. "J'arrive." *I'm coming.* A woman's voice. "Who is this?"

Robyn buttoned up her dress. "Monsieur Gaston Fabre, s'il vous plait," she said.

"What do you want?" The woman again.

A man's voice burst in the background, far away but loud enough. "Who cares what she wants? Open up! It's not like I have that many visits …"

The door clicked and rattled and finally opened with a squeak. A stick-thin woman in her sixties with a polyester apron assessed Robyn top to bottom, waved her toward the room on the right and locked the door.

The shutters were closed and kept the living room in penumbra. The room smelled of dried lavender and waxed floors. A fan hummed from a corner. There were two bulging shapes that were couches and a larger bulging shape on one couch that was Fabre.

Robyn introduced herself. Fabre extended his soft moist hand without standing up and invited her to sit across from him. He wasn't big; he was monstrously huge. Not fat; out of proportion. Blown up to a sphere filling the whole couch with a pair of intelligent eyes in constant movement. A gigantic humpty dumpty.

She sat at the edge of the couch. The shutters and windows were closed against the heat, Fabre explained. The woman came back with three tall glasses, a pitcher of water, a bowl of ice cubes and a bottle of Ricard on a plastic tray.

She poured the pastis, then the water, then added the ice cubes. "What do you want from my brother?" she asked, handing her a glass and sitting next to her.

Robyn stared into the fast melting ice and cleared her throat, then looked at Fabre. "I recently ... came into possession of a safe deposit box at the Banque des Deux Rives. I need some information to make sense of its content." She caught Fabre and his sister exchanging glances. "Unfortunately, the bank wasn't able to provide that information. They referred me to you." She took a sip of the cool liquorice drink, then another.

Fabre's sister shook her head. "They have some nerve."

Fabre lifted a rotund hand. "That's all right, Madeleine." He spoke in a soft soprano. "What information were you after?" he asked Robyn.

"Very basic," Robyn said. "Who opened the account and when, to begin with. Monsieur César mentioned some rules…"

The smell of burning onions crept from the kitchen and Madeleine hurried to it.

"César…," Fabre mumbled, and from a box he had on his lap popped something into his mouth. "In tune with the younger generation. Bunch of slugs. They don't know which way is up so they sit on their brains. Total waste of gray matter." He took a sip of pastis and finally looked at Robyn. "I don't mean you, of course." Another go at the box, a swift chewing. "You're …" His hands were trying to shape something out of thin air, as if words weren't available. "Did he make a pass at you? No?" He shook his head. "See what I mean? Totally hopeless."

Robyn couldn't help chuckling and said, "I think he's married."

"What's that got to do with it?" Fabre spread his hands apart, his eyes firmly on Robyn's. "It's just a matter of acknowledging beauty. Simple good manners." He winked at Robyn and laughed silently, the tremor shaking his whole body. "It's tough to be old and fat," he said, "but it's sad to be young and stupid." He shook his head. "Close the door, please," he said, his eyes on the kitchen where Madeleine was busying herself. "And pour us some more Pastis, if you don't mind."

Robyn pulled the door and reached for the ice cubes.

"Ice cubes come last," Fabre interrupted. "It kills the flavor to pour the Pastis directly on the ice."

When Robyn sat back and they were both cooling their hands around their glasses, he said, "I'm assuming your safe deposit box was in the middle storage room. The glass one." He nodded slowly when Robyn confirmed. "Of course."

Robyn waited.

"All I know is rumors. I was never more than a bank teller. But I worked there forty-eight years. Started wiping floors at seventeen, and moved my way up to bank teller." His eyes kept fluttering all around the room. "The social ladders in this country are very tough to climb, you know, so that was quite an accomplishment. And it's a very long time in the same place. I got to know a lot of stuff."

Robyn waited for the stuff, wondering if it would help her.

"But it's the first time I see someone come for the middle storage room." He scratched his cheek slowly, his gaze on Robyn.

The banging of pots and pans came from the kitchen, followed by sizzling and a deep-fry smell. Fabre gulped a couple white lozenges from the box.

"What's so special about the middle storage room?" Robyn asked.

"Apart from its controlled atmosphere? I don't know," Fabre said, managing to talk with his mouth full without sounding rude, "but rumor had it it was the bank's whole purpose. Protecting whatever was stored in those safes. All the rest—the other safes, the regular accounts and activities, were just décor, money-making at best. But there was some kind of house legend that said the bank was originally built according to certain specifications because of these things that needed storage. And then the founder died, and his secret with him."

He took a long sip of pastis. The ice cubes had long melted.

"Who was the founder?" Robyn asked.

"Charles Langlois. A merchant and ship owner. Did business worldwide."

"Do you think he had things to hide? Things he brought back from far away countries?"

Fabre shrugged. "You probably know more than I do. You saw what's in one of those safes." He took a long look at her. "I'm sorry, would you like a Calisson?" he asked, handing the box to Robyn.

"No thanks," Robyn said.

Fabre popped two or three in his mouth. "Don't like them?"

"Not sure I ever had any."

"You'd remember. It's a sort of almond-honey paste coated with sugar," he said. "Delicious. Make sure you have some before you leave."

She stirred her glass, wondering if she should get him back on track. She looked toward the window, but the shutters blocked the view, allowing only soft light through their angled slits.

The couch cracked as Fabre shifted his weight. "Now, why did you come?"

"As I said —"

"I want to know why you need help. All the time I worked at the bank I had this image of the owners of the middle storage safes to be super-powerful people who'd come one day to retrieve dinosaur eggs or a piece of the True Cross or who knows what. Certainly not a clueless woman who needed to ask her way to her possessions." Another Calisson in the mouth, then, "Why don't you help me help you? What kind of problem brought you my way?"

Robyn thought about Sybil and the prospect of returning to Florida without an answer; she thought about César and Toslav; she glanced at the life-long bank-teller with intelligent eyes and just enough money to sustain his cravings.

She summed up Sybil's attack, including the branding, gave him an idea of their father's letter and told him the vault contained a book with holes and the name and address of Sainte-Thérèse monastery. She left out her findings about the Voynich and the strong possibility that the document was its decoder. She wanted his untainted input.

"And you believe what happened to your sister is related to that book with holes."

She nodded.

"There's something else, right?"

She did not answer.

"I'd better not know, I suppose." He scratched his cheek again. "I don't know about that book with holes, Miss Gabriel," he said, "but I can tell you Sainte Thérèse monastery is where the last living member of the Langlois family—the bank owners—ended up. I can't think of her name now." He frowned. "Story was she'd been with a German officer. People wanted to shave her head during the Liberation, but they couldn't find her. All her family was killed in the Allied forces' bombing of the city — some people said it wasn't the bombs that killed them. She fled to the monastery." He shook his head, then lifted his hand and gestured with his thumb and finger barely spread apart. "The bank was this close to becoming State-owned in retaliation," he said, "but it didn't happen. Some kind of protection, way up there."

There was a roll of thunder. The room plunged into darkness.

"So, if the bank is private," Robyn said, "who does it belong to now?"

Fabre shrugged. "Different people, I think. We never saw them." He lifted an eyebrow. "Why don't you open the shutters and roll that table over to me."

Robyn looked to where he was pointing. On a hospital-type table shaped to fit over a bed stood a Dell computer — the kind that did its job without being impressive. She pushed the shutters open. Thick raindrops fell at intervals. The temperature was dropping. She rolled the table over. It was low, the screen at Fabre's eye-level. He grabbed the keypad and squeezed it on his lap, fired the computer and started to type.

Ten seconds later they were logged on to an official-looking website.

"Registre du Commerce et des Sociétés," he explained. "It will give us access to the bank's public records."

Forty seconds later they hit a dead end. The bank belonged to a trust with an address in Italy—Borgo S. Spirito 4 in Rome. The trust didn't appear in any public-record system.

The kitchen door opened and Madeleine filled the frame in a whiff of fried onion and wrath. "You're overstaying your welcome."

"It's okay," Fabre said to Robyn. "Don't pay attention to her." He turned toward his sister. "How's the boeuf bourguignon coming?"

Madeleine marched to the computer and unplugged it.

"Madeleine, you're ruining the memory."

"It's your memory that's ruined, my friend. Don't you know what they do to priers?

* * *

From Fabre's Robyn walked down to the harbor. It was time to face the hard part: seeing where Sybil had been found. The boat rides to Château d'If were canceled "due to weather conditions." She looked up at the blue sky. The thunderstorm had moved away. She kept walking on the quay, away from the throngs of tourists.

Then she found what she needed. A guy in his early thirties, sipping a beer in a tender boat. She snapped the top button of her dress open, counted a wad of bills, and went straight to him, a big smile on her face.

The guy's name was Philippe and he had nothing to do with his day. Two minutes later she was sitting on the Zodiac's fat black floater, gripping onto a hard handle. The tender was half-flying over the narrow strip between the city and the Island of If, leaping off the waving sea, bumping on swells rolling in from the storm somewhere way south. The bow was raised high above sea level. Robyn's hair was swept in wild tangles. Droplets of sea water and tears washed her cheeks. The vibration of the boat resonated through her spine. Every now and then they hit the surface hard, sending a flash through Robyn's body.

The boat slowed, the high pitch turning into a bass, and its bow lowered. A small harbor appeared, with an empty docking area. There was a sign with bold red letters.

"The castle is closed to visitors," Philippe said, "but if you really want to go I can drop you off."

"Do you know why it's closed?" Robyn asked.

He shrugged. "There's been some accident, I heard. The place was full of gendarmes and paramedics a couple days ago. Maybe that's it. I don't know."

The boat was rocking gently on the waves. "Do you still want to go?" Philippe asked.

Accident. "Yes."

He swerved the boat along the dock. She steadied herself against the floater and jumped ashore, then looked up.

"Straight up," Philippe said. "You can't miss it. I'll be right here." He reached into a cooler and opened a beer can.

15

ROBYN CLIMBED UP the flight of stairs carved in the rock. The sun was way up in the sky, a vertical blade of heat bouncing off her shoulders and skull. She walked with her gaze on her body's short shade, glancing up at intervals, squinting at the bright stones.

The stairs ended on an open space enclosed in walls and covered in flagstone, a sort of terrace. To the right was a row of small rooms with iron bars and a covered pathway leading inside the castle.

And right in front of her, a gate.

It squealed open. She stopped in the middle of the flagstone terrace. A trail of soil led to the castle, through the covered pathway. She followed it. The inside was dark and cool. The sound of shuffling came through.

She got to a small cell behind thick walls. A man in a navy blue uniform was sweeping dust toward a pile of stones. A cigarette dangled from the corner of his mouth. Ashes fell on the pile of stones. The pile of stones was next to a large hole in the ground. The man looked up at Robyn. Startled. Dropped his gaze to the hole. Frowned. Looked up again.

"Je suis la sœur," Robyn said. *I'm the sister.* Her voice came out coarse. Her hands were a little shaky. Her mouth was dry and her throat ached. She took two careful steps toward the hole as if treading there might hurt Sybil. Blood pulsed wildly in her ears. She looked into the hole. The dry well.

Three feet wide, six feet deep. Its bottom, lit by a spot lamp right above it, was filled with stones. She held onto the wall and the hardness of it made her shiver. She looked at the pile of stones next to the well, each one a weapon. She was on the verge of implosion.

The man brought two shaky fingers to his cigarette, pulled one long stroke and exhaled through his nostrils. He lifted a foot, pressed the butt against his sole and stuffed it in his shirt pocket.

Then he took his cap off and scratched his head. "There is no respect for anything anymore," he said in French. The cap was navy blue with a gold embroidery, *Guide*. "It's not my job, but I'll do it. Someone has to clean up this place." He pointed to a stone bench. "Why don't you sit down?" he said. He stank of sweat and cheap cigarette but had a warm, rocky voice. She remembered what the gendarme had said about him. Crazy. He didn't seem crazy to her. "Would you like some time alone?"

"No," Robyn said. "Thank you." She glanced at the bench. Her feet would not move. She braced herself and stroked her arms, unable to get her eyes off the hole. "So that's where they found her?"

He put the broom against the wall. "That's where I found her, yes," he said and right away she felt some kind of intimacy between them. "When I did my morning check I noticed the stone that covers this well was sort of upraised."

She looked at where he was pointing. Next to the stack of rocks was a large round stone, carved at the edges to fit the well, with a metal ring sealed in the middle.

He toyed with his cap. "The stone is sculpted to close the well seamlessly," he said with a movement of his hand suggesting the flat floor. "I noticed it was sticking out and I knew at once something was wrong." He did a clicking sound with his mouth, pulled out a tooth pick and started working through the dark stumps that filled his mouth haphazardly.

He said he had managed to lift the stone and found the well full of rocks. He'd pulled out a few. "Then one of them was all tangled with hair. Wouldn't come up, either." He shook his head slowly. His baby blue eyes filled with tears. "Never seen anything like it in my whole life…"

There was a long silence.

Robyn was both attracted to and repelled by the well and the pile of stones. Her skull ached, her chest constricted. She felt dizzy. "Why would anyone do that to Sybil?" she said, almost to herself. "She didn't know anyone here–been here just a few days."

He cleared his throat. "You know these cells here were used for heretics–Protestants." He bit on his toothpick some more.

Robyn stayed silent, and he continued. "You know what they did to another set of heretics back in the twelfth century? The Cathari?"

The Cathari.

She did not answer.

He was shuffling his feet, as if wondering whether he should go on.

She was thinking the Cathari, a dim flicker in the history of religions, couldn't keep coming up by chance. What would his input be?

He quit shuffling his feet.

"What did they do to the Cathari?" she finally said, to get him going.

The question loomed until he finally answered, "Well, there were all sorts of horrors. A favorite was to take a prominent Cathar, throw him or her in a well, preferably dry, and fill the well with stones, to cause suffocation and finish the job. The fall usually would not kill, only hurt enough to have the Cathar screaming through the whole ordeal. Then the screams would be muffled by the stones. Then they'd finally stop and the crusaders would tell the population to ponder the lesson."

Robyn felt nauseous. She leaned against the cool wall.

"Your sister did not go through that," he said, matter-of-factly. "The wells I'm talking about were much deeper."

He broke the toothpick in two and put the pieces in his shirt pocket with the cigarette butt. "I told the gendarmes, but …" He shrugged, turned around and mumbled, "Just a thought."

It couldn't be just a thought. "What made you think of the Cathari?" Robyn said before he reached the door.

He turned around. "The pine processionary caterpillar."

"The…?" She started thinking the gendarme may have been right about him.

He came back and started talking with more agitation, using his hands. "I pulled the stones one by one, as fast as I could," he said. "When the head and face were cleared, I thought that if there was a chance she was still alive, at least now she could breathe." He shook his hands. "I don't know much about medicine. Her cheeks were cold but not… not like a dead person's." He said that with an apology in his voice. His hands calmed down. "I ran to the emergency phone and called for help," he continued, "and when I came back, there was a large pine processionary caterpillar crawling out of the well." He went quiet for a beat. "That's what started me thinking."

An awkward silence followed, broken by an engine roaring in the distance. *I should go back to the boat*, Robyn thought. Philippe must be wondering how much longer she would be. She didn't want him to lose patience. She couldn't risk staying stuck here with the guide. "I should go," she finally said.

"You don't get it," the guide said. "The caterpillar." His eyes searched hers. It was not the gaze of a crazy man.

"I don't," she admitted.

"There are no pine processionary caterpillars in the summer."

"Right," she said. She glanced at her watch. *Five minutes.*

"Except," he said, his finger pointing up, "that because of the climate change, there are some time shifts now. The insects are all screwed up by this climate change, and in some places they've been crawling down the trees in the summer."

"I see."

"But not here."

"No?" *Four minutes.*

"Not on this island." He shook his head. "No pine trees here. I checked the few bushes we have, just to be thorough. Just in case caterpillars had built nests in there. Nothing."

"It could have been on one of those stones they threw on her."

"The caterpillar?"

"Yes."

He looked at her with indulgence and said, "This sort of caterpillar lives in large colonies that build very distinctive nests on pine trees. Like big cotton balls? I'm sure you've seen them."

An engine again in the distance, maybe two. "Right." Two minutes.

He looked at her. "You still don't get it, do you?"

"No."

"This means your sister was somewhere very particular, some place where the caterpillars, which normally develop in the winter time and are out in spring, operated a time shift. And she was in this place long enough for the caterpillar to somehow get entangled in her hair or her clothes. A pine forest. One of the rare pine forests where caterpillars operated a time shift."

He was beginning to make sense, but how exactly she couldn't tell yet. "And?" she said.

"And she was brought here for a reason." He raised his eyebrows as if to make a point. "Why here? The access is difficult, they could have been caught, they were not aiming at ditching the body away— sorry to offend you, but had she been dead, she would have smelled sooner rather than later in this heat. There are visitors here every day." He spread his hands. "It's as if they were looking for the body to be found. So that got me thinking." He paused for effect. "Why here? Why bury her in the Château d'If as if to make sure she would be found? What kind of statement were they trying to make?" He paused again, then he asked, "What is the first thing that comes to mind when you mention the Château d'If?"

"The Count of Monte Cristo," Robyn said.

"Theme?"

"Revenge."

He nodded. "There you go." He hammered his words. "Revenge. They brought her here because they wanted to state that they acted out of revenge."

Revenge. Aleister had slipped and mentioned payback. The guide had her full attention now.

"Now the well. That was less obvious, but I knew for sure I had come across a torture like that."

"Come across?"

"I studied History." He looked down at his feet, a little embarrassed. "Long time ago."

"I see," she said. It was all still a little blurry for her, but he was on some line of reasoning that deserved exploring.

"It hit me in the middle of the night. The Cathari. That was a torture inflicted to Cathari. The message here is, *We're doing this as revenge against what was done to the Cathari.*"

He was finally making sense. "Did you tell this to the gendarmes?" she said.

He shrugged and left without a word.

She stayed a long time in the tiny cell, not touching anything, not even sitting on the bench. The guide seemed to have vanished for good. She squatted next to the hole, tried to picture her sister in there, the suffocation, the anguish. Finally she touched a stone, then lifted it, turned it around. Put it back down. *Clunk*. She took another one, then another, and another. Each one had hurt Sybil. Some were heavy. A lot were small and sharp. A couple rolled as she dropped them. The noise shot through her spine.

She was looking for answers, but only hurting herself.

She stood and walked to the door of the cell and before she made it outside the sunlight was dimmed. Two bulging silhouettes blocked the door.

One of them was dangling handcuffs. "You are under arrest."

16

THERE HAD BEEN no sign of the guide or of Philippe and his tender boat. Robyn had no idea what she had done wrong. Trespassing? That couldn't justify the handcuffs. They cut through her skin and with her hands in her back she couldn't steady herself. She bounced off the hard seat of the boat, unable to hold on to anything, but tightly squeezed between two police officers, a man with hairy hands and a fat woman. Her tote bag was taken from her. The ride was roughened by growing waves. The storm was making its way back toward the shoreline. The boat finally edged along the quay of the old harbor, toward the entrance, far from downtown.

She was shoved into a car that wheezed through a couple narrow streets lining a cathedral. Walked into a crumbling building two centuries old. Stumbled down stinky steps. Taken to a cell.

The heavy policewoman removed her handcuffs. "A poil."

Robyn didn't understand.

"Take all your clothes off."

"I'm an American citizen," Robyn said. "I demand that my government be informed."

The cop rolled her eyes. She pulled on a pair of surgeon gloves and started patting Robyn up her bare legs. Robyn shrieked and pulled back.

"Du renfort," the cop called out.

Her male teammate came over.

"Where's Safira?" she asked in French.

"Not her shift," he answered.

"Ah shit, that'll do. Grab her."

The cop with hairy hands grabbed Robyn's wrists. The woman spread Robyn's legs apart until she couldn't move. The rubbered hands patted every crease, under the bra, under the arms, squeezing the waist, then back between the legs. Then the man pulled her wrists down to her feet and the rubbered finger searched her anus. Robyn gaped but no sound came out.

"She's clean," the cop said. They left and locked the cell.

Robyn slid on the floor, braced her arms around herself and stayed curled up for a while.

Then the thought of Sybil forced her upright. She straightened her hair and her dress. Tried to make sense of things and couldn't.

* * *

The sun was low when she climbed up the stairs from the cells, handcuffs back on. This time her escort was a young athletic female cop.

"I'm an American citizen. I demand assistance from my government," Robyn said to her.

The cop smirked, pushing her down a hallway, through a door, into an office, on a metal chair. The cop left the office.

Robyn was sitting next to a desk piled high with heaps of files. On the other side of the desk and the files stood a man in his tired fifties who didn't bother to introduce himself. He was tall and large by European standards, with a crew cut and blue eyes.

Robyn's hands were still handcuffed behind her back, forcing her to sit on the edge of the chair. "I'm an American –"

"Shut up," the man said calmly in English. He was pale, with red blotches on his neck. He lowered his voice, and spoke between clenched teeth. "Listen carefully. Your sister mixed with the wrong crowd. Happens all the time. Forget about who did this. There's no way to know." His accent was not local. Not French. Not even European.

His accent was Mid-West polished with Ivy League.

Robyn shivered.

He walked around the desk and shoved a stack of files to the side. Sat on the cleared space and the desk cracked. He bent toward Robyn and whispered. "Now, your sister came to retrieve a document.

Please understand this document was in the unlawful possession of your father.» He articulated every word as if drilling a simple concept into a hazy mind. "It is the ownership of the United States Government. You have until tomorrow evening to bring it to the Consulate General." His eyes were as menacing as his speech was soft.

Robyn shivered again and hoped it did not show.

A faint knock on the door and the athletic female cop came in with Robyn's tote bag. She unlocked the handcuffs, gave Robyn her bag and looked at the man. "Monsieur le Consul, our apologies. Overly zealous officers. There won't even be a record of her trespassing." She winked. "She's all yours, we've never seen her."

The consul. What was going on?

"We appreciate your understanding," the consul was saying. He wrapped an arm around Robyn and pushed her toward the door. "Oh." He froze. "The seizure," he added as an afterthought.

"Right," the cop said. "Let me get it. Gendarmerie finally relinquished it. Wasn't easy, believe me." She went down the hallway. The consul's arm was heavy on Robyn's shoulder but she didn't attempt to shake it off. The cop's footsteps muffled down and stopped. There was some metal door screeching open and shut. The thump of something stamped, once, twice. Footsteps and the cop came back with a thin blue file under her arm. The consul extended his hand.

She handed it to Robyn.

Robyn stuffed it in her bag and zipped the bag closed. The cop was watching. The consul's arm tensed around her, but that was it.

Robyn thought about kicking him off and shouting for help. Then she thought about the body search and what the cop had said. *She's all yours, we've never seen her.* With a wink.

They went down the stairs, the consul on her left, into a parking and drop-off area. Thunder rolled in the distance. The consul pointed to the left. "My car is this way," he said, voice civil, tone polished. His right arm nudging her closer. "You are in possession of stolen artifacts," he hissed. "Give them over and we'll forget about everything. Don't, and there's nothing I can do to help you."

There were a few uniformed cops in the courtyard, and a taxi coming in from the back, to Robyn's right. The taxi slowed and looped in front of them and prepared to stop. The consul hesitated. Robyn slowed down. He pulled tighter. The taxi stopped in front of them.

The back door opened. A lawyer, just out the courthouse with his black robe wrapped around his arm, jumped out. His gaze locked on Robyn's. He seemed to hesitate, then held the taxi's door open for her.

"Merci," she said to the consul, "et au revoir." She tried to shrug him off but his fingers dug into her arm.

The lawyer looked puzzled.

She shrugged harder.

The lawyer frowned.

The consul let go.

She jumped in the taxi, shut and locked the door. "Hotel La Bastide," she said. "Vite." The taxi spun away.

The file contained two sheets of paper. One had the address of the Banque des Deux-Rives. It was typed. And the other was in her father's handwriting: Monastère Sainte-Thérèse, La Sainte-Baume.

Same as in the vault.

The vault.

César had said to empty it by tonight, and he wasn't joking.

She leaned over and gave the taxi driver the address of the bank.

The cell phone blinked. New message. She opened it.

It was a picture. Robyn's heartbeat paused. She zoomed in, her fingers trembling. It was Sybil, gagged. There was a newspaper on her chest. Robyn zoomed some more. New York Times. She zoomed and scrolled to the date. Today.

Her ears buzzed. She called Sybil's phone. It rang and rang and went to voice mail.

She called Tom's phone. Voice mail, direct.

She went back to the incoming messages. The message was from Unknown Number. She opened it again. There was a short message under the picture.

Not a word to the police or to anyone, or she is dead. Continue what you are doing and wait for instructions.

She looked out the taxi window, her heart pounding. *Don't panic,* she thought.

17

MACK TYPED THE translations until dawn, hoping for more, but copying only religious considerations. At five he showered and prepared strong coffee. At six he drove to the office.

From seven to ten he read reports, memoranda, spreadsheets and drafts of regulations, and made hand-written notes in narrow margins. At ten he snapped at his intercom to let his secretary know he was officially in.

The rest of the day was spent working conference rooms and hallways and phones. He never held outside meetings if he could. Waste of time. Waste of power. Waste of turf advantage.

The overall atmosphere at the New York Fed was hushed to the point of feeling outworldly. It culminated in the beautiful dining room complete with Maitre d' and emblazoned silverware. Over time, it had brushed on Mack. At work, he usually voiced dissent or recommendations with a polish that outsiders could mistake for weakness or hypocrisy. But today he was on edge, and he didn't give a fuck. He went through the motions with the subtlety of a pit-bull, the back of his mind polluted with one thing: Barton, and how to get *him* to do his damn job. He was having dinner with him tonight. Two a.m.

He left the office at six, walked a couple of blocks to get a beer and clear his mind.

He got home around seven-thirty. No kitchen activity. He went straight upstairs. Natalie's door was shut, with light seeping under. He paused on the landing. He felt suddenly tired of putting *all* the fires out. There was so much a man could do. At the same time, seeing what his own daughter was turning into… he couldn't even find the word. He marched into his bedroom.

The TV was blasting. Elaine was propped on several pillows, wrapped in a yellow robe, her thin hair around pink rolls, her purple toenails spread apart by tissue. There was a dirty plate on her night-stand, and a can of diet coke. She worded "hello" and focused back on her favorite soap. He remembered then. *Pizza night.*

He took a shower. At eight he was ready. Still way too early. Barton had said two a.m. *It must be at one of his clubs*, he thought. The address meant nothing to him.

He'd been up for close to forty hours now, working throughout the previous night on the diary. He fixed himself a gin and dozed in front of the living-room TV.

Five hours later he was staring through a taxi's window at wrought-iron gates with the sign "Green-Wood cemetery" on top. The address was right, so this had to be it. And it kind of figured that the freak would invite him here. Mack pulled three twenties and waited for change.

The driver slipped the bills in a pouch, zipped the pouch and pumped the gas pedal. He looked at Mack in his rearview mirror. "Everything all right?" he asked.

Mack stepped out without answering. No point arguing. He shut the door in a firm but controlled gesture, accompanying it care-fully all the way, not just slamming it. And looking at the cab too, but seeing only the distorted reflection of the cemetery in the window, shades of black against the void of the glass, with the shining streaks of the fence and the shadows of the trees darker than the sky. The night was stuffy and the street deserted and when the cab was gone he could hear himself breathe. Two a.m. around a cemetery in the dead of summer.

The gates were partly open, just enough for a man to fit through. No lights in here, but a torch somewhere in the distance, to the left and slightly up, flickering as if it were appearing and disappearing behind bushes. Which it was, as he found out when he took the winding blacktop alley in the general direction of the light, relying on the glow of a big reddish moon to keep his step on track.

The park smelled of freshly cut grass and something sweet. He could almost enjoy the walk and the prospect of the upcoming meeting. He was going to whip the weirdo's ass, for sure. Didn't know yet what he'd been up to in France, but he was going to show him who's boss.

There were white square shadows propped against the trees—small houses with pillars. Mausoleums, that's what they were. Above-ground interment. He should probably start thinking about what he wanted for himself and the family when he was dead. He'd add that at the bottom of his to-do list.

After a last curve the torch appeared unhindered twenty yards away, with a blazing flame that fed on some kind of gasoline, if the smell was anything to judge by. Same as in Bohemian Grove, a sure Barton touch. Mack stood in the glow. The cemetery had become some kind of black hole around him. All he could see was himself.

He'd broken his rule of never conducting business outside his turf, but if Barton thought his Halloween setting was going to unsteady him, he was greatly mistaken.

He turned around, peering through the shadows but failing to see anything. Just making himself seen as if this were some mob meeting where the other guys would want to be sure he was clean. There were no telling sounds, nothing distinctly human, only flurries and rustles. Underbrush animal life. "Hello? Anybody there?" he finally said. The thick vegetation killed any echo. He couldn't help snapping his fingers. "Barton?"

A torch lit somewhere deeper into the park and he followed the clue. Right and left, marble crosses gleamed under the moon. A slight breeze picked up, a rustle ran through the high trees.

The light he was aiming at suddenly grew fiercer, then split. Another hundred yards and he was looking at six or eight torches lighting a mausoleum as if it were a suburb house with a party. A short flight of marble stairs led to the entrance, each with an encryption that had to be Latin. The frontispiece was boldly engraved BARTON. A family mausoleum, then. Strange. Barton didn't strike him as a family man.

Mack climbed the stairs two by two. The door was slightly ajar and he paused just long enough to consider whether the skull adorning it might be real or not. Then he pushed the door wide open with the tip of his shoe and brushed past the torches mounting guard on each side.

A heavy smell of cooked wine and foul meat assaulted and

nauseated him. He turned toward the wide open door, caught one last breath of near-pure air, then turned slowly back to the house of the dead. The room he was standing in was small, no more than eight by twelve feet. There was a marble bench against the wall opposite the door and paintings of stiff men and women in Victorian attire all around the room. No windows or other doors, just narrow stairs leading down, with a yellow glow that could pass as inviting. He went down.

In the middle of a room twice as large as the upstairs, surrounded by coffins on marble stands and lit by chandeliers, Barton sat at the high end of a trestle table covered in black linen, gold plates and matching cutlery. He was dressed in some silky black judo suit crossing smartly on his chest, enhancing the patrician features – the slightly bowed nose, the arched eyebrows, the high forefront. He glanced at Mack and silently motioned him to the other end of the table.

Mack didn't feel so self-assured all of a sudden. Something about the place and the smell. He wondered if the smell actually came from the food as he had first assumed or from the coffins. With all the preparations corpses underwent, they shouldn't smell, he hoped. So it had to be the food. Not good either. He tried to rid himself of these thoughts and focus on the job at hand. As long as he needed Barton, it looked like he was going to have to do with his whims. Might as well get used to them.

He took three long steps and sat in a large, antique-looking armchair with twisted wood and fancy tapestries just like the one Barton was sitting in. He was facing an empty plate and a full glass of wine. A silver dish filled with a brownish stew steamed in the middle of the table above a dish warmer, attracting a horde of fluttering insects that looked like moths. He didn't have much of an appetite to begin with, but now he was getting downright queasy.

Barton raised both hands and spoke in a loud voice, but all Mack understood was "Domini Inferno" and "Satanas", a variation from Bohemian Grove probably, where the deity was addressed to in English and sounded more like a natural thing. And although they hadn't yet spoken, Mack pretended to be perfectly fine with that. As if it went without saying that homage had to be paid to Lucifer before any word could decently be uttered between mortals.

When Barton was done Mack repeated the traditional "God is man", rubbed his hands and added "Thank you Barton", as if the help had really outdone themselves today.

Barton looked at him and said, "You do like ortolans, don't you?" Mack had no idea what Barton was talking about, so he said, "Sure."

"I assumed you did. You'll like this recipe even better. The flesh of the birds is left to rot on the carcass, but not quite to the point where it actually falls off the bones. As you would do for game, you know?" He took a large gold spoon and dug deep into the gold dish kept warm by the tea-light candles. With his other hand he motioned for Mack's plate. "Ortolans without bones, what's the point?" he chuckled.

Mack nodded silently like the connoisseur he wished to be. He eyed his glass of wine, wondering when it would be okay to smell it as a pro just to take a break from the stench.

Barton poured a generous serving of lumps in a thick brown sauce. Hesitated, then added some more. Handed the plate back to Mack, who looked at the lumps and couldn't quite make out what they were in the dim light. Barton had said birds. Like quails, probably, but smaller. A few moths followed his plate. He wondered if they were moths after all.

Barton helped himself and rubbed his hands over his own full plate. "Ready?" he said, then grabbed his napkin, bowed his head over his plate, covered it entirely under the napkin and started making crunching noises.

Mack stared at him, trying to understand what was going on. He took his fork and fidgeted in his plate. The foul smell was unbearable. Barton was still hiding under his napkin, so he took a sip of wine. Felt stupid.

Then he figured it was about time to get down to business.

He cleared his throat. "So Barton, how about telling me what's up, huh?" He slugged half his wine.

Barton stayed under his napkin, and his voice came muffled when he asked, "How are the ortolans?" There was some more chewing, then "Make sure you wear that napkin, huh McIntosh? What with all the bones the juice really spurts everywhere."

What had gotten into him when he decided to put Barton on the project? And what was it with Barton calling him McIntosh? He cleared his throat again. "Look, I appreciate your getting out of your way... the meal... the ..." He looked around, trying to find something worthwhile praising, and seeing only coffins. "Everything... but..."

"Don't worry, it's under way," Barton said, suddenly emerging from the linen.

"What?"

"We're securing the deal." He plunged back to his spurting ortolans.

"Oh, good, good." That would never do. He needed facts. Dates. He went at the wine again. "Any tangible prospect?"

Barton lifted a corner of the napkin and reached for his glass, sipped and plunged back. "You sure speak like the fucking banker you are, don't you, McIntosh?" he finally said.

The McIntosh bit was meant to annoy. Mack ignored it. "And like any fucking banker, I like a neat deal, and a timely delivery."

"I've outsourced the contract," Barton dropped.

Mack felt a shot of electricity through his entire body. Barton had lost it, for sure.

"You there?" Barton asked.

"I'm listening."

"Good. I knew you'd understand." It looked like he had finally finished his ortolans or whatever the hell they were, because he took the napkin off his head, wiped his face with it, and rinsed his mouth with wine. "I had the Cathari exercise payback time. It makes them feel good, and I like to keep a good relationship with the competition. And in the mean time, a nice little pressure on the Gabriel girls. I'm sure they got the message."

"Who are these people? What do they know?"

"The Cathari. And they know nothing."

"The Cathari? What kind of freaks are they?"

"Tsk tsk tsk. Let's not get carried away, my friend. Just because you don't understand doesn't mean it doesn't make sense. Quite the contrary, I would say."

"You don't get me that Logonikon with minimal damage, you're toast."

Barton sighed. "I'll grant you this, McIntosh. Outsourcing sucks. I did my own share. Quite fun, actually." He licked his lips. "I'm expecting a return on investment this coming week-end."

"Nothing ... illegal, right?"

"Fuck," Barton guffawed, "like you care!" He slapped his lap like he hadn't heard anything so funny in a long, long time. "Like what *you* do is legal?" He threw himself back in his chair, then cut the laughing and said, "You really think you *are* the law, don't you? Just because you're the bloody Fed?"

Mack cleared his throat and folded his black napkin carefully on the table. "I thought we weren't going to have any of that bullshit, Barton. I thought I'd made that clear." He stroked the napkin flat. "You know what a SAR is? A Suspicious Activity Report?"

Barton's eyes flashed on Mack, then softened. He poured himself another glass of wine. "I am so disappointed in you, McIntosh."

"It's a nasty beast that can freeze your accounts worldwide." He snapped his fingers. "Just like that."

Barton was staring at him as if he'd just had an epiphany. "All the initiation is really lost on you, isn't it?"

"It so happens a dear friend of mine is about to issue SAR's on all your companies, Barton. Looks like your mamma didn't teach you how to wipe your ass properly. You leave trails. You stink."

"Let me ask you a question, McIntosh. What does a twat like you care about the Voynich manuscript or the Logonikon? It's spiritual." He took a long look at Mack, his eyes half-closed. "You wouldn't be stupid enough to fool me, would you, McIntosh? Or am I missing something?"

"He's withholding the procedure for now," Mack continued. "One word from me and you're a goner."

* * *

Robyn looked at Sybil's picture again. She was staring sideways into the camera. She seemed groggy. Probably drugged. Her hair was pulled back in unkempt strands. White fabric covered her mouth in a loose gag. Her face was yellowish. Was it from the old bruises, or was it the picture? She seemed to be wearing a light blue top. Her bare arms showed. The newspaper covered the bottom half of the picture, on her chest.

Robyn zoomed on the sides of the picture. Grey background, like concrete.

She read the message once more. *Not a word to the police or to any-*

one, or she is dead. Continue what you are doing and wait for instructions.
Continue what you are doing. Get the Logonikon… then what?

The door of the bank opened before the taxi came to a full stop. César came out, walked to the driver's window, paid for the fare and told him not to wait.

Robyn followed him inside the bank, down the winding staircase, through the round, submarine-like door and inside the vault. She gave him the key. He retrieved the chest from the safe-deposit box and handed it to her without a word.

Back upstairs the bank was dark. All the metal shutters were pulled tight in front of the glass windows. César lifted a phone, punched two digits and said, "She's ready."

Then he turned to Robyn. "We went through your belongings in your hotel suite," he said. "There didn't seem to be anything of value. You do have your passport with you, right?"

"What do you mean, you went through my things?"

"We're exfiltrating you. If there's anything in your room that you can't live without, we'll retrieve it. But clothes, toiletries, suitcase—all that stays in there, to buy time." He reached inside his jacket and pulled out an envelope. Flipped it open. It was full of cash. Euros and dollars. He handed it to her. "Just in case."

Exfiltrating? She stuffed the thick envelope in her bag. Who were these people?

"We will escort you to the place of your choice. Then the burden will be yours."

A burden, yes. *Continue what you are doing and wait for instructions.* How was she going to secure Sybil's release? Why the hell wasn't Tom around now that she needed him? She was going to get killed, and so would Sybil.

"Time is running out, Ms Gabriel. They're after you."

"Who's they?"

"I have no idea. But they're very powerful. The bank never had such pressure since its foundation in 1914."

1914. Two years after the Voynich was said to be discovered.

César tugged her elbow. "Ms Gabriel, please, this way." He led her down another winding staircase. Identical to the one that led to the vault.

The staircase reached a landing, followed by a corridor that twisted slightly.

César turned around. "Would you like me to carry this?" he said, looking at the chest. "It's heavy. It's a fifteen-minute walk."

She wasn't aware of the weight of the chest, but she handed it over and kept following.

The corridor became a narrowing gut. César stooped. Robyn kept going, the picture of Sybil gagged constantly in her mind, hoping now for another text message that would tell her how to get Sybil back. The newspaper was the New York Times, which meant she was probably in the United States. Was César an accomplice? Did he make up the story about pressure on the bank? Anything was possible. But then, why wouldn't he just kill her now? And why bother with an envelope full of cash?

To entice her to follow.

They reached a metal door. The sound of splashing waves came through, and the smell of iodine. They were at the bottom of a hill that belonged to the bank, next to the sea. It couldn't be easier to dispose of a body here. She started thinking *kick, dive*. She started thinking *how do I keep the Logonikon out of the water*.

He handed the chest to her. "That's it," he said. Now he had his back to her. He unlocked the door and pushed it open.

They were in the deep end of a long cave, with a black strip of sea flapping against the narrow quay. Alongside the quay, a speed cruiser rocked.

Its endless, thin hull was like a dart, interrupted only by a compact cockpit with four large seats. There was a skipper sitting in one of the seats. He glanced at César and the roar of the engines filled the cave.

"Forty-seven Lightning Fountain," César yelled. "The tank is full. You have a range of about three hundred and twenty miles at full speed. It runs with twin Mercury seven hundred engines. You can cover twice the distance if you drop to fifty miles per hour. Tell him where you want to go—Spain or Italy are your only options. Then you're on your own." He shook her hand. "Good luck."

Robyn gave the boat an appreciative look and climbed inside. Maybe this was going to work, after all.

"You can call me Patrick, and I don't want to know your name," the skipper said. "Where are we going?"

"Spain."

César waved goodbye. The metal door slammed behind him.

"What port?" Patrick stood behind the steering wheel, legs apart, shoulders straight.

She dropped in the seat next to him. "I'll tell you in a minute."

He showed her the cabin door. "Get in there and don't come out till I tell you to."

She didn't feel like arguing. She didn't think she was in a position to, or that she had any interest in assessing who was in charge. She went down the few steps to the carpeted, dimly lit luxurious cabin. She sprawled on the white leather couch and pulled her cell phone. Started dialing Tom's number. Then she hung up. César had scared her with all his maneuvers to hide her departure. She wasn't going to ruin the careful planning with a phone call that could be traced or even overheard. She pushed the cabin door.

Patrick motioned her to stay down. Brought the engines to a purr and said, "What do you think you're doing?" The Fountain was at the tip of the cave, edging toward the open sea.

"You have a cell?"

"What?"

"A cell phone. Give me your cell phone."

He reached in his back pocket and said, "Don't come out". He handed her the phone. "You have half an hour before the coastline is comfortably far. You'd better know where you want to go by then." He slammed the door and gunned the engines.

She dialed Tom's number. He didn't pick up. She left him a message, "Call me back at this number. Please." She hoped the phone number was displayed. She lay on the bunk and closed her eyes, the phone in her hands. The heaving waves rocked her. The growling of the engines and the boat smell soothed her.

"Where are we going?" Patrick asked.

She jumped. She must have dozed off. "Rome." She looked at the phone. No message. Checked hers, just in case. Nothing.

"Last time I checked, not in Spain."

"Rome, Italy."

"Last time I checked, not a port."

Asshole. "Ostia."

18

WHEN ROBYN CAME out of the cabin it was still dark but a halo was forming to the East. The Fountain boat was now going a mere thirty knots, she figured. Approaching the coastline.

"You sure you want to go to Ostia?" Patrick said. No hello, not a glance at her. Just a snapped question.

"Of course I'm sure."

He nodded. "Of course you're sure," he said slowly and loud enough to cover the noise of the engine. The Fountain glided toward the string of lights ahead. "Can I ask you a question?" he shouted after a moment.

"Sure."

"What's your final destination?"

She didn't answer. Because he shouldn't have asked; and because she didn't know. She'd spent the short night thinking. Dissected the past four days, calling to memory every little event, every clue. She was frustrated at not being able to visit the monastery their father had indicated. There had to be some answer there, an answer she may not have for a long time. But there was one thing she could do in Rome before going home. And she wasn't going to tell him.

"Because," he said, "Fiumicino is right north of Ostia."

"Fiumicino?"

"The airport."

"Right."

"So?"

She went for the obvious answer. "Fiumicino then, fine." There would be no shortage of taxis there. "How far from the terminal would that be?"

This time he glanced shortly at her. "You can walk it."

An hour later she dropped in the back seat of a battered Peugeot, her nerves shot by three espressos gulped standing up at the bar of a café on the harbor. She'd asked the owner to call a taxi to take her to Rome and settled for his cousin's private car.

"Borgo Santo Spirito Quattro," she said to the cousin, Tino.

He came up with a fare of fifty euros.

"How long?"

Tino pulled a face. Hard to tell. "Forty-five minutes?"

"Tell you what. It's thirty euros, forty minutes, and an extra euro for every minute below forty." She saw him frown in the rearview mirror. "Works?"

He shrugged. "Forty euros and an extra euro like you said."

A jet roared above them, lifting its nose toward the West. "Okay. Forty. Let's get moving."

It was still a little early for morning traffic. The Peugeot darted on the autostrada. They hit the city around eight. If there was something to see, it was lost on Robyn. Tino took the one euro per minute deal seriously. She kept an eye on the time. Transatlantic flights took off in the morning. She hoped she would find a late flight.

She tried to imagine where she was going. This was the address of a trust owning a private bank, so she was probably looking at a mailing address only. A high rise building with offices, a bunch of sleek mailboxes with way more names than rooms in the building. What would she do then?

She didn't even remember the name that had popped up on Fabre's computer. He had typed in the bank's name in the website of some official French register. Accessed the by-laws and financial info. The sole owner of the bank was an acronym with an address in Rome.

Tino was honking his way through the thickening traffic. He swerved between delivery trucks, braked in front of mopeds, rushed through traffic lights of the wrong color. He demonstrated a rich usage of words and gestures of all sorts. Robyn picked up a couple favorites that didn't include any of the vocabulary she had learned.

Finally he raced through a tree-lined street, made a couple sharp turns, and slammed the brakes. "Twenty-eight minutes," he said. "Fifty two euros."

Robyn looked through the window. A stately, nineteenth-century building, several stories high, with large windows high above the street on the first floor and a front door cased by pillars and topped by a statue. "Is this it?" she asked.

"Borgo Santo Spirito, Quattro," he said. He narrowed his gaze and read, "Curia Generalizia".

Not what she expected, but not surprising either. She placed the tote bag on the floor. It was stretched to ripping point around the chest. "Keep this with your life," she said. She showed him a wad of bills. "Wait for me." She snapped the car keys from the contact, jumped out of the car and as she entered the world headquarters of the Society of Jesus, buttoned her dress up.

Ten minutes later she was seated across a priest in civilian clothes with a cross pinned to his grey jacket and some intricate band on his right ring finger. His hair was very short, his eyes without expression behind the metal rimmed glasses. "I shall take your name and file your complaint with our Private Affairs Secretariat," he said. He scribbled on a thick, off-white sheet of paper. Folded the sheet and slid it in an envelope and left it there on the table, crossed his hands and said, "Anything else?"

"Could I have a receipt of my complaint?"

"I'm afraid not."

"Why?"

He straightened in his chair as if the two-minute talk had been a marathon negotiation, took a deep breath and said, "To begin with, we have to verify if this bank is indeed our property." He tilted his head in response to Robyn's rising eyebrows. "You yourself say you don't remember the name of the owner. Allow us to verify."

"The address…"

"…Could be a mistake." He stood. "Then we will cross check your account of the facts with the policies in place in order to determine if there is a possibility of wrongdoing in the handling of your account. After which, you will have to provide us with documentation of said wrongdoing." He was showing her to the door, a smirk on his face.

"Nutzer?"

"I beg your pardon?"

"Does the name Nutzer mean anything to you?" she asked.

"Nothing," he said and walked away.

Tino was in the closed car, sweating. She handed him the keys, and the wad of bills. He started the engine and amped the AC.

"Fiumicino, pronto," she said.

"Harbor?"

"Airport."

"Same deal?"

"Same deal."

She hadn't gotten anything out of the ice-cold priest. But she had one piece to add to the puzzle: the bank that stored the document that started this whole ordeal was owned by Jesuits and built around the time the Voynich was discovered. And no one had tried to kill her yet.

* * *

Mack couldn't get Barton to tell him what had happened in France, and he left Green-Wood cemetery with a bitter taste that had nothing to do with the untouched food. He should have had the upper hand with his brilliant SAR scheme, but Barton always had an edge over him. He couldn't nail it. The guy was a freak, a loser, but Mack had not yet gotten what he wanted from him. But he would.

It was not five in the morning when he got home. The women were still asleep. He went to the kitchen to fix strong coffee. Empty shopping bags were scattered on the floor. The coffee machine started gurgling. He stacked the bags neatly. Then he poured his coffee, no milk, no sugar, in a large insulated travel mug with Traders Do It On The Floor in gold letters, and went straight to his desk. Pulled out the translations, fired up the computer, and started typing with two fingers.

He filled in page after page of religious considerations again, until he got to the date of August 23, 1914.

I sent the key to Charles Langlois today, with a note to safeguard it and the chest with his life, until I or the Curia Generalizia provide him with further orders.

The mention of the Curia Generalizia was only meant to preserve an appearance of normalcy, as they have no idea what happened in China. Given their gross misconceptions of the country, it would have been a mistake to inform them. I alone will keep the coded contract here, and with the decoder on another continent, there is no chance anyone will ever read it. With the departure of my brother in arms Paul Nutzer, I alone will have access to it should need be. I trust that in the next year or so, the contract will have been executed, the loan repaid and the documents unnecessary.

The New York Times ran an amusing article this morning.

The translation ended there. Mack opened the last diary and flipped the pages backward, until he got to the last written page. Two newspaper clippings were nudged in the crease, so thin they didn't add any thickness to the notebook. The largest one was folded and had underlined passages. He flattened it open, leaned back in his chair, mug in one hand, clipping in the other, and read.

An opening on how the American money market had just undergone an unprecedented crisis.

A summary of the war situation in Europe, and how it led European countries to sell their foreign securities for cash, then gold, at a growing pace as the war prospects strengthened.

A demonstration of how this would have battered the economy, leading the American bankers to export gold.

Mack took a sip of lukewarm coffee. The United States were being stripped naked of their gold, and if they could not meet the lawful demand of the European countries, that meant they were bankrupt. *"Amusing article?"* he thought with contempt. *"For all I know, those freaking catholic Jesuits could have been behind the war itself to serve their own twisted interests."* However, the matter had been settled, as was illustrated by the second article inserted by Simon in his late July entry.

The article praised American banks and the Administration of the US Treasury for the handling of the crisis, crediting both for meeting their obligations and bringing the markets back to business as usual. *Henri Simon had played his role too*, Mack thought, *and that was why he found the article amusing.*

The United States had been strengthened by the crisis, the article asserted, comparing the situation to that of 1895, when the country had to borrow gold from the Morgans and the Rothschilds to replenish the legal reserve.

The legal reserve was the minimum amount of gold that the United States was required to own in order to be able to face any demand of gold in exchange for dollars. It was linked to the printing of paper money. Each dollar bill symbolically represented a fraction of US gold, and the US treasury was bound to exchange dollars for gold, at least up to the amount of the legal reserve. If the US gold reserves became dangerously low, not only was the economy doomed, the credibility of the country itself was at stake. *Who knows*, Mack thought, *maybe its existence*. Pre World War I, the United States was not a super power. The European countries were.

The last passage was entirely underlined, and Mack could not believe what he was reading. The article went on to explain that this time, the pressure to meet the demand of gold fell upon private holdings.

In the narrow margin, the hand that had filled the notebook had scribbled in English, *I wonder if anyone will be curious enough to enquire about the sudden stock of private gold*.

No, Mack answered to himself. The United States had been saved by private gold, and no one would ever ask a question.

There was just the smaller clipping left. Two inch by two, it was a miracle it had not fallen off the diary yet. Mack pushed it under the banker's lamp. It was an obituary.

One Henri Simon had been found dead in his hotel room. Cause of death: natural. Date: August 24, 1914.

Mack ran a finger up and down his cheek. "I ain't no private detective," he muttered, "but I know the only damn natural thing about this death is the heart stopped beating."

19

ROBYN'S FLIGHT FROM Rome to Miami was five thousand miles, eleven hours non-stop. Six hours of sleep, five hours of thinking. One security check. No sign of whoever had kidnapped Sybil.

Continue what you're doing, the message had said.

In Miami she rented a car and put the chest in the trunk. Before hitting the highway she pulled into the parking lot of a superstore. She'd been wearing the same dress since the second morning at the bank. After that she'd been to Fabre's, from there to the Château d'If, from Château d'If to jail. Then back to the bank, across the sea in a boat, with a priest in Rome, across the ocean on a plane. All in the same dress.

She didn't know when she'd be back on her boat. She had to plan for several days. That meant one pair of jeans, one pair of shorts, a pack of six white T-shirts, a grey hoodie, a pack of assorted color thongs and navy canvas sneakers. She threw in a soap bar and a deodorant stick, a toothbrush and toothpaste, a hairbrush, mascara, and she was good to go.

On the highway she stopped for gas. There was a food stand inside. She ordered a burger, extra pickles, no cheese. It seemed the right thing to do. It seemed since no one was there to tell her to eat, she had to look out for herself. The first bite settled high in her stomach. It seemed the second would never make it through. There was no third bite.

Back in the car she called Parker. "I'm going to need a decent drink and a bed."

There was the background noise of wind and engines, then Parker saying, "When?"

"Whenever this piece of crap gets me there."

"Where are you?"

"It's a hybrid," she said, pulling a face at the plastic dashboard. "Engine kicks in whenever it wants. Rest of the time, it's like driving a bumper car at the fair. Drifting sensation included. I'm in the everglades, all I know. See you later."

The GPS gave her an initial ETA of 6pm, then started creeping forward to adjust to her speed. But when she hit the outskirts of Tampa shortly after 5, traffic took over, and the ETA kept pushing back.

Then she got a text message, Unknown Number.

In the Voynich manuscript hides our treasure.
Find it, and instructions will follow.
You have six days to complete your mission.
We are watching you. Not a word to anyone or she'd dead.

Something to do at last. Some hope. Some negotiating ground. She looked for the last message, with the picture. It was gone. She scrolled back up, looking for messages from "Unknown Number." Nothing. She shut her phone off, then back on.

The message she had just received was gone as well. As if she'd never gotten it.

Sybil's kidnappers gave her six days to find a treasure supposedly hidden in the Voynich, and she couldn't tell anyone. She would need Parker's help. If she told him about Sybil, would they know? She wouldn't risk it. She'd lie to him, and leverage his help.

By the time she got to Parker's the sky was softening. His apartment was smack in the middle of downtown Tampa. Ybor City. A district with old buildings renovated to look antique and strings of laid-back bars. She parked and checked her phone, just in case. No new message. She set it on *vibrate* and slid it in her back pocket.

Parker had said third floor and the third floor had one door on each side. The door on the right had a wreath and a welcome mat and a name under the doorbell. The door on the left had a miniature camera embedded in the top right corner and no name anywhere.

Robyn went to the left.

The door opened on Parker standing in a tight Buccaneers t-shirt and shorts, with one hand on the knob, one hand pushing his hair back, and half a smile, as if he wasn't sure whether it was okay to be happy. "Good to see you," he finally said. He lifted her bag and glanced at the chest. "We'll take a look at this later," he said.

She nodded. "Good to be here." She really meant it. Wherever Parker lived there was always something cooking, and the smell of fried onions, baked bread, tomato sauce, basil or chocolate cake grabbed you as a welcome and stayed like a farewell long after you left.

He'd moved here recently. The apartment was an open plan with the kitchen area taking half the space and the living room turned into a workplace. An L-shaped desk held three desktop computers. Printers, faxes and radios were neatly aligned. A coffee table disappeared under piles of folders. No armchairs around it. In a corner next to the master bedroom, Parker was setting Robyn's bag on a sofa cleared just for her. Piles of books were stacked on the floor and the flattened upholstery bore straight lines.

She sat at the kitchen counter and wrapped her arms around herself. Parker got busy preparing margaritas. They were quiet. The phone was quiet. Her stomach was a knot.

She watched him fix the drinks. She would need his help to get to the Voynich. *Not a word to anyone or she's dead.* She tried to stop thinking for a while. His hands were calm. Every one of his gestures had a purpose. His fingers were strong in a lean way. His fingernails short, maybe bitten. Hair on the tan skin, but not too much. Not too curly either, or too straight. Just right.

She swiveled quickly around. "So how'd the diving go?" she said, because that's what she would normally worry about.

"Why don't you tell me about your trip. Sybil. And the rest." He handed her a margarita.

They both said "Cheers," out of habit, and took a long draft. "Update first," she insisted. She still needed time.

"Piece-of-Eight and four-real cobs," he answered. "Some jewelry, too. Nothing much, but we're getting there." He put his glass down and heated a large pan of water, then pulled a long white thing out of the fridge and dumped it in the pan. "I have a good feel."

Good. It would be easier to convince him to work with her on something else if all was quiet on the home front. "Any problems with the crew?" Robyn asked.

Parker shrugged. "Na."

"What?" she asked, so he wouldn't suspect her mind was elsewhere.

"Just this Vance. Got a funny feeling about him. Don't take this personally."

Personally? "Which one is Vance?"

Parker took another sip and set his glass on the table, real slow, as if he didn't want it to make any noise. Then he sort of smacked his lips to dry them, squared his eyes on her and said, "The one you were sleeping with."

Vance. The love shots. Last week. A lifetime ago.

"Asian. Large shoulders." Parker's eyes were narrowing.

"Right. The guy from Yale," she said. "What about him?"

He shrugged. "Dunno. Funny feeling, that's all."

Robyn nursed her drink to give him some time. They were childhood friends but he always had a problem talking about her relationships. Or one-night stands. She waited a little, but it seemed he had said everything he wanted to say. *Funny feeling.* She really didn't give a shit.

She started telling him what had happened in France. She looked into her glass most of the time, so she could focus on information and leave out emotion. Focus on what he needed to know to help her and leave out the rest. Parker was a good listener, didn't interrupt, only grunted occasionally. Didn't think anything was outrageous. Just soaked it all up.

Every now and then he turned around to stir whatever was cooking. It smelled like fish. At some point he stood and said, "Keep going" and got busy with milk and flour and spices and olive oil. She summed up her father's letters, the vault and the document. "Why don't you take a look now," she said, standing from her stool and getting the chest from her bag. She pulled the book out. Handed it to him.

He flipped through it while she continued, then put it in the chest without a word. He listened to her while looking at the inside of the chest, the blades and the lock.

She told him that one of Tom's buddies came back with a decoding for the four last lines. That there was a reference to some twelve American cities, and also that in all likelihood it had been written by someone named Nutzer and someone named Simon, both Jesuit, and they had written it *For The Glory Of The Dragon*, maybe in Marseilles, in 1912.

Some things he already knew from the Skype sessions, but she repeated, for clarity, and to sort things out herself as well.

She mentioned the guide's theory about the Cathari, she told him about Toslav's threat, about the American Consul, and finally she told him she left because of French official pressure. She just said pressure. Nothing specific. It was as much as she could tell him, she thought. Everything except Sybil's kidnapping and the messages.

Parker kept grunting.

She told him that she didn't have time to visit the monastery and that she'd like to go with Sybil, if she was still up to it when she'd be better. At that moment her eyes welled up but it was okay to be emotional now, so she let it be. She also told him about the crypt and the catacombs and Aleister but skipped the bed part. She just said he'd been trying to piece things together as well. Last thing she needed was Parker pissed off at her sleeping habits again.

Parker turned the mixing bowl in full swing and its high pitch filled the room. Maybe he was pissed off. Maybe he did sense something was wrong.

What could she do? She finished her drink. Too sweet. Eyed the bottle of tequila. Six days left. Six days being someone's puppet and she sure as hell had no guarantee she'd get Sybil back safe and sound.

Parker pulled another bowl and broke eggs with his left hand and began beating whites with his right. The yolks disappeared. The whites got nice and fluffy. Parker kept beating. Finally he turned the beater off, took another egg, put it on the beaten egg whites, and watching it hold high, said, "Small bubbles make for a stable mousse."

Robyn stayed silent. Most people had some sort of hobby to let out stress. She had karate. Parker had cooking.

He said, "I like to get down to the principles that hold things together."

He asked her to repeat what Tom's friend had said about the four last lines. So she repeated, from memory. The two Jesuits, the American cities, the glory of the Dragon, Marseilles, and the date. April 1912.

"April 1912?"

"Right."

"And when was the Voynich supposedly discovered again?"

"1912."

"Anything you forgot to tell me?"

Yeah, Sybil's kidnapped. She told him about the visit to Fabre's.

"So his sister's scared to death, pretty much. But he didn't have anything to tell you."

"Just that legend about the bank being built to protect whatever was in the middle storage room."

"Right." He threw little balls of dough in boiling oil. Went to the dining table and started typing on one of his computers. "Name of the bank again?"

"Deux-Rives."

He typed. Grunted. Went back to the kitchen, pulled the fritters out. "You like accra?"

She looked at the screen. Same website Fabre had been on.

He put a dish of fritters on the kitchen counter and went back to the computer. He highlighted the trust's address and said, "There's my baby." Opened another website and pasted the address on the search bar. "Bingo." Closed the connection. "The bank is owned by the Jesuits."

"Yep."

"That's it?"

"I went there. To that address."

He stared at her. "You didn't tell me."

"There's been a lot going on." She grabbed the bottle of Tequila and filled her glass.

He threw a fritter in his mouth. "Aren't you eating?"

She gave the fritters a try.

"What else did you forget to tell me?" he said.

"Tastes like the Caribbean," she said.

"What's that supposed to mean?"

"Warm and spicy and like the sea's all around you." She took another fritter.

"Okay." He opened his hands like he was surrendering.

"Let's start with the beginning," she said. "The colophon on the Voynich bears the date April 1912."

"And the bank was built…"

"Inaugurated 1914."

"1912 is a grand year in the history of the Jesuits. The colophon names two Jesuits. The bank belongs to the Jesuits."

Parker liked to get theatrical. So she didn't interrupt.

"1912 is the year the Titanic was sunk," he said.

She poured herself some more Tequila.

Parker raised a hand. "Before you get all upset, listen." He was pacing the kitchen. "You're familiar with the story, right?"

As historian, and then as treasure hunter, Robyn was more than just familiar with the story. But brainstorming was in order, so she said, "Keep going."

"In 1910, seven men representing the Rockefellers, JP Morgan and the Rothschilds met in Jeckyll Island in Georgia to establish the bases of a central bank for the United States. In 1913, the Federal Reserve Act was finally signed. But in 1912—"

"What happened to the Titanic?"

He stopped his pacing. "That's the story. The Morgans were indebted to the Rothschilds. The Rockefellers and the Morgans were engaged in different joint ventures. And the Rothschilds, totally infiltrated by Jesuit laymen, were the bankers of the Society of Jesus, aka the Jesuits.

The power of the Jesuits was so threatening that the Order was banned from several European countries and suppressed by the Vatican in the late 1700s. They're in endless need of money and infiltrate every banking system they can. Until 1973, Switzerland had a constitutional ban on Jesuit presence in the country."

Robyn knew all that. Parker was getting at something, so she didn't interrupt. And while he spoke, she tried to connect what he was saying with Sybil's kidnapping. It made less and less sense.

"The Jesuits have priests," he continued. "And they have laymen who are just as devoted to the Society as the clergy, only nobody knows who they are. They serve the order in whatever position they are. They take an oath binding them until they die, under which they will obey any order given by their master within the Society."

He gulped a fritter. Robyn nodded and said, "Without will or intelligence."

"In 1912," Parker continued, "the Titanic, owned by the White Star Line, a JP Morgan Company, set sail from Southampton. Her captain was Edward Smith, a Jesuit layman. Are you following me?"

Robyn indulged him. "The Jesuits have members obeying blindly. The Morgans own the Titanic, and because the Morgans are indebted to the Rothschilds, who are infiltrated by the Jesuits, the Jesuits exercise their leverage to have one of their men appointed as captain of the Titanic."

"Right. You're pretty sharp, for a woman," he joked. "Father Francis Browne, an Irish Jesuit and Smith's superior, boards the ship in Southampton. He meets privately with Edward Smith –"

"—the captain—" Robyn clarified.

"—The captain," Parker confirmed. "Then Browne is ordered by his own Jesuit Superior to refuse the invitation of a millionaire to pay for his fare for the whole round trip. He has strict orders to disembark at Queenstown. The rest is history: that night, Edward Smith sails the Titanic full speed into the North Atlantic, a route he's travelled for over twenty years. Where he knows there are many icebergs. He ignores eight telegrams ordering him to slow down. *Eight.* When the ship finally hits an iceberg, he deliberately neglects his leadership duties. Doesn't take action. His aide has to press him to give orders to lower the lifeboats."

"You're saying the Jesuits deliberately sunk the Titanic."

"I'm telling you Browne meets with Smith and is ordered to leave the ship immediately. And Smith is a Jesuit layman, sworn into obeying orders blindly. And I'm telling you that very night Smith, best captain for the North Atlantic at that time, makes mistake after mistake." Parker counted on his fingers. "Disregards warnings. Disregards orders to slow. Goes against basic safety rules. Allows half-full life-boats to be lowered. Didn't have enough life-boats to begin with."

"So Browne gave Smith orders," Robyn interrupted.

"And the result is over fifteen hundred deaths."

"JP Morgan had no interest in sinking its own ship. So it had to be about the passengers. Who was on board?" she asked.

"Poor catholic emigrants. Irish, French, Italians."

"They wanted to kill poor Catholics?"

"No. These were the cover-ups. In case clues eventually pointed to the Vatican, their deaths would deflect suspicion."

"So who then?"

Parker smiled briefly again. "Three men. Benjamin Guggenheim, Isador Strauss, John Jacob Astor."

"Okay." She was thinking of a handful of reasons why the Jesuits could want them dead. "And why?"

"They opposed the creation of a central bank in the United States." He let it sink.

Robyn said nothing.

Parker continued. "A US central bank, infiltrated by the Jesuits—they already control Rothschild—would have given the Society access to a bottomless pit of money."

"Keep going."

"A central bank pools the resources of private banks—the money of the customers of the banks, you and me." He was playing with the fritters left in the plate, grouping them all in one neat pile. "The way they sold the idea, was to say: in case one of the banks has problems, the central bank will pour money into it to protect the customers. To keep that bank from going bankrupt." He put a fritter on the side of the plate. "People kinda liked the idea. Back in the day, when you put your money in a bank, if the bank went bankrupt, you could kiss your money goodbye."

Robyn nodded. "So what did these guys think was wrong with a central bank?"

"What's wrong with it, and what Guggenheim, Strauss and Astor opposed, was the fact that private money, earned by hard-working people, would actually be shifted to the government." He put the lone fritter back in the pile and shifted the whole pile to the side of the plate with three fingers like claws. "Like taxes."

"Except taxes are approved by Congress," Robyn said.

"Right. So more like stolen money. The central bank lends money to the government. And all this money can be used however the Government wants. It's totally out of the public's control. The central bank, a private institution, lends money that it sucked from private accounts, to the government. And that's what happened the very year the Fed was chartered. It immediately lent millions of dollars to the government. Billions of today's dollars. With no control."

Robyn wasn't sure she bought the "no control" idea but it didn't really matter. Parker's ideas were sometimes over-the-top. Not subtle enough to cover the whole concept, but they always had the basics covered. "So you're telling me the Jesuits sunk the Titanic to kill three men who opposed the creation of the Fed."

Parker just nodded and locked eyes with her as if he wanted to make sure she really got it.

"And around the same time drafted a cryptic document that ended up getting publicity, while its decoder was hidden," she said.

"That's the part I don't get," Parker said. He finished his margarita. "But you can forget about the Cathari connection. These religious things are usually bullshit. Look for the money is what I always say."

She thought about his Titanic story. About the timing, 1912. About the text message. "There's only one way to know," she said. "Get to the Voynich."

"You mean Yale."

"Right. The Beinecke library."

"The one that sinks into ground in case of a nuclear attack."

"Didn't know that."

"It also cuts the oxygen in case of fire. Saves the books, and kills the researchers."

"Charming."

"How are you going to do this, Robyn? You think you can walk in there, pick up the Voynich manuscript and walk out?"

"I'll steal it."

"There's cameras everywhere."

"It was done before."

Parker sighed. "That was just maps. The guy hid them in his books. Or folder." He rubbed his face.

He was right. The place had three Gutenberg bibles, the Vinland map, the first Shakespeare folios, the Romanov family albums. Every single book or manuscript was priceless. It was a fortress. "Still," she said. "It can be done."

Looking at her, Parker squinted. "I guess you have the next venture all figured out, boss." He started clearing the plates. "What time do you want to head back to the boat?"

"No boat. We're heading North tomorrow evening."

20

THE NEXT MORNING, Robyn saw payoff from her first move to access the Voynich manuscript, when she'd sent an email from France to Beinecke Library.

With a few days to process the information, the librarian in charge knew who she was talking to. "Shelf mark?" the woman asked out of excess formality.

"ms 408".

There was a beat on the line, and a slight sigh. "When would you be coming?"

"Tomorrow."

Another pause, as if she needed to think it through, then, "Okay. Four o'clock."

* * *

Mack was back from a meeting with his staff, and he needed to relax and wake up. Wake up, because the sound of people talking and talking had gotten the better of his lack of sleep. Relax, because these meetings wasted so much time and accomplished so little that his thoughts had drifted to Natalie and her addictions—over-eating, under-eating, over the counter drugs, prescription drugs, plain illegal drugs, doctors, shrinks, and everything else Elaine was probably not telling him about. He felt cheated somewhere, and also powerless. Work usually helped to forget, but not today.

There was not much he could do about his staff, either. He'd hand-picked the best, and they were as good as they were going to get. The Fed didn't pay well. People worked here for prestige. If he told them to cut the BS out of their presentations, they'd find another job the next minute. It was just like at home. There was just so much he could demand, so much he could expect.

His secretary walked in, carrying a silver tray. He felt so worn out he almost asked her how she dealt with her children, but he didn't know if she had children. And if she did, what were her education standards anyway?

Then she said, "Someone from the library called and said the item you requested would be available tomorrow at four p.m." and Mack forgot about staff and children and reached for the Maalox in his drawer.

The library was the Beinecke, the item was the girl.

Later, he'd tell his secretary to cancel the next day's appointments.

Now, he had phone calls to make, a plan to map out, bribes to distribute.

* * *

Robyn and Parker started off by downloading Beinecke's security system. The two likeliest hazards were theft and fire, and they found ample documentation on how the library protected itself. Interviews, minutes of board meetings, contractors websites, press releases, html of technical descriptions meant for industry conferences. It was all there, spilling out of Parker's printer.

Beinecke was a closed stack, meaning its volumes were consulted onsite. Anyone leaving with a document was stealing it. Anyone stuffing it in a bag was stealing it—and damaging it. Theft was tackled with more cameras than for the Superbowl. Every possible angle was covered. "There is no way they are watching the security cameras all the time, and I bet you more than half of them are decoys," Robyn said. "Besides, it's been done before." She was reading from the case of the man who had cut off maps from the rare book reading room and walked out with them. He'd been caught only because he dropped a blade on the floor.

She didn't mention to Parker that there had been a serious increase in security since then. Her face would be on every camera. She'd be tackled by security within minutes. "The idea is to get the Voynich *out* before they catch me."

"I'll generate noise," Parker said, "keep the focus on me. You'll just text me when you have the Voynich, I'll keep the guards busy. Give me five to ten minutes to get everyone excited around me. Then it'll be up to you."

The Voynich was bulky, six by nine inches, two hundred and forty pages. She'd have to hide it on her and walk out unnoticed. She'd take her large tote bag. She'd also pack a phone book to place it in the box holding the Voynich before leaving. Her bag would look heavy coming in, it would look heavy coming out. The box would feel the same to the staff member helping her. This would buy her the thirty seconds she needed to pull this off.

Over coffee she took a look at how Beinecke tackled other hazards.

In case of an earthquake, the building would absorb the shocks through the forty-four hydraulic stilts rooting it to the ground.

In case of a nuclear attack, the stilts would collapse on themselves and the whole building would sink underground.

In case of a fire, a special blend of gas would be immediately discharged, lowering the oxygen concentration enough to impede combustion but not enough to prevent breathing. Because the discharge of gas had to be sudden to stop the fire, the downside was the increase of atmospheric pressure and possible resulting damage to contents. To prevent that, large air vents connected the building directly to the outside, opening and closing at appropriate times during the discharge of gas to lower atmospheric pressure without letting air in.

"Got it," Robyn had said. "We won't need the phone book."

For the next two hours they pored over six blueprints freshly printed and taped together, memorizing the location of the air vents.

"You think this is going to work?" Robyn said for the third time.

Parker made a *maybe, maybe not* face. Then he said, "Real question is, *What's the risk?*"

Never seeing Sybil alive. "Jail. A huge fine. And a permanent ban from all libraries." She folded the six sheets of paper like a map, accordion and then across. "We're not technically going to steal. We'll give the manuscript right back. We're borrowing. And libraries are places where you borrow." She flattened the creases of the folded blueprint between her fingers.

Parker insisted they drove so they wouldn't leave a trace. Given what was happening, he said, no precautions would be too much. *If only you knew,* Robyn thought.

They took the EZ pass and the portable GPS from the car and stuffed them in a kitchen drawer. They squeezed both their cell phones in the kitchen drawer with the EZ pass and the GPS. Parker said they would emit signals showing them as being in Tampa.

He left to buy two go-phones he would pay for with cash.

While he was gone Robyn's phone rang. A long number starting with 334. France. She picked up.

It was the pseudo-shrink from the hospital in Marseilles, and he was trying to locate Sybil's treatment center to transfer them some records.

Robyn tried to think. "What kind of records?" she asked, to buy time. "I got everything when I checked her out."

"Psychological evaluation. For her memory loss. I have drawings of her recurring nightmares. In one she sees hanged women, their feet in buckets, and the rope running from one bucket to another. They seem to be in separate rooms, the rope linking them."

Like the drawings on the Voynich manuscript! Where could Sybil have seen that? What did she know…?

The pseudo-shrink was going on, "And a man with a scarred face and a snake tattoo on his chest."

Robyn's heart pounded. Aleister. She felt nauseous thinking she'd slept with him.

"Hello?" the man said.

"What did the police think?" she asked.

The pseudo-shrink cleared his throat. "Can't hand it to them. Too many ethical issues. When you can, let me know what hospital to send them to."

Robyn hung up and stayed dazed. She didn't know what to process first. That Sybil had known something about the Voynich manuscript. Or that Aleister had molested her. And she didn't know if she was more disgusted by Aleister or by herself.

She called him.

"Love... how are the worms behaving?" he slurred.

"Just tell me where and when Aleister. Stop playing games with me."

"I'll take you anywhere, anytime. Get your sweet ass over and let me show you."

"Goddammit Aleister, if you touch my sister once more, if you send me one more of your fucking text messages, I swear I'll burn your fucking Logonikon."

"Your sister. Right, I confess to the sin of lust with her. Nothing more. Are you jealous? We should try a threesome..."

Her hand squeezed the phone.

"... but messages... I don't know what you're talking about, my dear."

She yelled. "My sister for the Logonikon. Right?"

"Are you in trouble, dear? I haven't the faintest idea what you're talking about."

She slammed the phone on the kitchen counter. The screen cracked, but stayed together.

A chirp. New message.

Another mistake like this and you won't see your sister alive. You do not know us, don't try to outsmart us. Go to Yale and do what you must.

She stuffed the cell phone back in the kitchen drawer. When Parker got back she was still trying to figure out the big picture.

They took César's cash so they would not need to use their credit cards. They entered each other's phone number in the go-phones. Robyn added Sybil's and Tom's.

There was only a slight risk that Robyn's visit to the Beinecke library would be recorded anywhere and connected to any other database. It was a chance they had to take.

They packed a basic change of clothes each. Robyn found a cardboard box in a closet, emptied it and fit the Logonikon into it, then secured the box on the back seat of the Mazda. Parker threw his tool box in the trunk, and some blue coveralls. When night eased down on the street and they were ready to go, Parker said something about setting the alarm in his apartment.

"I need to pee," Robyn said and ran upstairs. She snapped her cell phone from the kitchen drawer before Parker got to the apartment. From the bathroom she took the battery out so it would not emit signal. Then she walked in front of Parker as if nothing, the dismantled cell phone in her pockets, the grey hoodie covering her hips.

From I-75 North she pretended to try to call Sybil from the go-phone, for Parker's benefit. Then she tried Tom. No answer. She wondered if he too was gagged somewhere or if he was on one of his "out of network" missions again. She left a short message telling him about the trip to Yale.

"He doesn't care where we're going," she said.

21

LI MEI CARED very much where she was going. His spy phone software had recorded her call to the Beinecke library while he was still in Hanoi. He caught the first plane out and twenty-six hours later he was standing in the middle of Newark airport's crowd, checking arrivals. Continental from Tampa was expected on time, which meant Vance would come out in half an hour.

He sat at a food court table and dialed Toslav's number one last time. No one picked up. The man was dead. There had never been a doubt in his mind. Who had answered the phone two days ago? Who knew about the deal?

The Gabriel woman hadn't been using her phone either. That one was not much of a chatterbox. Except with this Michael Parker, and they would be together now.

People were talking. People who had no right were moving. Had he been too slow? Had he lost faith in the cause? Had he confused the cause with the journey? He felt he was playing his last card with the sister.

A long time ago, he had been so close. He had gotten a job at the Banque des Deux-Rives. A summer job.

It was about ten years after the missionary Paul Nutzer had died. He had been one of the two felons. He found the nerve to come back to China, not long after the events. Hidden. And he had stayed there until his death in the seventies. It took about ten years for his deathbed confession to be repeated to the Elders. By then it was the eighties and the Triad had been looking for clues for seventy years.

It was in danger of losing its purpose. Its members were now the third generation after the events, and although they did not question what their predecessors had witnessed, they were at a loss as to where to start. Then came the confession.

It gave details and an address and an idea that their mission was going to be long and painful and technical. The Elders didn't mind. They expected long and painful. And they would train Li to be technical.

Li was the right age for college. So he was sent to France. Told to study. Told to research the Banque des Deux Rives, a private bank in the French coastal city of Marseilles, mentioned at length in the confession.

Summer recess in French Universities lasted four months. One third of a year. A lot could happen in a third of a year. He took a summer job at the bank, during his first year. And during his second. And his third. A full year all in all.

Something happened during the third summer. An American by the name of Frank Gabriel and his wife died in a car crash.

The event was like a mini bomb at the bank. Because Frank Gabriel had been inside its vault the day before. Tall, blond, strong. Alive. Now he was pulp at the bottom of a cliff. Dead.

People had a problem incorporating the notion that someone they had seen alive and well, was dead a few hours later. They were also happy they were not the pulp at the bottom of the cliff. They felt important to have been the last ones to see the deceased alive.

These different feelings triggered endless talk. This was something Li had observed more than once, and in any country. Li had not seen the client, so he could not talk, but he rode the gossip wave. Listened to each and every tale about the man.

Because Li Mei did not believe in coincidences. In his world everything had a meaning. The direction in which birds flew while he was making a decision. A leaf on the stream. A cloud. So he gave the American's death a lot of attention. He listened to the gossip. He backtracked the man's visit to France. He found out about a monastery he had visited. He listened to more gossip. In the monastery lived a nun whose family had owned the bank. He listened to more gossip. The nun had been pregnant before being a nun. He did some research.

He found out the man was a geneticist.

He gave this a lot of thought, and kept his conclusions to himself.

He decided that now that the man and his wife were dead, he needed to keep a close eye on the rest of the family. The rest of the family was two daughters, living with the maternal uncle and his family.

Li was pursuing a lot of other paths at that time, and he worked on a tight budget. He had to be creative. He travelled to America and tapped the uncle's phone in Florida, where the girls lived. Nothing happened for years. No sudden flow of money. No move to a large house. No trips abroad. Nothing.

Then college came and the girls split. Double surveillance, double cost. By then he had earned a Ph.D. in the United States, on a scholarship. That was around the time when his mole at the bank, big fat Fabre, was fired.

Fabre called him his friend and Li Mei always sent him a huge box of Godiva chocolates toward the end of the year. Fabre would send a thank you note saying he'd punish himself with the Godiva when his holiday supply of Puyricard chocolates was out. The note always ended with a *Anything I can do, please let me know* type of sentence. So one day Li called and got the conversation rolling on that Frank Gabriel who had died and was there any chance Fabre could glance at his file? Just tell him if his account was still open? Li Mei was running out of funds, and he'd rather know if the Gabriels were out of the game.

Fabre had called back about a week later. Yes, the safe-deposit account was still active. Sybil and Robyn Gabriel were listed as co-beneficiaries.

Then the next year the thank-you note came back with no joke. Fabre had been fired. He couldn't afford the Puyricard chocolates anymore. He was grateful for the Godiva.

Li didn't send anymore chocolates after that. The expense was no longer justified.

Then cell phones were everywhere and his life got much, much simpler. With the right tools and a little time he fine-tuned a program that recorded all conversations between any two given cell phones. It wasn't that complicated.

His main concern was that he might end up overflowed with twin chatter. But it did not happen that way. Not at all. The Gabriel sisters kept their conversations minimal. There was a brush about one of them refusing to lend money to the other.

Li got seriously excited when one of the sisters called the other and read her a posthumous letter left by their father. The letter instructed them to go to Switzerland. The sister in need of money for some underwater treasure hunting said she wasn't going. First he thought that was good news, because it meant they would be on the phone talking about the whole thing all the time. But things went differently. They stopped talking. He tweaked his cell phone spy program to record any conversation to or from any of the twins' cells.

They didn't discuss the trip or the letter on the phone.

Li needed to know what was going on. He hired Toslav to follow Sybil Gabriel, but only in case and after she went to the bank in Marseilles. And he got in touch with Vance.

Vance considered him a protector, and he had been, in a way. Li had helped him get into Yale, for instance. But that was because Li needed a few well-prepared pawns, and Vance was one of them. Nothing more. Li had been particularly proud of his choice when Vance was cherry-picked to enter Skull and Bones, of all places. It was an excellent omen.

Li asked Vance if he could swim.

He could.

He told him to take a couple diving lessons and rush to apply for a job in Tampa.

He did.

Then Li told Vance to tell him if the boss, a woman named Robyn Gabriel, was up to anything else than looking for gold on the bottom of the Gulf of Mexico. He told him to stay close to the woman.

Vance stayed so close to the woman he called Li the minute she left the boat with her sidekick in the middle of the night because of bad news from the sister, somewhere in France. Vance could not remember the name of the city. He had sounded drunk on the phone.

The next morning Li got a visit from Toslav, and a good idea of what had happened.

Vance called again when the sidekick said that the diving was put on hold for a few days.

This meant one of two things. Either she wanted to be at her sister's bedside. Or she was hunting a different treasure. He hoped for the latter.

His hopes were fulfilled by a phone call from the treasure hunter to her friend Michael Parker, during which the Voynich manuscript was extensively discussed. This meant they were ahead of the game. Anyone else would have panicked. But Li had trained himself to think differently. He considered a problem was not a problem unless it had a solution, and he kept in mind that every setback was a victory in the making.

With these two principles guiding his thinking, he devised a plan that appropriately used the enemy's force.

He got the historian turned treasure hunter to work for him. It only took the kidnapping of her sister by a mobster triad. The triad gave him seven days to pay. He gave the woman six days to deliver. He was a man of honor. He'd pay the triad and he'd free the woman, if her sister did the job right.

When another automatically recorded conversation between Robyn Gabriel and a librarian at Beinecke library confirmed ms 408, aka the Voynich manuscript, would be at her disposal the next day, 4 pm, Li Mei took the first flight out of Hanoi to New York and told Vance to get there too. They would both drive to New Haven.

He checked the arrivals again. Vance's plane had landed.

Half an hour later Li registered Vance as the driver of their rented car and sat comfortably in the passenger seat. He started taking two cell phones apart. Traffic was dense. Vance was focused on the road.

"You'll be wearing a microphone," Li said, "embedded in the cell phone."

Vance glanced in the rear view mirror, switched lanes. "Okay."

"They won't search you, will they?"

Vance chuckled. "Of course not, uncle." He kept checking traffic, right, left, behind, relaxed yet focused.

"You like driving?"

"I do." Big smile on his face. Vance could be a little laid back, a little careless. Corrupted by the West. What would the Elders have thought about him? Li would have told them that the end justified the means.

"Any news from the woman?"

A frown. "You mean Robyn?" Li was quite sure his hands had tensed on the wheel. "No, nothing."

Li stayed silent for a while. He put the phones back together. "What I need you to do today is very simple." He clipped an earpiece in place. "And very important." He put a phone on Vance's lap. "Say something."

"I can handle that."

Li didn't like the dreamy smile he saw on Vance. He briefed him on the mission, and the smile disappeared.

22

ROBYN TRIED TO stretch. Nineteen hours in Parker's Mazda RX since they left Florida. They stopped only for gas and food. She checked her phone once from a bathroom stall, just in case. No message.

They shared the driving. Stick-shift was alright. When all this would be over, she might get herself a car.

One more hour to go. From Parker's tool box she took a small screwdriver, pliers and plastic straps and tucked them in her pockets. One more hour of pot holes and traffic on I-95 North. To make it to New Haven, Connecticut, Home of Yale University. Home of the Beinecke Rare Book and Manuscript Library. Home of the Voynich manuscript.

At four they entered the small New England city under thickening clouds. They drove along elm-lined streets, Baroque and Gothic buildings, red brick, stone, hedges.

"Never liked it, never will," Robyn said. "There's something about Yale, don't ask me what."

"Maybe this?" Parker asked.

He hit the brakes in front of a brown and pinkish building, bulky and unadorned. Irregular stone and stiff colonnades on either side of a dark entryway. Maple trees shadowing it like a cave. "The Tomb," Parker finally said.

She said nothing. There was a Cadillac DTS idling, a driver inside. She was burning to glance at her phone.

They drove off. "Skull and Bones headquarters," Parker dropped.

They parked two blocks down and stepped into the heat. Parker locked the car, glanced around, crouched and nudged the car key behind the wheel. "Old habit," he said as they walked away. "Stuff happens. You're searched. You lose your clothes. You never know."

Good point, she thought, thinking about the French police search.

The portion of Wall Street, New Haven that ran along the library was for *Authorized Vehicles Only*.

Fifty yards into the street, a cop's motorcycle was parked slam in the middle, level with a clearing to the right, a stone plaza glaring in the sun, a monstrous expanse of unforgiving granite, with the library occupying its half left side.

All the parking spots in the *authorized vehicles only* section were reserved. "That a library or the goddamn New York Stock Exchange?" Robyn said.

The cop was next to his bike. Hands on hips, his back to them.

They slowed to a stroll. Parker put his arm around Robyn's shoulders. Their mirror sunglasses shielded them. She scanned the streets. Spotted the cameras. The cop turned around slowly. They used their hands as visors. Looked straight at the blinding plaza to the right. The cop straddled his bike. He rumbled away. They put their hands down and walked into the plaza. Stopped against a low wall surrounding a lower-level stone courtyard.

Parallel to the courtyard, Beinecke Rare Book and Manuscript Library stood on four trapezoidal legs one story above ground level. The wall around the ground floor was one large glass panel. Above, no windows. A pewter block of large panels and rigged frames. Facets chiseled as though a diamond, giving it the appearance of a mineral chest. A gigantic Paleolithic coffer.

Parker made a face. "I don't want to know how much this cost. The uglier, the costlier," he said, and went toward the pillared building perpendicular to the library, shooting pictures with his phone like a bored visitor.

Robyn pushed the library's revolving door and entered a temple dedicated to the worship of precious books.

The light was dim. Sunshine seeped through the fine marble panels that were the outside walls, as if through stained glass. Behind three janitors and security guards silently shuffling papers and keys on a long reception desk, an amber-colored tower of ancient books rose six stories high, protected and magnified by a glass encasing. Directly behind the reception desk, a large bronze panel with gold inscriptions gave access to the tower of books, like a giant tabernacle.

The Holy of Holies, Robyn thought.

The key to Sybil.

Five days left.

Behind the receptionist, the large, square bronze door slid one yard to the right. A guard came out and turned a key in the wall. Before the door slid back in, Robyn caught a glimpse of beige walls, a heavy metallic door and an electronic combination lock.

Behind the glass, posing as a bookcase, a vault.

Once again.

3:30 p.m. She had time. On each side of the entrance, a large flight of stairs. She went up to the large mezzanine running along the four sides of the building. There were display tables with not-so-rare editions. Shelves with temporary exhibitions. Carpeted areas with leather couches and small tables.

In the center, the tower of precious books, with an empty space all around it. Robyn leaned on the railing. Saw a Bible and a small volume about the Decalogue. Beyond the display, metallic shelves were stacked with books, cardboard boxes and files. There was an inside wall. A small door that could be locked. Probably stairs behind it. Maybe more storage.

Back downstairs, she slid her student ID card across the reception desk. "I'm here to see Ms Campbell."

The receptionist took the card, glanced at it, tapped it against the marble desk. Clicked it flat. Turned to a computer screen and ran his fingers on a keyboard. "You'll have to come back." He slid the ID card back to her. "Ms Campbell had a family emergency." His eyes still on the screen.

Robyn didn't touch the card. "Let me rephrase. I made arrangements to access ms 408. Anybody can pull it out for me."

He picked up an old beige phone and punched a key. "Miss Gabriel is here for Ms Campbell," he said, "and I told her... Oh..." A glance at Robyn, a scratch of the head. "Uh-huh," several times, then "Thanks." Put the phone back down and wiped his hand on his pants... "Someone'll be with you at five."

He stood and turned his back to Robyn and got busy with his

cell phone. Looked up at the tower of books as his call went through. "Hey. They're letting me out early. Love ya."

Robyn picked up her card. Looked through the glass wall across the plaza. No Parker. Checked her cell phone. No message. He must be in one of those buildings now, figuring out something for when she'd done her part. She updated him on the change of schedule and killed the next hour in one of the leather couches of the mezzanine.

Just before five, two guards started herding visitors out the door. She went back downstairs. The receptionist glanced at her sideways several times. A tight T-shirt would do that. But still.

From a staircase leading down, a few serious people with heavy bags came up. Daylight filtered. Robyn peered down the stairs. The reading room circled around the courtyard she had noticed on the plaza, with large glass panels for walls.

The security guard stood and stretched and turned to his buddies. "Ready?" he asked.

Only then did he take notice of Robyn. "For some material, reading is after hours. For security. The place is locked and the staff can…" He seemed to look for his words. "They can assist the researcher better."

Keep a close eye on her, Robyn translated. "I thought everything was valuable here. I thought you had only manuscripts and incunabula."

"All I know is, some stuff, they do it after hours. Not a lot of it. Just some." He paused. "You wouldn't imagine the number of freaks." He scratched his nose then seemed to consider picking it, but his finger finally dropped to the corner of his mouth. "But you're okay," he said, chin pointing to the phone. "You'll just be locked in with the librarian. No need for extra security."

He followed the guards to the back. Their footsteps resonated. There was the clicking and rattling of lockers and garbled conversations. Then a door again, locked tight.

Then nothing.

Robyn texted Parker.

Forget about keeping the guards busy. They sent security home.

A hushed footstep, tired and uneven, came up from the reading rooms. "Ms Gabriel?" The voice could be male or female, young or old. There was no telling. Robyn looked down the staircase.

A frail, hunched man with thick glasses said, "This way, please." No taller than five feet. Bald and so skinny his skull and cheekbones protruded hurtfully. The impression of malady was balanced by his outfit: pinstriped, pleated and cuffed pants held by black suspenders, starched white shirt with sleeves rolled up. His nametag read L. Bowden. "Young lady, I don't have all night."

The entrance of the downstairs area was fenced off with a mesh curtain. A bunch of keys took care of it. Bowden locked them in.

He took her to a small reading room with just one table. "Sit here." A request form and a ballpoint pen were on the table. "Fill this out."

His head bobbed as he read the form just inches from his eyes. "Stay right where you are." His hunched silhouette rocked around out of the reading room, through the glass wall, the courtyard, and the other glass wall. Finally disappearing through a door.

Would he let her handle the Voynich? Probably not. Would he let her be alone with it? Against the rule. She'd have to improvise.

Rules. One reason she left the academic realm. But there had been more rules to follow and paperwork to fill out to collect coins in the open waters of Florida than to access the most mysterious manuscript in the world.

She went to the door of the reading room. Scanned the ceilings and walls of the larger, common reading area. She took notice of air ducts and summoned the blueprint to memory. There was a door in the outside wall that had not been on the blueprint. But the building did not extend beyond that wall, and the door was ordinary. A last-minute addition of a closet, probably.

Comparing the blueprint to aerial maps, she and Parker had agreed on the South-East conduit. South-east of where she stood was a large grille on the upper part of the wall. Plenty of tables nearby.

No sign of Bowden yet.

She crossed the wing, climbed on a table. Every second would count. Two screws, one on each side of the air vent. She pulled the screwdriver from her back pocket and loosened one screw. She fit her fingers in the grille and turned it away from the opening. The grille rattled against the ceiling. Plaster powder dusted her. She brushed it off and hurried back to her assigned reading room.

Still no Bowden.

Parker would be in his blue coveralls now, pliers and shears dangling from his waist. This was going to be easy. She felt sorry for the little old man. Once Parker would buzz his okay she would tie Bowden to the mesh curtains with the plastic straps. Blindfold and gag him. She'd try not to hurt him.

Then she'd push the Voynich as far as possible inside the air duct.

Bowden marched back, holding a cardboard box flat with his two hands outstretched. He set the box on the table. There was a bright, large yellow sheet of paper. *R. Gabriel* in thick permanent marker. Someone had prepared this for him. His sight was too poor to make out the shelf-mark taped on the side of the box. Ms 408. The Voynich manuscript.

"I forgot my gloves," he said. "Wait." He seemed to hesitate. Didn't move to take the box with him, though.

Robyn took a good look at him. The last thing curators wanted was the oil and acid of fingertips on their precious manuscripts. Surely he knew she would be tempted to take a sneak peek at the manuscript once he left. Maybe worse. It wasn't as if it never happened.

Too many things weren't right. First Campbell with a family situation. The after-hour viewing. The janitors sent home early. And now Bowden forgot his gloves, and was about to leave her *alone* with *the most mysterious manuscript in the world?*

But then she remembered how easily the man had stolen the maps. Some things never change, she thought. *Relax, this is going to be easier than you think.*

"I won't touch it," Robyn said. She crossed her arms and sat back in her chair. Bowden nodded and trotted away.

She peaked out the room and saw him shut a door behind him, beyond the courtyard.

She opened the box. There it was. Her heartbeat picked up. A thick notebook with no inscription on the cover. She opened it randomly. Felt a rush of adrenaline as she recognized the strange writing and the eerie drawings. *Later.*

She closed the box and ran with it to the table nearest the grille. She climbed on the table and glanced again through the two glass walls leading to and from the courtyard.

Bowden was way back there, hitting a switch. The natural light dimmed. Purring filled the room. Shutters rolling down. Darkness grew, until it filled the room entirely. No artificial light came on.

Stretched on her toes, she nudged the box far inside the conduit. Put the grille back in place. With just one screw to hold it, it swung down. She pressed it back in place. It fell again. She crouched and felt the table for the screw. Her heart started pounding. *This is never going to work. The lights will come on and Bowden will press some emergency button.* She found the screw and held it with sweaty fingers. *They'll get to the Voynich before Parker.* She couldn't find the hole. *They'll kill Sybil.* She found the hole and pushed the screw and it went right in. Loose. No bolt on the other side. The grille seemed to stay in place for now. She texted Parker: *Done.*

Now back to the reading room. I'll pretend he's not only half-blind, but forgetful. I'll say I never saw the box. When he turns around, I'll grab him. She stumbled back to her table. Reached out for the desk lamp and felt its contour in search of a switch. There it was right under the bulb. She turned. It clicked. No light came on. Turned again. It clicked again. Still no light.

No Bowden.

The beam of a flashlight played on the walls and floor of the reading room. "Over here," she called. The flashlight blinded her for a few seconds, then went off. "Mr Bowden?" she called.

She stood. She called louder, "Hello?" And was blinded once again, much stronger. She raised her arm to protect her eyes. The beam of light lit the ceiling, then twirled. The flashlight, aimed full blow at her head, landed on her raised arm. Her elbow seemed to explode. She gasped. She kicked, but missed. Enraged, she pulled her screwdriver from her pocket and, holding it in her raised fist, stabbed into the darkness.

She met something hard. Heard, "Shit". Stabbed again. The screwdriver lunged into something soft and resistant. She pulled it out in a downward, cutting motion.

A scream of pain exploded inches from her, breath foul with cigarette and alcohol.

Then a million stars exploded as the flashlight came down on her head once again. She hit the floor. The flashlight went dead. She scrambled to her knees. Tried to stand but was too dizzy. She fell back on her side.

A gurgling sound startled her. Liquid, poured. The smell of gasoline. She crawled away and bumped into a table. Darkness was still complete. She couldn't help staring wide-eyed. A lighting match flickered. It left a wide trail on its way to the ground. Flames burst with a roar, and a tall male silhouette appeared in the light of the closet door. The door closed behind him.

* * *

The flames spread inside the library, following the trail of spilled gasoline. She waited for the inhibiting gas to kick in, not sure what to expect. No alarms went off. No visible or audible discharge. The fire spread.

Behind her, the mesh curtain was locked. She ran to the door she had thought to be a closet, through which her attacker had fled. Pulled and pushed. Locked. Felt the handle and around it, along the frame. Nothing. Locked from the outside.

Her eyes began to sting. She coughed. The roar of the fire picked up, smoke from the burning carpet throwing the room in a haze. She flattened herself on the floor and called the frail librarian once again. Nothing. She stopped wondering about him. One answer: he was in on it. More questions. No time to think.

The Voynich manuscript would burn unless Parker was almost there. She pulled her cell phone, pressed the call button.

No network.

23

MACK WOULD HAVE had network from where he was, just a few feet away, parked on High Street. Except he didn't have a cell phone. He didn't need one, because he planned, and he didn't want one, because it was plain dangerous. He let the engine of the DTS run and the air on. Kept an eye on gas level. He'd forgotten how hot it could get in New Haven. Not that he'd been around a lot in August. That was for geeks.

Geeks and weirdos like Barton, who'd spend their free time locked in gloomy caves or outside at night, learning and repeating meaningless gibberish and really believing in its power. Barton mentioned going somewhere exciting next week, Mack couldn't remember where. He said he'd get the Logonikon over there. Right.

The Logonikon was right here, or nearby. Had to be, because the search of the vault in France yielded an empty safe. The Gabriel girl turned out smarter than expected, and gutsier, but Mack had her all figured out. Yale was his turf, the boys in the Tomb were his gofers, and she was falling right into his trap.

He checked the time. By now the fire would be well under way. No fire trucks in the distance, no alarm of any kind. Trap closing.

Mack looked at the door of 64 High Street. The Tomb. He remembered his first time in there, way before Barton's time. The pride. The embarrassment of having to tell your whole sorry sex life to a bunch of guys laughing their asses off. The marvel at their own stories.

Then later, much later, when he joined the Federal Reserve Bank of New York, the initiation into keeping the secret, the knowledge that its guardianship was split between the High Priest of Bohemian Grove, and the library of their Alma Mater, designed as a huge vault, hiding secrets in plain sight. Mack relished knowing that Barton's beliefs were built on sand, while his own duties held the country together. Barton believed a scam. Mack knew the truth.

He drummed his fingers on the wheel, impatient for his boys to come out, job done.

* * *

A sudden rumbling alarmed Robyn. She turned around. Half the ceiling had collapsed. The air grew thicker. Her lungs felt parched.

She felt her way to the door, took a large step back and gave the door a nasty side kick. Her heel made a dent. She aimed right next to the dent and kicked the door again, faster, stronger. Slammed into it. Her foot went through. She pulled it out, slid her hand in it, felt the area around the handle.

No lock.

No bolt.

Nothing.

The smoke getting thicker. The heat still bearable.

She kicked higher into the door. This time her foot went through immediately. Another kick a little lower and the hole was big enough. She groped through it. Felt a simple bolt and turned it open.

Not a closet. Not even a room. A corridor.

She closed the door tightly against the fire and the smoke and she stumbled through it. Her cell phone screen lit a smooth straight path. She ran.

The corridor had two angles, then a flight of stairs straight up to a yellowish glow. Up the stairs a door was open on excited voices.

"Where is the manuscript?"

Robyn startled. It was Bowden's voice. She went up a few steps. Stopped before she reached the light cast from the open door.

"It wasn't there." The voice of a young man, a little out of breath.

"*In* the box, stupid! I checked myself. Go back!"

"There was no box."

"First reading room," Bowden shouted.

"Sshh. The new guy's here. No box, I swear. I looked everywhere."

"Damn idiot. I'll get it myself. You did knock the woman out, right?"

"I think so."

"You think? Clean up that blood on your neck and come with me. And don't miss her this time."

The young guy argued about the fire being too strong and the clothes needing to be soaked before going back and him needing a knife just in case. A door or a window was opened upstairs. Sweet warm air rushed down the stairs. The two men decided to wet their clothes and bring some equipment.

The outside noises were close. There was an open exit, street level. Fifteen steps up. She'd have to dodge the young guy and Bowden and god knows who else. Going upstairs now wouldn't be good.

Going downstairs to get the Voynich out of the flames *and then* come out would be worse.

She went downstairs.

24

LI MEI WALKED down High Street and spotted the car immediately, right across from the Tomb—that was how they called the place, Vance had said. A tan Cadillac DTS, engine running, water oozing from the AC system. As he walked passed it, coming from behind, he saw that the driver was alone, had short hair and a thick neck. Li did not make the mistake of staring. He just glanced behind his shoulder, once. As he did, he noticed the man's nervous glances toward the door of the Tomb and to the front, toward him.

Things were getting complicated. Having the woman's sister hostage may not be enough.

Li had been loitering in the library, careful to not be spotted by the woman, when he heard the receptionist tell her she would be shown the manuscript after the library closed. He had to leave at five, with everybody else. During his short walk from Beinecke library to the Tomb, he talked to Vance on the phone, in Vietnamese. Vance told him he'd heard of an underground tunnel between the Tomb and the library, and he'd try to sneak in. Li decided to stick around.

He pulled out his earpiece and played with the screen of his customized cell phone. Pretending to place a phone call. Or to listen to music. The earpiece clicked. The soundtrack connected him to Vance inside the Tomb, clear except maybe for the soft rustle of the fabric of his pocket against the microphone. Vance had not made contact with the woman yet. Li turned right at the first corner and waited.

* * *

Mack's thoughts wandered to a man who had just made a right after passing his car. Classy and all. Fiddling with one of those ear things people who had cell phones were slave to. Overdressed considering the heat. He glanced back and Mack got a better glimpse at him. He was Asian. That explained the suit. Maybe he was a teacher in residence. Or a recruiter for a Japanese company. These guys were bright and disciplined. No wonder they made it in the States. Mack would rather work with them than with Europeans—Brits like Barton. After the man disappeared around the corner, the street was back to hot stillness.

* * *

Robyn scrambled down the stairs and followed the corridor. Got to the door and pushed it. Flames had engulfed the rear part of the library. Smoke was thick. Over the roar, she heard shouts and pounding. The fire crew. She ran alongside the wall, trying not to breathe, until she bumped into the table she had pushed to reach for the air vent. She climbed on it and pulled on the screen. It came right out. She grabbed the box and jumped down. Crouching low against the smoke, the box in her arms, she ran back along the wall to find her way to the door. Shouts again. Not the firemen. Bowden and that guy, coming back. She waited for the door to slam shut after they entered the library. They coughed their way in the opposite direction, toward the table where Bowden had set the Voynich, away from where the fire started. In the heavy smoke, they did not see her. She made it to the door. Closed it slowly after her. Then ran to the first corner and texted Parker. *In corridor to bdg s of bnke.* The message would air when she would have network.

She ran the next leg of the corridor, up the stairs, to a brightly lit room. And bounced against a hard mass of muscle.

25

MACK WAS BEGINNING to lose patience. The sky had turned pink, then dark blue, and was now pitch black. He had killed the engine and opened the windows. Gusts of warm wind whirled inside the car. Distant lightning flickered. The fire sirens stopped, replaced by police.

Bowden should have touched base a long time ago. He should have given him the Voynich and the good news that the girl was taken care of.

* * *

Robyn looked up. Had a flash of large shoulders over her naked body, of long love-making and expert hands. She couldn't quite place the guy, though.

"What's a woman doing in here?" he said. Familiar voice, unfamiliar intonation.

The Tequila shots.

It was him. The Asian features, the dimple, the way the teeth overlapped slightly. The square fingers. His smell. Every single detail was him. But the frown was unfamiliar. So was the question, *What's a woman doing in here?*

Vance. That's his name. Shit. The diver Parker didn't like. What the hell...? She looked straight at him, then lowered her gaze. "I won't press charges. Just let me go." With the box under one arm, she reached into her pocket for her cell phone.

"Press charges?" He took one step back, as if to assess her, then a second step, and looked at the box.

A draft signaled an open door.

He glanced behind him.

She lunged and hit him hard on the nose with the cell phone. He cursed and brought both his hands to his face. She kicked his crotch, a sideways kick, quick and powerful. He stopped cursing and gasped, knees bent, mouth open.

She darted to the door and pressed the call button on her phone.

* * *

Li's earpiece transmitted a clear conversation between Vance and the woman for a few seconds. Then her voice faded. What was going on? He raised the volume. Piercing shouts, then ruffling, then nothing except hurried footsteps. He peaked over the corner toward the Tomb. The woman was running toward him, on the opposite sidewalk, a box under her arm, shouting in a cell phone. *What was she doing here?* Much later, five, maybe ten seconds later, Vance followed, limping a little. Wasted more time to stop and look both ways and seemed to only then decide to go after her. A young man ran out of The Tomb and passed Vance, clearly chasing the woman. Li stepped into the street.

* * *

Robyn ran on the sidewalk, opposite from the Beinecke. She pressed her cell phone against her ear. "Where the hell are you?" Stamping followed her.

"Beinecke. They shut the area. Get to the car."

The car would be a block or two to her left. The first left was an alley off the sidewalk, between two rows of buildings. She took it.

* * *

When the door of the Tomb opened, throwing out crude light and the girl, Mack swore. Had to control himself. To top it off the girl was clutching a box. The Voynich manuscript.

A young Asian guy he didn't know came out and walked in her direction.

The Skull and Bones guy Bowden had gotten to help spilled out of the Tomb and ran past the Asian guy, after the woman.

The young Asian guy broke in a trot and followed.

When the overdressed Asian man materialized and darted after them, Mack reached for the Smith & Wesson 638 Airweight in the glove compartment.

From the beginning this whole deal had been mishandled. Time to straighten things out.

Mack counted to two and with the small revolver snug in his palm, followed on foot.

* * *

Robyn stopped at the end of the alley and tried to assess the territory. She stood at the angle of a square bordered by buildings on three sides and a street on the fourth, opposite her. A dark mass lined the building across her, on the other side of the square. Bushes, or small trees, about six feet high.

Footsteps closed in behind her, clear in between distant thunder. She turned around. Pitch dark, with the distinct rhythm of steps. She couldn't make it to the street.

She ran across the square and slid between the sweet smelling vegetation and the warm wall, breaking some branches, scratching her face, making too much noise—scraping, stomping. She stopped and let herself slide to a crouch against the wall, clutching the box on her lap. Her vision adjusted to night. With only tree trunks two feet from her, to her right she made out the alley, to her left raised ground that must be a flower bed, the street behind it, and a wall maybe thirty yards opposite her.

She tried to steady her breathing. Her eyes were riveted to the alley, where the footsteps had come from. She hoped no one would spot her. Hoped the darkness enveloped her.

A guy was coming her way. She slid the box behind her back, under her T-shirt. Pulled her cell phone out. Texted Parker, her eyes on the guy.

S w sq hurry

Would that be clear enough? Maybe. Maybe not.

Silent and athletic, the guy scanned the square, ran to its end, looked right and left into the street, then trotted back her way. Slowed. Stopped right in front of the thicket she was hiding in. Squatted.

His features were only silhouetted, but the whites of his eyes shone in the dark, and he was looking straight at her.

He didn't move. He didn't say anything. He just brought a hand to his neck and rubbed it slowly. Lightning struck, freezing his features in grey contrasts. Platinum hair. Ashen face. White rage.

He stretched his left hand. "Give it to me." His right hand held a knife.

Loud thunder again.

The guy licked his lips.

She pressed herself against the wall, the box in her back.

The guy lunged and the blade settled against her throat.

She tried to kick him off but the blade dug deeper. The guy's eyes were crazed, and as he reached for the box in her back she recognized his cigarette and alcohol breath. She glanced at the bloody slit in his neck.

"You're gonna pay for that, bitch," he said.

Lightning intermittently flashed the square, cutting out a silent silhouette behind him. The silhouette dived and snapped the guy out of the bushes. Both stumbled on the gravel, then stood. It was Vance in front of the guy, bare hands spread out, ready to fight.

The guy's blade gave a nasty shine. He started a circle, as if playing a game.

A powerful crack, like that of a whip, tore the silence, and the guy jerked back.

* * *

Li put his gun in his rear pocket. The noise may have been lost in the rising storm, confused for a falling board, a slamming door.

* * *

In front of Robyn, the guy fell with his arms spread apart. His head bounced on the ground and steadied sideways, his eyes locking on Robyn's, an air of surprise about them.

In the strobes of lightning that followed, thunder exploded and thick dark blood gradually stained his T-shirt, then the ground. The square fell dead silent again, for just a beat, or maybe longer.

Vance yelled "Run", and disappeared.

Footsteps rushed her way. She glanced at her cell phone. Her fingers trembled. One new message. *Stay put.*

On her right, the steps neared. Pleated pants, polished shoes. They stopped ten yards from Robyn. Or was it from the guy? The footsteps resumed, methodical, then stopped level with the body. The tip of the black shoe pushed and rolled the head.

* * *

Mack had hid in the darkness of the alley, one hand in his pocket, gripping the gun. Way down the square, the Skull and Bones guy, who'd come out from the Tomb and followed the girl, had crouched in front of a bush, then dug into it. The young Asian guy, who'd also come out of the Tomb, started a fight with him. That's when Mack saw the older Asian guy pull out a gun and take down the Skull and Bones guy. Technically, Mack's guy. Mack got a good grip on his own colt and waited. Now the killer walked really slowly across the square. Stopped next to the fallen guy and with his foot played with the head.

Before Mack could pull the trigger he was blinded by headlights. He blinked and re-adjusted.

* * *

From the left of the square came a sudden roar. Robyn didn't need to look. It was Parker. The blinding beam of his headlights cut through the pitch dark square. The car screamed up and down the flower bed. Robyn ran toward it. Couldn't resist glancing at the man.

He was rushing toward the alley in the long awkward strides of someone not used to running.

The Mazda skidded to a stop on the gravel and the passenger door swung open. Robyn ran for it, her eyes still on the man now in the middle of the square. As he crossed the beam of the headlights, a gunshot snapped, the man's head jolted back and a pinkish flow squirted out of his skull. His knees bent and he folded like a rag doll.

Another gunshot resonated. Gravel sparked. Parker killed the headlights. Robyn reached the car door, threw the box with the Voynich manuscript on the rear seat and jumped in. Parker U-turned, headlights still off. Gunned the car straight toward the street, up and down the flower bed. He hit the brakes just before the sidewalk. Gunshot again. The car bounced into the street, and another gunshot tore over the storm when he swerved into the street. The RX roared from first to second gear, then third. Robyn looked behind. "There's no one," she said, "but the rear windshield took a hit."

Parker downshifted to second. The engine screamed. "Brake lights gave us away," he shouted. "Can't take the chance. Hold on." He made a sharp left turn and Robyn was pressed against her window. Then he shifted back into third. Fourth. "We should be okay now," he said.

She looked back. "Still no one," she said, but kept looking.

He was using his breaks now, easing through the blinking yellow lights.

She turned around and buckled up. They were following signs for I-95 South. "I don't get it," she finally said.

* * *

As Li drifted into unconsciousness, shame filled him completely.

He had missed the occasion.

He was not having an honorable death.

* * *

Mack felt helpless as the car vanished into the street, out of his reach. He was always one step behind the girl. He couldn't believe she had escaped his trap. And with the document.

The storm moved north and the rain stopped, leaving the city dripping under a clearing sky. The power was still down. The square was silent. He could make out the two bodies, ten yards apart on the moonlit gravel. He walked to the closest one.

It was the only man he had ever killed. He felt both belittled and justified. He felt he should not think about how he felt. He frisked the man's pockets and found a wallet, a passport and a cell phone. Took all of it. He ignored the other body and left the square. He placed a call from the first public phone he found. The passport was Vietnamese, with a valid visa. He spelled out two names: Li Mei,

Robyn Suzanne Gabriel. Gave their birth date and place, as stated on the passport for the man, and, for the girl, as he remembered exactly from the prior research he had run on her, out of routine, early on in this ordeal. The request was extremely urgent, he said. He said the woman was suspect of killing the man. He needed to know everything about the man, and he needed the woman to be located. Just located, nothing else. Then he hung up.

Sirens sounded toward the square. He made a wide detour to get to his car, breathing in the cooling air.

On his way he crossed fire trucks swarming toward the library. Bowden had made it out, some way or another, and re-activated the alarm. It wasn't supposed to turn out that way, but Mack could easily think of a way to spin the story. *Deranged woman sets fire to library–Steals precious manuscript – Murders two – Crash kills woman, destroys manuscript.* It was even better than his original scenario of having her killed by her own arson. By moving the death outside of the library, there'd be less publicity, less enquiries. Things were turning out nicely.

During the drive back to Sunken Heights, he thought about how he would put things to Pritchard. He hoped he'd get his information overnight, so he'd talk to him with things pieced together.

An alien had been killed. You could cover up stuff that happened to nationals. But here there would be foreign countries involved. An investigation. Who was monitoring him? How much did he know? Had he spoken to anyone? Who was the young Asian guy who'd run away? How much did *he* know?

And the girl and the driver, running free with the document and its decoder. He hoped to get to them before it was too late. Before the unthinkable happened.

26

THE WORST WAS not the constant shaking of her hands. Or the stench of smoke on her clothes and hair. It wasn't even the pulsating pain in her skull, sharp enough to make her nauseous.

No, the worst was the visual memory of the dead guy's stare on her, his eyes surprised by death. It wouldn't go away.

And Vance's presence there.

Parker's silence didn't help. He'd been driving a steady 70 miles an hour. If you drove within the speed limit in this part of the country, you stood out. Last thing they wanted right now. Things were bad enough with the bullet hole in the window. That was about all he'd been willing to say. She didn't even care what part of the country they were in. Although the names on the road signs were familiar, they meant nothing to her right now.

"I don't get it," she said again.

The answer snapped. "You just sleep with the wrong guys."

"Who says they're the wrong guys." She looked through her window.

"He was a mole, Robyn." He slammed the palm of his hand against the wheel. "I knew it. There was something wrong about him."

"A mole for what? The guy's an idealist. He wants to open hospitals in rural China, for chrissakes. That's why he studies hard and works hard."

"And he's hard about you. Great. When did he tell you that Chinese hospital crap? After sex?"

"I'm the one who barged into Skull and Bones' headquarters. He didn't know I was going to be there. *I* didn't know I was going to be there."

"There are no coincidences."

"That's probably what he's thinking right now. That we hired him because he's at Yale, that we knew he was Skull and Bones, and that we were going to use him one way or another."

"Bullshit, Robyn. You know it."

"He saved my life today."

Parker swerved the car to the fast lane. "I thought I did." He raised his voice. "What are you trying to say?"

"You did save me. And so did he, before you came. This guy had a fucking knife against my throat when Vance came out of nowhere and…" She shut up before emotion had a chance to take control. "Doesn't matter," she said.

"The hell it does. You like the wrong people."

"I didn't like him."

"You were sleeping with him."

"Exactly."

Parker slammed the brakes. They eased back in the flow of traffic and passed a police car ambushed behind a thicket.

She said, "You sleep with people you like, you may end up loving them."

* * *

Parker fiddled with the ham radio and settled on a channel where nothing made much sense to Robyn. "Code," he explained, and raised the volume. After a few minutes he picked up the mike. From the tone of his voice he was asking questions. He used nonsensical words and digits. Answers came from different voices, crackling through the speakers, meaningless to Robyn. Then someone said, "Dude. They may want you 10-7. You'd better drop the hammer".

"Full of vitamins and pulling the big one," Parker said. They exited the highway.

He took small roads. Stopped for gas. Bought a loaf of bread, frankfurters and beer. Robyn added writing pads and pens. They ate in the car. Silent. By then she'd figured they were in the thick of Pennsylvania. In the bathroom she reassembled and checked her phone. The one she had taken from Florida.

No messages. She took the battery back out.

Finally Parker said, "The Fed police is chasing us."

"The FBI?"

"The Federal Reserve Bank of New York police."

"What's that shit?" Robyn asked.

"Yeah, I know. Don't know what their jurisdiction is, and it probably is just inside their fucking building, but with all those anti-money laundering laws, you never know where the next blow is going to come from."

"Why would *they* be after us?" she said.

No answer.

She glanced on the back seat at the box with the Voynich and the box with the Logonikon. Chemical components ready for chain reaction.

Thirty minutes later they were on a dirt road. Then the dirt road dead-ended at a picket-fence gate.

27

"COUSIN'S FARMLAND," PARKER said. "No house around." He got out of the car.

Robyn's hand went to her pocket. She felt her phone and its battery. Did she have time…?

Parker was fumbling with the gate, his back turned to the car, his broad shoulders outlined by the headlights.

Should I tell Parker? "They" would never know. Or would they?

He was coming back to the car. She avoided his stare.

They drove through a wood, then in between farmed fields, and got to a barn.

Its large door opened silently. It smelled of dust and summer heat. Parker reached to the right of the door and clicked a flashlight on. Handed a lantern to Robyn. Large planks formed the walls. Swallows ruffled in the beams. A few hay straws were scattered on the otherwise empty floor. He stopped the beam of the flashlight on some hayforks and a wheelbarrow and planks neatly propped against a wall. "Ready for harvest," he said.

Behind the planks there were trestles and in less than a minute they had a table. They got the boxes with the Voynich and the Logonikon from the car and set them on the table next to the lantern. Robyn pulled the Voynich out first, carefully. Its box had been roughed these last hours but as far as she could tell it didn't seem to have affected the manuscript.

"Cool," Parker said, turning the pages slowly. "Wanna get some sleep first?"

She set the Logonikon next to the Voynich. Ripped the stack of white writing pads open. Spilled the pens on the table then aligned them neatly. Wiped her hands on her pants. Ignored Parker who had pulled the wheelbarrow and slumped into it and was now looking at her.

Standing up, she took the first page of the Logonikon and applied it on the first page of the Voynich.

"Need help?" Parker said.

The precise perforations revealed some isolated symbols. "I'll have to do this alone," she said and copied them on the writing pad. "It's symbols. I can't dictate. See what I mean?" she said without stopping her work.

After a while Parker said, "When's the last you heard from Sybil?"

She didn't lift her eyes. "I thought you were sleeping."

"I was thinking."

I don't want this conversation. "Same difference." She tried to focus but realized she had copied the same symbol twice. She swore, erased, cross-checked.

Next page.

"I don't remember you guys having *such* major communication issues," he said.

She put her pencil down and took a mean look at him. "You wanna have a *talk* or you're just trying to *distract* me?"

A shocked look shadowed his face and for an awkward moment she thought she had hurt his feelings. Then he pulled a huge grin, did a *keep going* type of gesture and said, "Just checking your reflexes."

She continued jotting symbols down, then said, "The problem is Tom."

"Blame it on the guy."

She shook her head. Truth was, Sybil had gotten more distant when she started dating Tom.

"What are you doing?" he asked when she took a page of the Logonikon and set it with the one she had used, but without applying it to the Voynich first, then did it again with the following page.

"Some of the Voynich pages are missing. The Logonikon is complete, so whenever there is a missing page in the Voynich, I skip the corresponding page of the Logonikon."

"Anything make sense yet?" Parker asked.

She did not look up. "Course not." She turned another page of the

Voynich, took another page of the Logonikon. Copied three symbols.

Parker's silence became thick. She looked up at him, and waived the notebook. "It's still cipher," she said. "I need to convert these symbols."

He sniffed loudly.

"I'm hoping there is a conversion chart somewhere in here. I'll let you know."

"I'll be in the car." The barn door banged behind him.

She didn't have the patience to be sweet. Not now. She ploughed back in. Over two hundred pages left. She did it all in one stretch. Focused, focused, focused.

Some pages had less than five symbols or letters. Some had more. Most had digits. She copied them all neatly, four per line, five lines per pad, leaving space between the lines to write down the transcription into letters, later.

When she reached page 113, she knew she'd make it. The Logonikon revealed a conversion chart: symbols on one side, Latin on the other. She copied the chart and continued applying each page of the Logonikon to the corresponding page of the Voynich.

She was into her second one-hundred page writing pad when she reached the end of the Logonikon. There was only one page of the Voynich left, and that one had already been deciphered:

"Drafted by Simon and Nutzer, s.j.,
For the power of the twelve American cities,
And the glory of the Dragon
To be sheltered in Marseilles, April 1912."

She turned to the conversion chart. Two columns. One of symbols, one of letters. Almost too simple now.

Under each of the symbols on her notebook, she copied the letter that it represented. After a few pages, she could tell the language was French. She made out some words, but mainly she was focused on copying. And thinking what her next move would be. When all the symbols would be converted it would only be a matter of grouping the letters into words.

Sometimes she would hit a series of consonants and digits. She wondered what she would do with that.

Throughout the night she took one bathroom break behind the barn and used it to power her phone just long enough to check messages. No network. *I need to get out of here. ASAP.*

When the morning ashen light seeped through the disjointed planks she was done. She sat against a wall, a sunray on the writing pad, and drew vertical lines between letters, making out words. She read over, and despite the missing pages, she got the big picture. The note in the back started making sense, especially the twelve cities. The strings of consonants and digits made sense. Not all her questions were answered, but she had a plan.

She went outside. Parker was napping on the back seat, his feet sticking out the window. She knocked on the car roof. "I'm going to Austria," she said.

28

PARKER DIDN'T OPEN his eyes. "Sure, boss, I'll take care of business in Florida," he sneered.

"You have a passport?" She asked.

"No. It puts you in the system."

"Then what are you complaining about?" She went back inside the barn and packed the Voynich and the Logonikon in their boxes. Brought them to the car and put them on the passenger seat. Parker was still pretending to be asleep.

She took the wheel and slammed the door. "Keys please," she said. *Five days left.*

"We ain't going nowhere in broad daylight," Parker said.

* * *

They sat in the barn, waiting for the sun to set. She had tried to argue, but Parker's point was two stiffs in New Haven, a killer running loose, and them being in that shit because she couldn't help herself.

She thought, *Five days left, Don't tell anyone* and figured one night and four times twenty-four hours could still take her a long way. Then a prom picture of Sybil jumped into her memory, replaced by the picture sent by the kidnappers, and her eyes welled.

"So?" Parker said, pointing his chin to the notebook.

She handed him the pad.

He glanced at it and handed it back. "It's in Italian."

"French."

"What does it say?"

Don't tell anyone or she's dead. It better mean, *Don't tell anyone we kidnapped her,* because she needed Parker, his logistics, his brainstorming, and if she couldn't use him, she could just as well forget about saving Sybil anyway.

She said, "It's an agreement by which one party entrusted its riches to another."

"A loan?"

"Something like that."

"What's the big deal?"

"This document records the numbered bank accounts on which the fortune was deposited. And the access codes, called keys," she said, waving her notebook.

"Wait a second. Backtrack. You are saying that on top of recording a loan, this records the bank account on which the money was deposited?"

"Not just any bank account. Numbered bank accounts."

"Meaning…"

"The accounts are not in the name of a person, but can be accessed by anyone who has the account numbers and the access codes to the accounts, which they call keys."

"And this information is in there?" he asked, pointing to the notebook.

"In plain English now."

"How much?" he asked.

"Seventeen carloads of gold and gems."

He scratched his head. "Seventeen carloads? It's a joke. Who measures gold and gems by the carload? The whole thing is a joke."

Robyn had felt that way too, hours before, deciphering. Now she saw how it all was beginning to make sense. "Gold, silver, emerald and diamonds. Jewelry and works of art too, but recorded for a lesser value. Because of the difficulty to trade them, as opposed to gems."

"Which means looted."

"Probably. But the bulk of it is gold in various forms, mainly bullions and coins."

"What coins?"

"It doesn't say."

"But it's in an Austrian bank."

"Part of it, yes."

"Where is the rest?"

"Don't know," she lied. The document mentioned the cities where other deposits were made. Twelve American cities. "Several accounts are mentioned, but the specifics are complete only for the Austrian account. The rest is probably recorded on the missing pages of the Voynich." That much was true.

"So that's why you want to go to Austria."

She thought, *And to Europe to get the rest of the codes in exchange for Sybil*, but just winked and said, "It'll help paying our loans back. Numbered account. No names. Just three codes called keys, a bunch of letters and digits."

"Why three?" he asked.

She had wondered too. "Tell me what you think."

"The account is accessible only when the three keys are presented together?" Parker asked.

Robyn nodded.

Parker's gaze focused somewhere beyond her as he thought the process out loud. "With a numbered bank account, and one key which works like a pin, it should be enough. Unless… unless the money belonged to three individuals, or companies, or one company with three officers… Yes, that's it. Like the codes to launch the atomic bomb. One man alone can't do it. Got to have the right codes presented together. A joint decision."

"Right," Robyn said. "At the time the document was drafted, the keys must have been distributed among three individuals, each of whom needed to give his consent for any movement on the accounts." She looked at him and waived the notebook again. "For some reason the three keys of each account were recorded here. In a cryptic document, an unbreakable cipher. I'll bet you anyone with the three keys can claim the accounts as his own. To the bank it's just the same if it's three people each with their key or one person with the three keys. They'll execute the order. No questions asked. That's the beauty of numbered accounts."

She nodded, her analysis comforted by Parker's. "The Voynich manuscript gives out all the information to legally retrieve the fortune. And with the Voynich on one continent and the Logonikon on another, the info was safe enough."

"But the Voynich was found in Italy, right? That's damn close to Marseilles," Parker said.

"That's where Wilfried Voynich *said* he found it. But nothing proves it. The Jesuits in Italy always denied selling him books or manuscripts. The first time the Voynich manuscript was made public, it was at a Chicago exhibition."

"Along with the Hapsburg family stuff. There you go," Parker said. "Voynich didn't know it, but he was showing around the Hapsburg bank accounts. That's why you have the Austrian bank." He slapped Robyn in the back. "You are one damn of a treasure hunter, you know that?"

No, not the Hapsburg fortune, she thought, but couldn't tell him. Not yet.

For some reason, the money was sitting there since 1912, according to the last page of the Voynich, and no one had claimed it. Maybe a key was lost. Maybe one of the parties died without passing along their key. But it still was there, or Sybil would not have been kidnapped.

She wouldn't have been attacked in the first place, and Toslav would not have such eager buyers, and the consul in Marseilles wouldn't have been so Machiavellian. Robyn had been nothing to them, just a roadblock to a huge fortune, maybe more. One of them was using her now, and she and Sybil were still nothing. They would probably not come out of this alive, but Robyn would fight till the end.

She wondered what part in the story their father had played.

* * *

By the time Mack reached Sunken Heights, he had his strategy right. He would start off by handing an eight-page, double-spaced memo to Pritchard summarizing the history. He'd go on with the sorry story of the recent failures. Because Pritchard was a political beast, his reaction would be ass-covering. So Mack would shoulder the blame. But because of their respective positions, a blame on Mack would be a blame on his boss, Pritchard. That was where it would get tricky. He would have to make Pritchard understand it was not about him or even the Fed. Because it was way more than that.

It was about the nation's power.

After Pritchard understood that and was beyond playing the blame game, he'd better have the guts of a Paul Tibbets, or better, of a kamikaze. There were times in History when a country needed heroes, and this was one of them. Mack would say something like that to his boss, before he went back to Washington to report to the very top and burn his career.

The more he thought about it, the more he knew this was the only way to go about it.

He turned into his driveway, mentally writing the introduction to his memo, and activated the garage door opener. Nothing. He'd forgotten to change the batteries again. He left the engine running and went inside the house, leaving the front door open. By the time he got to the garage he had the intro nailed down. He activated the door switch. Watching it roll up, he visualized the focal points of the memo. Once behind his wheel, he had the whole thing figured out. He'd be done in an hour. He put the car in drive and took his foot off the brake. Something kept it from springing forward. He gave a slight acceleration. A small bump, a crushing feel, made its way from the wheels to the pedals, to the steering wheel, to his whole body. He glanced at the open front door. He froze.

He rushed out of the car. Behind the front right wheel, a white furry mass was flattened in the middle, something dark spilling out. *Oh no.* Mack's stomach quivered. *Austin.* His hand unsure, he lifted the bunny's head. It was stilled by death. Mack's vision blurred. He petted the bunny one last time. *I killed two people today,* he thought. Then he got a grip on himself. First things first. He glanced at the upstairs windows. Natalie's bedroom was dark. *Good.*

He took a shovel and a plastic bag from the garage and wrapped the bunny before its blood and guts were all over the gravel. He dug a hole in the flower bed and stuffed the warm bundle at the bottom. Shoveled earth back on top and spread mulch, then put the shovel back on its rack, rolled the Cadillac in the garage, cleaned his shoes with rags and tiptoed into the silent home.

He washed his hands, splashed cold water on his face, slid into his empty study and started typing the memo. Two fingers, right, left. Slow, but steady. No hesitation. No typos. He read it over. It was all there. The brilliant scheme from way back, and the recent messy story. He saved it under its first word, Classified, inside the folder labeled 00, next to the pdf scans of the diary, their handwritten translations and their typed version, Notes.

He decided to let it sit a little. He'd have a coffee, and take a shower, and then he'd read one last time, to make sure he got everything right before printing it.

He went into the kitchen and there was Natalie, crouched before Austin's cage, swinging the door open and closed. Squeak.

Squeak. Squeak.

Squeak.

29

HE FOCUSED ON ignoring where Natalie was or what she was doing, grabbed the TV remote and snapped Bloomberg on. Funny how sound could make the whole difference. The room was almost welcoming now. He started on the coffee. Soon the gurgling got going, the smell too, and everything seemed normal again. He popped bread in the toaster and asked Natalie if she wanted juice.

She said sure. She stood and took two long strides and perched on a bar stool across from him.

He breathed better now and was able to focus on the news. When the ads came on he got the butter from the fridge and started working on his toasts.

"Aren't they cute?" Natalie said about something on TV.

He glanced up, froze for a beat, then concentrated on adding more butter. He spread it back and forth until it was evenly soaked inside the slice. Then he started on the second slice.

"Dad?"

He glanced up again, then back to the buttering. On the TV screen, the Energizer ad played. A line of bunnies, drumming.

"Maybe we should get Austin one for Christmas."

He grunted.

The screen switched back to business news.

"You think he'd play with one of those?" she said. "I mean, he's not a cat. Not sure he'd interact. Could be funny though."

The little appetite he had was gone. His knife kept going back and forth on the toast. In between the TV blurtings it made a scraping sound.

She said, "Maybe I shouldn't wait til Christmas."

"Why not?" he finally said, and started cutting his toasts diagonally once, then again. He was looking at eight triangles of toast stacked up two levels thick. He gave the plate a forty-five degree twist, then pretended to turn his attention back to foreign markets.

"Cause bunnies don't care about Christmas."

He popped the first triangle in his mouth, forced it down his throat with coffee, moved on to the next.

Half the plate gone without him saying anything, she said, "And also bunnies don't live that long." She kept staring at the TV screen and added, "You know." She turned to look at him, quickly.

He managed to keep a straight stare, a constant chewing.

She grabbed the empty orange juice container, slid off the bar stool and turned around to the recycling box. She took all her time folding the container and squeezing it in. He could have sworn she was glancing at him every now and then. *Guilt will do that to you*, he thought.

He couldn't stand it anymore. He went right past her and put his plate and mug in the sink. He mumbled he was going to take a shower and walked out of the kitchen.

He heard her snap the TV off. The screen whooshed. The house turned silent. By the time he was upstairs he figured she had started playing with the door to Austin's cage again. Squeak.

Squeak.

30

PARKER'S COUSIN SHOWED up at the barn around midday, gave a thoughtful nod at the car, and drove them to his mother's. He didn't say more than ten words. His silence spoke of understanding and family duty.

The mother said Parker was his dad's spitting image. She fed them farm chicken and corn and watched them eat in silence. She offered rhubarb pie and ice cream. They asked about a shower. She gave them thin towels and coconut shampoo.

Then Robyn handed Parker a wad of bills from César's envelope, Parker went outside for a serious talk with his cousin and the cousin went to town. He came back ninety minutes later with the keys of a seven-year-old Dodge pickup truck that was guaranteed to handle a trip to California and back several times.

Robyn and Parker weren't going to California but no one needed to know. Parker was driving back to Florida, with the Logonikon and the Voynich. That was simple enough. Drive south.

Robyn was going to Austria. That took a little more planning. They did some travel research, at both ends of the price spectrum. Then Parker upgraded the go-phone to handle international calls. That took some spinning on his part, and Robyn didn't quite get all of it. She got busy memorizing parts of the access keys to the bank account.

Parker dropped her at a small international airport with only private jets. César's envelope did wonders. She took off for Saint Martin in the West Indies in the next half hour. From Saint Martin she caught a charter flight to Paris. Change of price, change of comfort. From Paris she flew into Munich.

She walked into Kitzbuehl Volks Bank, Austria, at 1 p.m. on Monday, four days left on the ultimatum, no news from the kidnappers. The bank was a three story half-timbered building with stained glass windows lined by geraniums. Inside, it smelled of apples and pine, the carpeting was thick, the counters were blond wood and there was a sitting area in the middle of the hallway with a carved Tyrolean chest.

But it was a bank all right, with clerks busy doing mysterious tasks, high consoles, deposit slips, pens on metal strings, a long line of customers at a stern counter. Two opaque glass doors were engraved with names. One set of double, full-wood doors bore a brass sign, *Direktor*.

If all went well, Robyn would soon access a nice chunk of the money, but the kidnappers hadn't been in touch. How was the exchange supposed to happen? Until she heard from them, she'd have to improvise. She'd park the money in the bank account their father had opened in Switzerland "in case things went sour in the United States", their uncle had explained when they were old enough. There wasn't much money on the account. It had seemed to her very Old World, this type of planning as if for war or civil unrest. Now, she wondered.

She took a deposit slip and started scribbling. The line at the counter was making progress. There was some serious stamping going on, voices up a pitch. A brunette with a shrill laugh pocketed her receipts and stayed glued to the counter, small-talking the clerk. The next customer walked up and joined the conversation.

A small bank in a small town.

Another clerk walked through the hallway, nodded toward her and went through the *Direktor* double doors. Came back out a minute later with a thin file under his arm, said "Ja, Herr Winkler," and left the door half open.

Robyn caught a glimpse of a modern desk and a gray-haired man with suspenders and the sleeves of his white shirt rolled up. He was extremely busy reading a ski magazine and didn't notice Robyn until she shut the door behind her.

He looked at her over his glasses. "What can I do for you?" He spoke English to her, as if she was so obviously foreign. His magazine hid the bottom of his face. His desk was immaculate, with only the flat screen of a computer facing him, the wires neatly tugged away, a Montblanc fountain pen and a three-by-three light blue post-it notes cube. On the left, a window with the cobblestone street and the Alps in the background. Behind him, ski pictures on the wall, and in a corner next to the door, a coat rack with half a dozen Tyrolean hats.

Robyn pulled a chair and sat right in front of him, elbows on the table. "I want to access my account," she said.

He took a second good look at her, then folded his magazine inside out, to keep the page. He pulled a tray holding a keyboard under his desk. "Account number?"

She told him.

He made a face. "How old is that account? Not even sure it still exists under this nomenclature." He typed anyway, his eyes on the keyboard. Then with one finger he pushed his glasses all the way up on the bridge of his nose and frowned at the screen. "And you are?"

"I am a number."

He cocked his head toward her. "Really?" He rolled the r far too long. Then he looked back at the screen and his glasses reflected some blinking on the computer. He made a small grunt and said, "Nett." Then looked at Robyn over his glasses and said, "And what number, please?"

At that point the door behind Robyn opened and closed and she felt the ruffling presence of someone just behind her back. She glanced behind her shoulder and saw a dark suit and that was pretty much it. She looked at Herr Direktor.

"Standard procedure for numbered accounts," he said. "Witness. I'm sure you're familiar."

Two days ago numbered accounts were a movie gadget to her. She wasn't going to argue the specifics. She began reciting the first key, a line of nineteen digits and letters. She had memorized the spaces too, but apparently he didn't need them. She stopped and he looked at her with an air of utter amusement and said, "Next?"

She punched the last number called on her cell. Took her wallet. Pulled out two strips of paper. One had one of the keys. The other the number of the bank account in Switzerland. She slid the first one to him.

He frowned and punched in the numbers. Robyn reached for her cell.

The dark suit behind her extended a hand. "No telephone."

Herr Direktor smiled.

She turned around to get an idea of who the dark suit was. A thin moustache and a beer-belly. "I'm being assisted by my lawyers," she said. "Standard procedure." She turned back in her seat and smiled at Winkler. "I'm sure you're familiar."

Then she took the cell and activated the loudspeaker and said, "Ready."

Parker's voice came out loud and clear, spelling out the last key, digits and letters.

Winkler punched in the numbers. The computer whirred like this was really a hard task and Winkler looked outside the window to the mountains, then back at the screen.

He clasped both hands on the desk and looked really jolly and said, "Sorry, wrong identity." He drummed his fingers on his immaculate desk. The man behind her sniffed.

Winkler seemed too content.

She picked up her cell phone and talked in it as in a walkie-talkie. "Did you hear this?" she said, and to save the embarrassment of an answer, said, "I demand to see the screen."

He angled it toward her. There were three thick white lines against a blue background, and the lines were filled with asterisks. A red rectangle with some German writing blinked beneath.

"Let's do this again," she said.

The director raised an eyebrow and looked at his keyboard. Then he pulled it from its tray, eased the cords out and slid it to Robyn.

She punched the first key, the one she memorized, then the second, the one she had on paper. They'd decided on that procedure with Parker. Two keys with her, but only one on paper, and one that she wouldn't know, but Parker would. This way the account was safe. She'd call him once everything was clear at the bank and all she needed was the last key. "Repeat, please," she said in the cell.

Parker repeated the key and she typed carefully, looking at the keyboard, taking it slowly because the keyboard layout was a little different than what she was used to, and there was no way of checking on the screen if she typed right.

When she punched the last digit the red rectangle blinked again.

Winkler coughed in his fist.

What did she get wrong? She had the name of the bank and the account number right. So her interpretation and deciphering of the Voynich were not faulty. She and Parker went over the keys several times, to make sure there were no mistakes. She was quite confident in her memorization of the key, but there was always a risk of error there.

Winkler glanced at his watch.

She could ask Parker to double check the first key, Logonikon against Voynich. But that would mean coming back tomorrow. Too risky.

The first key.

It wasn't the first key.

Parker had memorized the first key, but they agreed on calling him last, when everything was in order. That was it. There was an order. It was Parker's key first, then the one she memorized, then the one on paper. That was the way it was written on the Logonikon. Just like the Chinese chest, everything had an order, and there was no point trying to force things.

One key could not be substituted for another.

She erased the three lines of asterisks.

She asked Parker to spell out his key again. Typed really slowly again, because stress was making her fidgety. Then her two keys.

Pressed enter.

A small white rectangle blinked and the computer chimed.

What now?

"My turn," Winkler said. He turned the screen back toward him, grabbed the keyboard and punched four digits.

Then he went pale.

Really, really pale.

31

MACK TOOK A long shower, did a few push-ups and shaved. Already he felt better. In charge. Ready for the day ahead. He got dressed, wiped his brightly polished shoes, buckled his belt. He was in the mental state of a winner now. He had taken his time, and it was paying off, he felt.

He was wrong.

The long shower and the time taken to choose the right shirt, the right cufflinks, the right tie, had given Natalie time to do some thinking of her own. The process had started with a chat session from her laptop in the kitchen.

> *Nat: hey*
> *Xoxo: heyy sup?*
> *Nat: life sucks*
> *Xoxo: yea I know*
> *Xoxo: …hey?*
> *Xoxo: everythin ok?*
> *Nat: mack drove over Austin*
> *Xoxo: wtf?*
> *Nat: i know*
> *Xoxo:??*
> *Nat: idk, it just happened*
> *Xoxo: wtf r u talking about*
> *Nat: mack*
> *Nat: my father*

Xoxo: yea
Nat: drove over Austin
Xoxo: that's far
Nat: my bunny
Nat: remember Austin? my bunny
Nat: he drove over it with his fucking car
Xoxo: omfg
Nat: effin bastard
Xoxo: did he do it on purpose?
Nat: no
Nat: i don't think so
Nat: i didn't see it actually happen.
i saw him bury Austin
Xoxo: shit
Nat: yea he was next to his wheel so
Xoxo: idk what to say, I'm so sorry
Xoxo: it sucks
Xoxo: how old was your bunny again
Nat: old
Nat: but that's not the point
Xoxo: he was like family
Nat: no it's not that.
Nat: it's about mack.
Nat: i just don't get it. you kno, he didn't even come to tell me and shit.
he put him in a garbage bag and he buried him without even telling me
and then at beakfast he's like nothing hapnd. what am I? a fuckin baby?
Xoxo: i know my dads the same
Xoxo: you just have to get over it. some things don't change.
Xoxo: good things come out of bad things sometimes
Nat:???
Xoxo: wait and see.
Nat: wtf
Xoxo: gtg sry hun
Xoxo is offline.

Xoxo was her friend Anna's id since seventh grade. Anna was the only person Natalie respected, so she pondered her advice. That led her to her father's office, to the locked cabinet with its key in the top drawer, and to the computer turned on with the CLASSIFIED docs conveniently located on the PC's desktop.

All while Mack was treating himself to a careful shave, an invigorating shower.

And while he was busy donning his business uniform, his empowering attributes, Natalie's thinking translated into the following email:

Hi Parker,
You may remember me from school. Or maybe not. I dropped out. Anyway, I really liked your stance on any subject matter. If you're still into conspiracy stuff, I have s/thing that may interest you.
See attachements.
N.

Mack entered his office to review his memo one last time. He sat at his desk feeling too confident to notice the warmth of his chair, or the faint scent of strawberry shampoo.

He read the document. Perfect. Nothing to change. He hit print, shut down his computer, and left for work.

* * *

Her eyes on Winkler's ashen face, Robyn spoke toward the phone. "For the record, the procedure of accessing the account is complete. I am now requesting a balance statement." She looked up. "Herr Winkler?"

Winkler looked at Robyn, then above her head, and said, "Thank you, Gerhardt, the day is over."

Gerhardt left as quietly as he had come in and Winkler stood and pushed a bolt on the door. Robyn clasped her cell phone.

"Nothing to worry, miss," he said. His face had a shrunken look. He sat in his chair and stared at the screen, then finally grabbed the phone. Kept it in his hand as if weighing his options. Then he looked at her and said, "Nothing to worry for you."

He spoke German on the phone. First a long sentence where the words dragged on as if they might bring about something terrible. His eyes kept going from the screen to Robyn and back to the screen. Then he listened, his brow cupped in his left hand, focusing on a point next to the fountain pen. He glanced at her cell phone and said something about *Rechtsanwalt.*

She glanced at her cell. The battery was still half full. Parker was probably recording everything.

Then he rubbed his face several times, still listening to the phone. He sat back in his swivel chair, phone to his ear, eyes on the screen. But there didn't seem to be much talking on either side.

"I'm requesting a transfer," she said.

"That is impossible."

"Why?" She had an answer ready for the closing time bullshit he was about to throw.

"We need to liquidate the assets."

What assets? "How long?"

"They're closing the markets." He hung up.

"I didn't say sell. I said transfer the account." She pulled out the slip of paper with a Switzerland bank account number on it. Then she tilted the screen toward her and sat back and looked at it. The writing was all German. The screen was divided horizontally into four or five sections, as if there were different types of accounts, and vertically into three columns. The left column had repeat 1912. Must be the opening date. The center, wider column, was all written in German with some digits. And the column to the right had to be the balance. Nice long numbers, more than nine digits for sure. No wonder everyone got so excited.

"They're closing everything. No more transactions. Globally. Until this crisis is over." His glasses were steamy.

She must have missed something in the news. "What crisis?"

He looked at her and pointed his finger to the screen. "That one."

She looked at the screen. Looked back at him.

He rubbed his face again as if trying to wake up from a nightmare. "How did you get the keys?" he finally asked. Then he raised a hand and shook his head and said, "Don't tell me. I don't want to know."

A church bell rang outside. Even strokes. Five o'clock. Life was nice and simple and airy outside. It was getting oppressing and very, very complicated inside.

She pushed the Swiss bank account number accross the table. "Just transfer and I'm out of here."

He looked at her as if she were a stubborn child.

"If markets are closed then open a new account on your books for tonight and transfer the money," she explained. "We can move the funds to Switzerland tomorrow. I just don't want it sitting in this account anymore."

That's when he sat back really hard in his chair and had a sour smile and said, "You have no idea what you're talking about, do you?" Then he stopped looking at her as if she were a despicable interruption in an otherwise perfect day. He clapped his tongue and looked toward the screen and fiddled with the mouse and said "You see this here?" The arrow was pointing to two digits in the middle of all the German in the center column.

"Yes."

He expelled a dry cough. "You know what accrued interests are?"

Yes, she did.

"It's an interest rate applied each year and incorporated into the principal," he said. "Each year, the principal deposited is augmented by the amount agreed upon, and the interests are included in the following year's principal. Let's say you deposit one hundred with a 5% accrued interest rate, the first year you'll get 5, and the second you'll get 5% of 105, that's 5,25. So the following year you get 5% of 110,25. Ja?"

"Yeah."

"Well, in this case we have a 20% accrued interest rate. "

So the contract was still in effect. "Interesting."

He pulled on his edelweiss embroidered suspenders. "No. Not interesting. Total madness. Rrreckless banking. If you deposit 100, the first year you end up with 120, the following year you get 20% of 120, that's 24, you end up with 144. The third year, 20% of 144, that's over 28, you end up with 172." He had gone from ashen to crimson and was easing the tie off his neck. "What are you doing?" he said, looking at her finger still glued to the first line of the balance. "These are the entry numbers. One hundred years ago. The initial amount deposited. It gets more than doubled every four years. Times eight after eight years. Times sixteen after twelve. Times thirty-two after sixteen years. Times thirty-two by 1928 only. Shall I go on?"

"If you scroll down, will we have today's figures?" she asked.

As he grabbed the mouse a thin smile played on his lips, leaving the eyes out, all cold anger and exasperation. He moved the mouse swiftly on the pad. He had the square hands of a mountain guy but softened by office work. The pad had a logo – it looked like a globe with a circle around it but it was hard to tell because of the mouse.

Robyn looked at the screen again. A few pages much like the first one, rows and columns of figures and text in German, then the cursor on the right hand reached the bottom.

Winkler sighed. "The account was transferred in 1914." He smiled broadly now, and seemed to breathe better. He scrolled quickly back to the top page, and the arrow pointed to an area toward the top. "Yes, transferred," he said. "I should have seen that," he mumbled. "Not my problem anymore."

Her heart sank. "So what's the fuss all about?"

"The fuss?"

"Closing the markets…"

He looked at her and squinted. "Fascinating." He shook his head slowly and his whole body began to shake, then his mouth cracked open and Robyn couldn't tell if he was crying or laughing. He wiped his eyes and said, "Hilarrrious." He reached into the pull-out tablet supporting the keyboard and produced a steel flask, polished by design but matted by wear, the kind that was rounded to fit within a belt. He uncorked it with his thumb and it made a soft thump followed by a click. He gave it a hard look. Threw his head back and closed his eyes. Poured the liquid down his throat, and gurgled as he swallowed. When the last drop fell he kept his eyes closed and threw the flask back into the drawer.

Then he stared at Robyn and said, "It's about time the damn capitalist system meets its doom. The account was transferred, not closed. Transferred to the Federal Reserve Bank of New York. We pay you, they pay us."

The numbers didn't mean anything anymore. It was the dates. The dates pulled it all together. "What did you say?"

"Two years after the account was opened, it was pensioned to the Federal Reserve Bank of New York. Without moving any of the assets, by just the stroke of a pen, this account was virtually transferred to the Federal Reserve Bank of New York, who could claim it on its books."

"What assets?"

He glanced at the screen. "Mainly gold, some gems, some redeemed for cash."

"Where are the assets now?"

"They're effectively still in our vault, but they belong to the Fed. At a cost."

"Twenty percent, accrued."

"Correct."

"Why would they leave it in your vault?"

He shrugged. "To have gold readily available in Europe, for instance. What do I know?"

"Did the Fed use any of these assets?"

"That I cannot tell you," he said. "It is between them and us." He pushed the papers with her scribbling toward her. "Is that all I can do for you?"

"How can I claim my balance?"

"Your balance?"

She grabbed her cell phone. The battery was running low. "I'm demanding the balance of my account."

"Your account is the equivalent of the initial deposit in gold and gems. All corresponding commodities markets have been closed. No market value available today, I'm afraid." He stood. "End of the story for now." He unbolted the door.

Robyn turned the loudspeaker off and put the cell phone to her ear. "Counsel?" she said.

"Get the shit out of there," Parker whispered.

"That's what I thought," she said. "Thank you." She cut the connection and went around the desk and sat in Winkler's chair. Kicked her shoes off and propped her feet on the desk. "Nice office, Winkler."

32

ROBYN POINTED TO the mountain outside the window. "That where you ski?" Then she started flipping through the ski magazine, holding it at eye level.

The sound of Winkler clearing his throat, then the bolt sliding shut. "I am going to call the police."

"Sit down. We need to talk."

He grabbed the receiver of his desk phone. "I am going to."

"No you're not. You don't want a written record of any of this," she said, pointing to the screen and her notes.

He put the receiver down.

"You are going to grant me a loan," she said. "Immediately. Make it a very short term, high interest. Collateral is my deposit," she said, pointing to the screen. "Transfer the funds to the Swiss account. Next week, when the loan is in default, help yourself."

Winkler chuckled and shook his head.

"Relax. There is no worst case scenario. Next week you'll write it off. Whatever the market price."

Winkler looked through the window. "Next week, I won't be working here if I do that."

She slammed her fist on his desk. "I swear, you'll be dead if you don't."

His head jerked back in fear.

She took the Montblanc pen and ripped a blank notepaper off the three by three. Wrote down two numbers. "This," she said, circling the larger amount, "goes to this account." She slid the Switzerland bank account number over. "Consider the other amount your severance pay. Park it wherever you'd like."

He glanced at the note. Stretched his suspenders with his thumbs, clapped his tongue a couple times, sighed and made his way to the keyboard.

* * *

Ten minutes later Robyn was outside the bank. A bell struck something elaborate in the distance. Cars rolled past her, resonating over the cobblestone. The air, earlier stilled by heat, felt lighter. A gust of wind moved the trees like a wave over the mountain.

No new message. Was she doing this right? Was Sybil still alive? Were the kidnappers waiting until all the accounts were located and accessed to give her instructions? That had to be it, and she couldn't do that until she found the missing pages of the Voynich manuscript.

Last time she saw them was in the crypt in Marseilles, and Aleister had been right there.

He asked her to bring the Logonikon to Les Baux de Provence. Who would want the decoder—the Logonikon—if they didn't have the code—the Voynich? Aleister must have the missing pages of the Voynich, at least some of them, at least the useful ones. She hoped.

Sybil's nightmares and drawings pointed to Aleister as her attacker. Another reason to go there.

33

THE CLERK AT the Hertz reservation counter had driven the road to Southern France once, through Italy one way and through Switzerland the other way. Switzerland was less of a change from Austria, but an easier route. It was a full day drive, he said, either way. Robyn made it a full night, through Switzerland. At five in the morning she crossed into France and hit the Rhône river valley, its traffic heavy with trucks and tourist cars, packed bumper to bumper, everybody driving the same speed, the needle on the counter one notch above legal. Somewhere around Lyon her eyelids got heavy. She stopped for gas and caffeine and hit the road on the left lane.

At eight she reached Avignon and got a call from Parker.

"Goddammit," he said again and again. That was all he could say, *Goddammit,* while she briefed him on how she convinced Winkler.

"S'pose I should congratulate you," he dropped.

"I still don't know how our father got the Logonikon."

"Just get back home Robyn."

"Right."

"Are you in the car?"

"Just cruising around. The Alps, you know. Scenic." She looked outside the window at the olive trees and the sun-burned fields. "Green."

He grunted, then said, "The fire at Beinecke Library didn't make the news. They want to keep this quiet."

"Think so?"

"There's an investigation into arson or accident, with possible theft or not. Which means they're keeping their options open, de-pending on what you do."

"Uh-huh." She could tell he was upset.

"There's no report of the two guys in the alley. Federal, local. Nothing. Nada. It's like it never happened."

"Got your car back?"

"Not yet."

"You scared?" She clutched the wheel and then forced herself to relax. There was an uncomfortable silence.

"There's something else you need to know," he finally said. "And I don't like it that you're an ocean away. Get back here, we'll put our brains together, and we'll figure it out."

"What do I need to know?"

"I'd rather tell you in person. Want me to book you the next flight out of Munich? How far are you? Couple-three hours drive?"

"I was thinking of unwinding a little. You mind?"

"Like… come back in a couple days?

"Something like that."

"You're the boss." He hung up.

There's something I need to know, she thought. *I wonder what he's up to.*

34

SHE ENTERED PROVENCE at 9 a.m.. Three days left. What if she couldn't find the missing pages of the Voynich manuscript? What if they were elsewhere? *But where?*

A sign on the road. Saint-Maximin. Where the monastery was. Her father's handwritten note stuck in her memory. Why had he left that note with the Logonikon as well as with the lawyer in Switzerland? What if the missing pages of the Voynich were there?

She took the exit, followed the signs for Saint-Maximin then stopped and asked for her way. There was soft whistling and hands pointing way over the next fold of the mountain. An hour, easy.

An hour could get her to Marseilles and beyond. They were probably talking bike distance there. Then she understood. The road twisted on itself, wormed up to a pass and back down in the same fashion. She never got past twenty miles an hour. She never crossed a single car either, which was just as well given how narrow the road was.

At ten thirty she caught a faded sign off the road and climbed up a dusty trail for another ten minutes.

Past a wrought iron gate the trail continued up to a parking area lining a long, windowless wall that was one side of the monastery. The wall had the weathered look of a century-old construction, with a slight bulge of its lower third that indicated an upraised garden behind it. Above the wall, pine trees stood high, a couple fuzzy white balls caught in their branches.

She turned the engine off and walked to a large wooden gate that opened onto a graveled courtyard. White walls were pierced by a large door to the left with a cross on top. The chapel.

Right across from her was a smaller door with a knocker. She lifted and dropped the knocker. Waited. Nothing. Knocked again, several times. She strained her hearing for footsteps. Still nothing. There was an alcove within the door. She ran her hand in it. The alcove moved slightly. She pushed on its side, and it turned. The device was used in monasteries where nuns lived in seclusion and could be used to deliver mail or small objects. She felt the inside of the other side. There was a key. She knocked one last time.

No answer. Using the key, she let herself in.

The monastery smelled of wax. There was a large trail of mud on the polished tile, from the front door throughout the hallway and down a corridor. Strange. She called. No answer. Not a single noise. She followed the trail deeper into the monastery, through a curving corridor, to a door that opened on the cloisters.

No one.

This place is an empty monument, and I'm wasting my time, she thought. The key was there for occasional worshippers.

Then she heard some shuffling. Down the passageway, a nun was slowly walking toward her, signing herself repeatedly.

She walked toward Robyn, her head tilted. Her pace picked up a little and she straightened her stoop. She stopped three feet from Robyn. Her dress was pale grey, with brown blotches here and there. Strands of grey hair escaped her stained veil. Her pale blue eyes seemed to look straight through Robyn.

"You look… different," she said, looking at her hair. "How did you escape?" She extended a bony hand and took Robyn by the arm. There was a tremor, then a firm grasp, as she held on to her as to a raft. "Come."

She pulled Robyn out of the cloisters, into a park, then into the countryside scorched by the sun. Mediterranean pine trees, short and tormented, provided intermittent shade. "They're in the ice caves," the nun said.

"Who?"

"My sisters. They put them in the ice caves."

"The ice caves?"

The nun led her to a rocky trail. Then she let go of her arm and crossed her hands over her rosary. She walked carefully up the trail, her lips moving through a soft mumbling, her fingers sifting through the beads of her rosary. Every now and then, she shook pebbles off her sandals.

Then she stopped, let her rosary hang back in the folds of her dress and looked ahead. About one hundred feet from them, a door seemed carved in the hill. She took Robyn's arm again. Then she said, "Watch out", pointing to a column of insects making its way through the white trail. "Caterpillars."

Robyn stared at the stubborn progression. *Caterpillars.* The guide who found Sybil said she had one in her hair. *But it could not have happened on the island,* he said, *because there were no pine processionary caterpillars in the summer time. Only in some rare pine forests were they operating a time shift.*

Was this where it happened?

A few bees sucked on the thyme spurting through the stones. The air was vibrant with heat and the shrills of thousands of crickets.

"In the winter it gets really cold here," the nun said. "They would freeze water in shallow pools. Then they would break the ice and store it in ice caves like this one." She pointed to the low door in the hill. "In the summertime the caves remained cool, and fresh ice was carted every night to Marseilles, getting into the city by morning."

They were in front of the ice cave now. The nun pushed the door open. The temperature dropped. They entered.

Their footsteps resonated on stone. A corridor ran for about five yards, then opened on a large round area. Windowless. Robyn strained her vision.

Then she saw it.

A vertical shape, still. A human shape.

White.

Terribly white.

It was a woman, totally naked, hanging from a rope just inches above the ground, her feet inside a bucket, her back turned to them. The rope ran from the ceiling to the body, to the floor, to the next room.

"Come," the nun said.

Robyn couldn't make herself look at the hanging body. She kept her eyes on the floor. It was slightly sloped inwards, with a hole in the middle of the room.

They followed the rope into a narrow corridor. At the end of that corridor, there was another round room with a sloped floor.

And another naked corpse hanging over a bucket.

Just like the drawings in the Voynich manuscript. Rotund women in round chambers, linked to one another by small tubes.

And just like Sybil's drawings.

Then there was another and another, until they reached a larger room with five corpses hanging and a slot high up that provided some light. Robyn leaned against the wall, queasy, but what she couldn't get her eyes off were nine carmine, grotesquely dripping letters:

L-O-G-O-N-I-K-O-N.

She slid against the wall and wrapped her arms around her knees.

* * *

"It wasn't me," Robyn said. "It was my sister, Sybil, and she did not escape."

The nun took her hands. "Then where is she?"

"I don't know."

They were in a parlor. A room with polished tile, six chairs in a circle, a window. The sun setting on the park. The nun sat on one chair and Robyn pulled hers close to the nun's. There was a tremor deep in the nun's eyes as she looked into the emptiness of the room. She said her name was Sister Pauline. Her hands were on her lap, side by side, under control.

"When did this happen?" Robyn asked.

"It was Sunday," Sister Pauline said. She stroked Robyn's cheek. "Poor child, you are under shock. You don't remember. It was after vespers. You had barely gotten here."

She was still mistaking her for Sybil. The shock.

"You remember now?"

Robyn shook her head. "Sybil," she murmured.

"What is your name?" sister Pauline asked. "Sybil? It's a beautiful name."

"No. Sybil is my sister. My twin sister."

Sister Pauline nodded. "And you are?"

"Robyn Gabriel."

She startled. "Gabriel?" Her hands started shaking. She closed her eyes briefly, and whispered, "Of course."

Robyn's shoulders felt heavy.

Sister Pauline continued in a shaky voice. "Nuns come from all walks of life… and when they take their perpetual vows… it's like dying and being reborn. Their previous life is… over. For some, it has never existed. They need to shed it, in order to lead the life of purity and prayer they have embraced." She cleared her throat and continued in a steadied voice. "Monique… had a baby out of wedlock before she came to the monastery. Back in nineteen-forty-four." The nun looked out the window. "In those days, when something like that happened, it was common to seek refuge in monastic life." She lifted her thin eyebrows to her veil. "Especially for Monique…" She turned to Robyn. "The father was a German officer. Her family was prominent in Marseilles, involved in the Resistance. She did her bit. Socializing. Attending and giving parties, getting as close as possible to the enemy. To get information. Who was coming and going in headquarters? Was a meeting canceled at the last minute? That sort of thing." She fell silent. Dusk enveloped them.

Robyn thought, *More than a week alone with the corpses and the lingering terror. How much sense is she making?*

"There was this one officer. Very urgent. Very classy. Very interested in the family's library, too. Possibly looking for more than just romance in that family. A real mensch too, if he hadn't been on the wrong side. She got too close." Sister Pauline fell back in her reminiscing. How intimate had she been with Monique to know all that? Robyn wondered. Monique must be one of the victims.

"She got pregnant. And all her family was killed in the bombing of the railroad station the very day she was giving birth. Shortage of doctors, nurses. Some made it, some didn't. Next to Monique, there was an American woman. Her husband was with Varyan Fry's underground network helping refugees make it to Spain. Her baby was stillborn, and she stayed unconscious some time. The baby of Monique was healthful. When the midwife suggested swapping the babies, it was an easy decision for Monique. What kind of life would her child have? The bastard of a German officer… Monique's baby was reported stillborn on the hospital records, and the American couple went home with the boy."

Robyn thought about Sybil, and wondered what she had gone through here. She thought about the bodies hanging in the caves. Eight days now. Eight days that the nun had been reminiscing each one's story, probably.

Sister Pauline pushed her chair back and walked to the window, avoiding Robyn's gaze, looking into the night. "The Langlois family had pledged to safeguard a secret document," she said.

Langlois. The founder of the Banque des Deux-Rives. Fabre had told her about some family scandal, something that happened at the end of the war, and ended here, at Sainte-Thérèse Monastery. Sister Pauline had her full attention now.

"As the sole heir of the family, Monique was in charge of it. She should have given it to the monastery, along with all her belongings, but this was different. It did not belong to her. It was, rather, a responsibility. The document stayed in a bank. One day, a man paid a visit to the monastery. An American. He was a geneticist, he said, and he had found out that he was not the biological son of his parents."

A geneticist. Robyn's father was a geneticist. Her heartbeat picked up.

"He was born in Marseilles, at the end of the war, and his research for his biological parents had ended there. Someone at the hospital had suggested the monastery... And here he was."

Oh God. Her own father. Her father was Monique's natural son.

"Monique passed the secret along to him," sister Pauline said.

"What was the secret?" Robyn managed to say.

Sister Pauline looked at her and tilted her head. Unfolded and refolded her hands. They locked eyes for a long time, until tears welled.

Sister Pauline said, "I should call the police, shouldn't I?"

"You should."

"Then go. I'll wait for an hour, until the road is clear."

* * *

Robyn let the car glide down the dusty trail and then the winding road. Her headlights bounced off the shrubbery. My father, she thought. So he was really... the son of a nun and of a German officer. He must have been shocked when he learned. She felt detached, as if this wasn't her story. And it wasn't. It was her father's. She did not want to think beyond that. Not now.

There were a lot of things to think through. First off, she'd check facts. Dates. Her father was born on May 11, 1944. Was there a bombing of the Marseilles railroad that day? First things first. She'd call Parker, but not now. He'd get suspicious.

There was something else that Sister Pauline had said. That the German officer was very interested in the family's library. Why did she say that? How did she know? Then two things struck her simultaneously and she hit the brakes. But the road was too narrow to make a U-turn. And the police was coming, and she shouldn't be around. She had only three days left, if the kidnappers were still game. If nothing had happened to Sybil yet.

Her first guess was that sister Pauline was Monique Langlois. She said something about shedding your previous life. That usually meant changing names. She never said Sister Monique, only Monique. And she knew the story very well. Too well. Sister Pauline had to be Monique Langlois.

The second guess was that the German officer was probably after the Logonikon. Interested in the family library, she said. Hitler had been very interested in the Voynich manuscript, and if research led him to the Langlois family, he very well might have sent someone to investigate that closely. In 1943 the Voynich manuscript was still in private hands, readily accessible, exploitable with the Logonikon. It all made sense.

And it would have been for the gold, but he would have made it look like it was for the occult interest. The Anschluss meant he could get his hands on pretty much anything that was in Austria, if he knew where to look. Number or no number, he had other means than Robyn. All he needed was the name or location of the bank.

She'd have plenty of time to think about all this in the future. Right now, she had a score to settle and a deadline to meet. She was only half an hour from Les Baux-de-Provence and she was going there full speed.

"IT'S THE BOGUS account," Mack said, pushing his memo across the desk.

Pritchard stared at him. "The bogus account?"

"Right." Mack had been summoned and kept waiting outside Pritchard's office for more than fifteen minutes. He would let his boss do some thinking now. Pritchard had just returned from Washington, he said, and he was going back there. *Washington,* Mack thought. *Same old same old. They think they rule the world. But they don't have a clue. And Pritchard is just like them.*

From the detailed info he had requested on Robyn Gabriel, he knew that she had no known address other than a P.O. Box, no automobile registered in her name, only a motorcycle, was believed to dwell on a boat, or perhaps, occasionally, with one Michael Parker, a business partner. Said Michael Parker had an address in Tampa, Florida, owned a Mazda RX and was a Columbia alumni turned conspiracy theorist. Columbia didn't seem to be doing a good job at keeping kids on the right track, Mack thought. Maybe it wasn't a good idea to have Natalie go back there.

The car seemed to have vanished, although a search for it had started the very night Mack placed his info request.

Both Robyn Gabriel and Michael Parker had cell phones in their names. According to the phone company, Michael Parker's was located in Tampa, Ybor City to be precise, and had been there for days, inactive but emitting signal. Robyn Gabriel's had been emitting from Europe.

Since the morning after the disaster at Beinecke, Mack had been preparing for the worst by strategically spreading rumors. When the girl showed up at the bank in Kitzbuehl, Austria, two days later, he was ready.

As planned, the owner of the Austrian bank called him, frantic. His manager was on the other line, sitting across the beneficiary of a numbered account threatening to pull out her assets. That was supposed to never happen, he kept repeating. Mack called a couple buddies in the commodities markets, confirmed the rumor for a massive dumping of gold about to occur, and let them do the job. Markets were shut down globally for a few hours. Mack said that's all that would be needed. He was worried about lawyers being involved. But the girl didn't do anything. Just left. Strange.

And now he was summoned to his boss's office, asked to explain why he was meddling with commodities markets. Word got around quicker than he'd expected.

"The bogus account?" Pritchard repeated.

"You're privy to it, right?"

"Should I?"

Damn no, Mack thought. "Should you be asking me about my intervention to save the gold market?"

Pritchard exhaled loudly. "We must keep our ethics in check. Word is going to get around, we need to have an answer ready." His desk phone rang. He answered it. "I'll be just a minute," he said and hung up.

"They're asking for the balance. Accrued interests computed, of course, or I wouldn't be here."

"The bogus account?" Pritchard repeated a third time.

Mack paused a beat, let him simmer, then said, "It's a private account opened on our books."

"What are you talking about, son? There are no private accounts at the FRBNY."

Son. Mack shook his head and sighed. Stood and walked around the desk until he got next to Pritchard's armchair. Pointed to the computer. "You have our annual report in there?" he asked.

Pritchard typed a few words, moved the cursor around, clicked a couple times, and a pdf file loaded, with a green cover and an eagle and the words *Federal Reserve Bank of New York, Incorporated May 18, 1914*, and below, *Annual Report*.

Mack took over and scrolled down the first few pages until he got to the Financial Statement page. He pointed to a line toward the middle. "Liabilities, Deposits, Other Deposits: that's it right there."

Pritchard pulled out a pair of glasses and hunched forward. "Two hundred and thirty nine million dollars. That's a bullshit amount."

"It's one year's interest owed on a deposit made one hundred years ago. What's worse…"

"…The Fed does not pay interest on deposits," Pritchard interrupted. "Who the hell got you this job?"

"What's worse," Mack continued, "*accrued* interest. Two hundred and some million dollars is the interest owed on the first year of a deposit of over a billion dollars made in 1914. The total private deposit may even have been much larger than one billion dollars. Looks like our bookkeepers couldn't stomach counting after the first year. They left it at that."

Pritchard's jaws bulged two, three times as he clenched his teeth staring at the screen. "Who knows about this?"

"You. Me. My predecessor at the Bank."

"That's it?"

"That's it."

"Okay. Now you tell me why you picked up your phone and called about the gold dumping. Make it short, I have an appointment in Washington."

"They called the account."

"Who's they?"

"We're not sure yet."

"What do you mean?"

"It's numbered accounts. No ID."

Pritchard nodded. "How does it work in our case?"

"The person goes to the secondary bank—the one that transferred the gold to us. They present the keys. Then it's a basic transfer of funds. Electronic transfer *and* moving of gold."

"Moving of gold?"

"Eighty percent of the gold in our vault could go out of the country."

"It's foreign gold. Nothing we can do about that. Country wants it back, they take it."

"It's in the… other vault. The national section." Mack wondered how much he should tell Pritchard after all. "It couldn't be treated as foreign gold. Because it was a private deposit. Totally illegal, totally outside the scope of the Fed. But totally brilliant."

"Keep going," Pritchard said.

"It backed the value of the new Fed notes back in 1914," Mack explained. "At the time the European nations were draining us of our gold after selling US stocks and redeeming their dollars for gold. This private deposit guaranteed we would be able to face any demand. The thing is, the deposit being private…"

"…I've heard enough," Pritchard said, raising a hand to stop Mack.

Here comes the ass-covering, Mack thought. "However, you are right about the gold not being an issue per se anymore. We're out of the gold standard, thank God."

Pritchard muttered, "It's payback time."

"The issue we have is with the accrued interest rate," Mack continued.

Pritchard's voice strengthened. "I hear you. I don't want to know the amount. I don't want to know who the owner is. We can't allow this to happen. Are they American?"

"Who?"

"The people who are trying to access the account."

The people. A 25-year old beach blonde. "American, yes."

"Shit." He seemed to think. "Now again, maybe better. Do it."

"Sir?"

"Time to get creative, son." He stood. "Get us rid of them."

36

MACK STOOD IN the hallway, dazed. He could not get the FRBNY police involved. They carried guns, but there was no way he could get them to kill an American citizen on foreign soil in the next twenty-four hours. He had no idea where to find a hitter. All he could think of was Barton. The guy was a real nutcase, but that was all he had. The worst part was going to be to admit to Barton that yes, they should have got it right the first time. Yes, Barton's radical measures was the way to go. He went back into his office and dialed the freak's number.

"I need you to go after the girl," he said. "I don't care what fucking cool part of the world you're in. It needs to be done now. I want cold meat."

"Cold meat," Barton repeated and laughed. "Now you're talking like the bloody gangster you are, Mack." He laughed louder, then calmed down and said, "I love you Mack. You are *so* much fun."

"Will you find her?" Mack asked.

"Don't worry about that," Barton said. "She'll find me. I invited her. She'll come."

Nutcase all right. "What the hell?"

"To Les Baux de Provence. You've heard of it, right?"

Yes. No. Maybe. "I don't give a shit what you're talking about. My friend with the Suspicious Activity Reports is getting antsy, is all you need to know."

"Even you would be sensitive to the beauty of this night, Mack. I'm standing at the edge of the cliff, overlooking the valley. You don't mind the noise, do you?" He chuckled.

"What noise?"

"Trillions of crickets fucking. Can you hear it?"

Mack reached for the Maalox. *How did I end up with that freak?*

"I rented out the whole place. The villagers deserted their homes as if a hurricane was about to strike. In a sense, it is. 6ferno will perform, I told you, didn't I? The stage is on top of the mountain, where the castle used to be. It'll be grand, just grand. You should come!" He laughed.

Mack couldn't help asking, "How much did this cost?"

"A fortune. And I'm making twice that just by selling the TV rights. In case you wondered," he said, his tone down three notches, "it's all offshore accounts. Your little friends would have a hard time finding any of it."

"They'll find your money if I tell them to."

"Anything else?" Barton asked.

Atta boy. "The papers. I need the papers."

"You mean the Logonikon."

"The Voynich too. The bitch stole it."

"Wow. She sure fucked you, didn't she?" He laughed again, longer, then cut it. "Just like I said. There she comes."

37

ROBYN PASSED MANY exits with "en Provence" or "de Provence" append-
ed to their names. Hers was "Saint Remy de Provence". The road to
Les-Baux-de-Provence narrowed and wormed uphill much as the
road to the monastery. There was a dark mass that must be the village, and the road turned into a street.

Her headlights lit a sign for a public parking area. The car
climbed up the last stretch in a wheeze. She slid in a spot between
two vans and killed the engine, took a long drink of Evian and
wiped her mouth with the back of her hand. She put the plastic
bottle on the passenger seat, got out the car and stretched a little.
No one around. She put her bag in the trunk, locked the car and hid
the keys inside the rear wheel. After a few minutes, she heard some
stomping and rattling.

Across the parking lot, toward the village, a black figure with
shiny specks was taking long spider-like strides toward her. She
forced a tight-lipped smile. And she managed not to wince when he
was close enough for her to notice the stomping came from thick,
black leather boots strapped and buckled to the knees, and the rattling from a chain dangling along black pants like a demonic rosary.

The guy was tall, taller than Aleister, with straight raven hair falling on his eyes and shoulders, cheekbones jutting through spotted
skin and a mouth like an open cut. He stopped under a lamppost ten
feet from her. He was stooping a little, the way tall people do. His long
forearms hung limp on each side, slightly bent, his knotty hands still.

He looked at her and said, "Man." Then he scratched his head. "Over here." He turned around and walked fast away.

He crossed the parking lot and climbed a flight of stone stairs between two high walls, part staircase, part street, taking three steps at a time. She ran to catch up.

Her eyes settled on the back of his T-shirt, right on the tear of blood trickling from a sword impaling a girl with long blonde hair.

Their footsteps filled the night. The guy's stale sweat smell was sickening. Bare bulbs lit the way, and their shadows extended, doubled, then retracted as they went from one light to the other. They passed under a small bridge that linked two houses and after a straight-angle turn entered a courtyard. The guy unlocked a thick door and let her inside a pitch-dark house. She shivered as she brushed past him. She stepped on something soft, maybe an area rug. An artificial scent did a bad job at covering up something soft and sickening like mold. She took two steps in the dark and stopped. Behind her, the callous hand flicked the light on and said, "He'll be here tomorrow." The door shut and the lock turned twice.

She swung around.

The stomping was already fading down the street.

I asked for it, she thought.

There was a twin-size bed against the left wall, its head facing the front door. A small fridge and a range against the right wall, with a kitchen table covered in a yellow and blue plastic tablecloth. And in the center of the room, right in front of her, a pair of small sofas facing each other. She pushed one against the other, climbed over and curled inside. The fabric smelled of suntan lotion. For a split second she wondered who lived here. Then she thought of Aleister and wondered why she wasn't scared. She should be, she thought.

But she wasn't. And she knew why.

She had nothing to lose.

She didn't look up when the door opened the next morning. She was lounging on the sofa, reading some tourist guide book she'd found in the tiny bathroom. She had showered and had eaten breakfast out of an open box of *biscottes*. The rattling of a key in the lock startled her, but she was composed by the time the sunlight flowed in and Aleister's figure filled the frame. He pushed the door behind

him and said, "I'm terribly sorry you were locked in, Robyn. Lebrinski is a little slow minded. I had to leave and he got my instructions wrong." He took another step toward her and brushed her hair
lightly. "You're not cross, are you?" He sounded concerned.

She looked up and forced a smile.

He pulled his hand out of his pocket and squatted down toward
her. Shut her book close and pulled her chin toward him. She looked
at him straight in the eye and he smiled and chuckled a little. Then
with his eyes deep into hers, he kissed her, his fingers still pinching
her chin. His other hand grabbed her nape and pulled her closer. His
tongue searched hers and he grunted a little.

She closed her eyes and hoped he would mistake her shiver of
disgust for that of pleasure. He let go of her chin and, still kissing
her, grabbed her by the waist, stood and pulled her against him. His
breath brought back memories and the sharp stab of guilt. "You're
nice and tense," he said. "I like that."

She tightened her eyes and ran her nails against his back.

He chuckled and held her tighter.

"Pussy cat, are you?" he said and laughed softly.

Dragon, she thought.

* * *

Two waiters pulled their chairs. The dining room was empty. Robyn's
heart was pounding. The night had wiped out some of yesterday's
shock. Her numbness was fading, and she was coming back to her
senses. She still had twelve bank accounts and one cold-blooded
murderer to figure out. Two days left, if the deal was still on.

"They don't usually serve breakfast here," Aleister said. He spread
the linen napkin on his lap and sat back against the high chair. "But the
owner isn't in a position to refuse me anything right now." He pointed
to the large letter B's stitched on the upholstered chairs. "In case you
were wondering, that stands for Baumanière—not for Barton."

She looked at the chairs and the candles and the softness that
radiated from the bare stone walls. She had spotted the name of the
restaurant on their way in. L'Oustau de Baumanière.

"We have not been introduced properly, have we? Although I
believe we fucked mighty properly, haven't we?" He laughed louder

and then cut it. "Champagne," he said to the waiter. "We need to bubble this young lady up."

"Selection Baumanière?" the waiter said.

Aleister smacked his lips, glanced at Robyn and said, "Pink champagne."

"Very well," the waiter said. "Brut Billecart Salmon?"

Aleister nodded, still looking at Robyn.

She straightened herself and smiled, tight-lipped.

The waiter bowed and turned his head and someone behind him rushed away. "The chef suggests omelette aux truffes," he said, "followed by a pigeon au jus de—"

"No," Aleister said, "no birds. I'm tired of birds. Truffle omelet is perfect. What else?" he asked as the second waiter brought tiny glass tumblers filled in multicolored layers and decorated with a passion flower. It was feeling more and more like a last meal to Robyn. "Petals of wild salmon, caviar expression in an avocado cloud," the first waiter said to Aleister, bowing lower.

"Sounds good," Aleister said. "Now go."

The waiter startled then backed a few steps before turning. A sommelier in a dark red apron started working on the bottle of champagne with studied flourish. "Cut the show, we're busy," Aleister said.

Robyn squirmed in her chair while the sommelier served them deftly. When he vanished Aleister lifted his glass, looked at her and took a sip, then another, then smacked his lips and said, "To the Logonikon."

The word hung there like a menace while waiters set artful plates in front of them. Then a door shut after them and Aleister rubbed his hands and said, "How is your sister doing?" Smiled coldly and added, "Finally out of the coma?"

Robyn wrapped salmon around her fork, spread avocado mousse on it and held her fork in mid-air. "In a sense," she said. She shoved the food in her mouth and chewed rhythmically, her eyes on Aleister's teeth. Her mouth was dry and when she swallowed the food barely made it past the lump in her throat. "She's dead," she dropped.

His upper body tilted slightly backward in surprise, the eyes registered relief quickly suppressed and replaced by a pained frown. "I'm sorry."

"It happened last night. I got a call on my way here."

"I don't know what to say…"

"It's for the best, believe me."

"Really?"

"Yes. The shape she was in…" She let her words drag and searched his face. No expression. *You bastard, you know exactly what you did to her,* she thought.

"You must be devastated," he tried.

She shook her head slowly. "We were not on speaking terms. Hadn't talked in years," she lied. "Not that I don't care about her passing, but it's not like I'm going to miss her."

"I see." There was a long silence, then he added, "You are very brave."

"Brave?"

"Coming here after what happened to your sister…"

She shrugged. "Why is that? I was on my way here when I got the news. I made arrangements to leave later today for the funeral. Doesn't change anything."

"How do you know you are not going to bump into your sister's murderers here? The event attracts all sorts of cults. There were clues pointing to cult followers. The well, the branding…"

Her heart pounded. She had never mentioned the branding to Aleister. He had slipped. Or had he? She was at his mercy now, there was nothing he needed to lie about. Cold rushed through her body and she suddenly felt disconnected from reality. Her surroundings appeared unreal, a sort of décor for the play that was about to unfold. With the sense of reality, the sense of fear had disappeared, making anything possible. She managed a shrill laugh. "Oh no no no." Shook her head. "The well and everything? That was a set-up. To confuse the investigation."

He had barely touched his food. "Is that so?"

"I decoded the Voynich," she said. She looked at him squarely. "Nothing religious in there."

He cleared his throat and reached inside his pocket. Popped a black metal tin open. Ignoring Robyn, he lit a Camel Rare and pulled on it for a long time, exhaling slowly with his eyes half-closed, then took an equally long sip of the pink champagne, then went back to his cigarette.

"I'm afraid the parameters have just changed," he said. Another long pull on the Camel Rare. "The whole point of owning the Logonikon is to be the only one to have access to the Voynich." Long pull again, eyes half-closed. "You read it. Anybody could have read it now. It could be all over the internet as we speak."

"You have the missing pages. That gives you a distinct advantage over the rest of the world."

He tilted his head, as if to concede a point, but said, "Doesn't matter. No longer interested."

He may be sitting on billions, she thought, *but he doesn't know it. Which means two things. One, he's not the one sending the messages. Two, his incentive is low level.*

He finished his glass of champagne without ever losing eye contact. "Aren't you going to drink? You turning all shy on me?"

She reached for her flute, her turn now not to break eye contact, and drank in one long slug. She tilted her head for the last few drops and felt his gaze on her neck.

"I'm going to fuck you to hell," he said when she put her glass down. He had a way to play with his voice that made anything sound like a party.

38

"AND THIS IS the sacrificial altar," Aleister said.

Robyn looked at the table. It was made of thick marble, about hip height, six feet long, three feet wide, with two wide legs spanning its width, a thick candle on each side but no linen, just the bare white stone.

"Notice the groove," he said, running his finger along the side of the altar. "The table has a slight inclination that ensures the liquids are directed properly." A copper bucket hung from one the corners of the table, as it would under an oversize carving board.

They were in the crypt of Saint Vincent's church, on top of the village of Les Baux. They'd gone there immediately after breakfast, Aleister eager to show her the place. He'd explained with feverish eyes that the Christians had merely stolen the original worship sites of pagans, chosen because of their magical power, and built churches over the primal temples. There were telluric forces at work there, he said, and Christians were polluting them with their twisted presence. It was important for the forces of Light to restore the balance and worship the prince of darkness as close as possible to the womb of the earth. Or so Aleister said.

Hence, the crypts.

Lebrinski, who'd followed them everywhere since they came back from breakfast at Baumanière, listened wide-eyed, glancing at Robyn in frightened glimpses, keeping his distance but drinking every word his master said.

Aleister kept running his hand along the altar, a finger in the groove, and looking at Robyn. She saw the flicker of lust and shivered, remembering his body over hers on the dining table just a few days ago. A smile twisted his mouth. He lifted his chin, ran his eyes along her body, ran them back up slowly, stopped around her midsection, half-closed them and said, "Lebrinski, go get Rebecca. Ms Gabriel is going to need a baby-sitter until tonight." His voice was deep and with a shiver, almost to the point of breaking.

Lebrinski leaned forward, then back, then got a grip over his hesitation, turned around and started for the staircase. Stopped. "I can babysit," he said.

Aleister closed his eyes in exasperation and thundered, "Just do as I say."

Lebrinski thumped out the crypt and up the small spiral staircase in a rattle of chains.

Fifteen minutes later Robyn was out on the plaza surrounding the church with Rebecca holding her arm, dismissed by Aleister who mentioned some ritual to perform on his own in the crypt. The broad daylight made Rebecca's skin a sicklier white than it had seemed that night in Marseilles or inside the catacombs.

She was wearing a black robe that could have passed for hippie if the jewelry hadn't been an inverted cross on one ear, a stylized goat on the other, and a large silver skull dangling around her neck on a string of braided hair. Her hands disappeared in the folds of her robe.

She seemed fierce and determined and at the same time a little out of touch with reality. As if she felt bestowed with some outworldly mission she would carry out at any cost.

On the deserted plaza, as they both stood stunned by the light and the heat and the palpable strikes of the sunrays, Robyn's wheels began to turn. Surely she could get rid of this one with a couple of powerful kicks.

Then Rebecca pulled her right sleeve up. In her tiny alabaster hand, a small revolver shone. "I'm dying for you to give me an excuse to use this," she said. She aimed the gun at Robyn, then turned it a little. Didn't wince, didn't contract any muscle.

Fired.

She handled the recoil as if she'd done that all her life. The bullet ricocheted on the stones. A burning smell hung in the air. Robyn looked beyond where she had aimed. In the far distance, a shirtless guy unrolling cables looked up, then down, and went on with his task.

Rebecca played with the barrel and the security for less than a second, aimed back at Robyn, pulled the sleeve over her hand and said, "Let's go."

She took her to the studio Robyn had spent the night in. Robyn grabbed the tourist guide she'd been skimming that very morning and dropped on the couch, working hard on looking relaxed. For the next few hours nothing was said. The only noise was the turning of pages, Rebecca's irritated footsteps around the small room, and a rising hustle and bustle outside.

Two days left. How long was she going to be stuck in here? Robyn thought. "We'll hear the concert pretty well from here, I assume," she said, letting the book slip from her hands to the floor.

Rebecca looked at her, her mouth twisted in what could pass as a smile. "You're not going to be here when the concert starts," she said. "As a matter of fact, it's time I give you a tour."

Side by side like two best friends, Rebecca's arms folded so that the gun dug into Robyn's ribs, they went up the narrow streets to the plateau topping the village. The preparations for the concert were in full swing, centered on the stage, an ordinary metallic structure brought alive by a maze of cables feeding all sorts of lights and sounds.

A dozen men, fleshy, muscular, tanned or sunburned, but all shirt-less and all tattooed, shouted orders across the expanse. Technicians were bringing guitars and percussions on stage. Screeching noises started blasting. TV crews adjusted their cameras and headphones.

"That's for the masses," Rebecca said. "The feast after the ritual. But it's going to be cool anyways."

"The ritual?"

"The sacrifice to Belial. You'll find out soon enough." She looked away, beyond the scene it seemed. "Let me show you something. It's not going to make any difference now. Better sooner than later." She nudged her forward. The sun was lowering over the horizon but the heat was still thick. They both ignored the lingering glances as Rebecca led them past the stage. The platform was deeper than it seemed, extending far back. "Aleister will be leaving from the stage, pulled up by a helicopter like a black angel rising," she said with a sudden excitement. "After the sacrifice. They will play some classical music while he rises slowly. It's going to be grand. Just grand. They'll bring the altar up from the crypt for the sacrifice. Aleister wants that one. He says it carries just the right charge. Has the right proportions and design, too." She pushed her toward the cliff. "Keep going, don't be a sissy." They reached the edge of the cliff.

It wasn't a vertical fall right away. The terrain was steep, but with bushes and protrusions. Further to the right, directly behind the middle of the stage, a few steps were carved roughly off the rock. Rebecca pushed her again. "Go down there," she said. The steps weren't large enough for a foot. Robyn felt more comfortable going down sideways. It kept her from looking downhill, beyond the bushes, to the freefall nearly one thousand feet high. After ten steps there was a tiny landing and directly into the rock, a hole about six feet high, two feet wide. Pitch dark inside. "Go in," Rebecca said and reached for a light switch.

It was not a cave. It was a tunnel the size of a man, narrow and tall, bearing the marks of the chisel that had carved it. Corked off the mountain, lit here and there by bare bulbs, the corridor led downhill like the bowels of the earth. At the end was a wooden door. "Push it open," Rebecca said.

The door had no handle. It opened and swung back behind them. A yellowish glow fell from an old brazen chandelier. They were in a small room that smelled of cold incense. Across the room was another door, this one with a lock. The floor was flagstone, there was a solid oak wardrobe, a table, no chair, a painting of Christ on the cross and a kneeler. They were in a sacristy.

Rebecca pushed Robyn with the tip of the revolver. Robyn tried to resist, and heard the security click off. Rebecca pressed the gun in between her shoulder blades and opened the wardrobe with her free hand. Got some handcuffs out. Robyn tried to knock the gun off with her elbow while shooting a back kick.

The bullet grazed her arm. Rebecca hadn't thought twice before shooting. Probably hadn't thought at all.

"You're stupid, aren't you," Rebecca said. With surprising strength, she shoved Robyn to the floor. "Wrists together, behind your back, against the foot of the armoire."

Robyn inched back on the floor until she felt the softness of the wood against her hands. Her arm prickled.

Rebecca pressed the revolver against Robyn's temple. "Don't move."

There was no risk of Robyn moving. Rebecca was frantically trying to handcuff her to the wardrobe with her left hand, while her
right hand held Robyn's life at the mercy of poor coordination. After
a few unsuccessful attempts, the handcuffs snapped shut. Rebecca
shook them and threw the key on the floor, in the angle opposite
from Robyn.

"Lie down," Rebecca said, setting the revolver on the table. "Feet
toward the key."

Robyn stretched herself on the floor. Rebecca pulled on her feet
until her whole body was lifted and her arms were outstretched behind her shoulder blades. Then Rebecca dropped her and she stifled
a cry as she landed on her folded arms, crushing her joints, smashing
her hands, crashing the back of her head against the corner of the
wardrobe. She turned sideways to ease the pain.

Rebecca pulled on her feet again, this time leaving her body on
the floor. She was still far from the key. "The only reason I'm not
killing you now, is it's going to be so much fun watching Aleister
do it himself." She gave Robyn a bright smile, grabbed the revolver,
turned the light off and went out the swinging door, back into the
corridor that led through the mountain.

39

AT LEAST THE place was cool, Robyn thought after a while. And her legs were not hurting. Her arms were beyond painful now. They were totally numb. Her head felt like a sound box for her heartbeat, each pulse sending a jolt of pain through her skull. She was stiff. She wriggled, trying to find the least uncomfortable position. Settled for alternating between sitting and lying sideways. She didn't try calling. If help was going to come, it wouldn't be from the outside. It wouldn't be from anybody here.

Loosing sense of time, she drifted between memories.

The shrill sound of Sybil screaming with pleasure as the swing pushed higher and higher in the clear spring sky, laughter and thrill in a perfect mix, when they were ten. Years before, in the red-checkered kitchen, making brownies with their mother, her tiny index with a neat pearl of black dough while Robyn's face was smothered in chocolate—she'd run to the mirror to check if it was true, what they were laughing about. The way Sybil was always tidier than her, but seemed less happy too, always pointing to the reasonable thing to do, bringing up rules and recommendations.

Robyn wanted this back. She had survived her parents' brutal death, they both had, not without tears and sorrow and nightmares and fragility but with, eventually, a newfound strength. Sybil—it was different. Robyn had needed to part from her to become herself, but the idea of losing her twin was simply unthinkable. The idea of failing to save her was worse.

A thick ball filled her throat and she cried herself silently to a nightmarish sleep.

She was awake when the door to her left opened. The yellow light blinded her. Aleister stood in the doorway, wearing pleated dark pants and a black shirt. His spiderlike sidekick clad in black and boots and chains, Lebrinski, stood behind him, holding on his folded arm what looked like a priest's robe, only black, and in his free hand a pointed hat prolonged by a mask with eye slits. Something Klansmen would wear, but black.

Aleister looked around, picked up the key and kneeled toward Robyn. Brushed her head softly with his lips. Opened her handcuffs and rubbed her wrists in his warm hands and helped her up like a gentleman.

Then he dropped, "This Rebecca can be quite the witch, can't she?" and laughed softly. "We have some catching up to do." From the wardrobe he took some folded fabric, she couldn't quite see what, then he pushed her gently to the next room, shut the door behind them, slid a metallic bar across the door and flipped the wheels of a combination lock.

Dozens of candles were scattered on the floor, sending eerie flickers on a low, vaulted ceiling. The edges of the room disappeared in shadows. The incense smell was stronger here, and the humid air cooler. At times, mice-like scraping suggested some life in a distant corner.

In the center was a dark, rectangular mass. A table with two legs spanning its width, and a reddish circular shape hanging from one of its corners.

It was the large marble altar with the grooves Aleister was so proud about. The reddish shape was the copper bucket hanging from one of its corners and shining from the candle lights. The top of the altar, with the grooves, was in the dark.

They were in the crypt of Saint Vincent's church, and she couldn't keep her eyes off the altar. Like a black hole, it sucked in all the energy.

Aleister set the folded fabric on the table and took the vestments from Lebrinski. He opened a door in the wall that hid a simple, shallow closet. An inside light came on. Three thick wooden shelves separated the closet. Nothing on the bottom shelf. Aleister laid the vestments flat on the middle shelf.

And Robyn couldn't keep her eyes off the top shelf. In the flicker of the candle lights, gleamed the triptych displaying the lost pages of the Voynich manuscript.

Her pain vanished at the sight. She just had to grab it, and maybe give a fight, but it was all there, still within her reach.

Aleister said to Lebrinski, "Keep guard." Lebrinski walked to the door of the sacristy and wriggled the combination lock that held the metal bar in place. Apparently satisfied, he turned around, stood firmly with his legs spread, folded his arms across his chest, and looked at Robyn.

"Keep guard upstairs," Aleister sneered. "Get out, lock us in, and stay on the other side of the door."

Lebrinski shot a mean stare at Aleister, crossed the crypt in his rattling, spider-like gait and disappeared up the dark stairs.

The door creaked open and shut. A bolt slammed. There was some more rattling.

"The chap has something about chains," Aleister said. "I sort of like that." He closed the gap between him and Robyn, towered over her without touching her and said, "Maybe I should ask him for one?" Then he grabbed her right wrist and pulled it up, twitched her arm slightly and brought it to his mouth. "Yes," he whispered softly, "chains would like that little body." He bit the inside of the wrist, sucked on it and let go.

Robyn didn't dare rub her aching arm. *Don't show the guy you're down*, she thought. The fear that had dissolved earlier was rising back in a wave of panic. She was locked in a crypt with a monster intent on having his way with her and downright crazy about his new butchering table. The only exit was a door bolted and chained from the outside, with a nutcase standing guard, and another door bolted with a combination lock and opening unto a cliff.

As if this wasn't enough, she'd made sure no one she knew had any clue where she was.

"So where's my Logonikon?" Aleister's voice was icy. He was still inches from her, breathing down her face and neck.

"I thought you weren't interested," Robyn managed to answer in a steady enough voice.

"Wrong answer," Aleister said. "You were supposed to bring it."

"I don't recall that," Robyn said.

"We'll refresh your memory later." He kissed her neck and pushed himself slightly from her. "But first let me settle something." He pulled his cell phone out and punched a few buttons. His body suddenly exhaled the stale sweat smell of nervousness. "Mack," he said in the phone and shut his eyes briefly. "I'm with our little hero." Pause. "Yes." Another pause. "Don't count on it. You played with me, you lost. The deal is off. Call back your Fed dogs or I'll feed you to my bloodhounds." He hung up and smiled coldly at Robyn. "Where were we? Ah yes. Bringing back memories."

Robyn's mind raced. Fed dogs? What did that mean? Who was this Mack? What deal was Aleister talking about?

He ran a finger down her neck. "We were in that hotel in Marseilles." He pushed her against the altar. "We had some fun." He kissed her neck. "You were wearing this adorable little lace thing. Ah," he said, seeming to suddenly remember something. "Wear this." He pointed to the folded fabric on the table and stepped back from her. He cracked a match. A large halo engulfed him, then the match died. He cracked another one and started lighting candles on a chandelier above the table.

Robyn unfolded the fabric. It was a black lace tunic, like the one she'd worn that night at the bar with him. That night at the hotel. Sybil's tunic. She put it back on the table and started taking her clothes off, slow, slow, so she'd have time to think while he was busy with his candles. He wasn't even looking at her. She folded her jeans and her white T-shirt on the table. *Relax. Breathe.* She took her sneakers off. She slid the tunic on.

"Put your clothes on the floor," Aleister said.

She aligned the sneakers between her feet, took her folded clothes and crouched to set them neatly on the sneakers.

Under the altar, the thick blade of a carving knife shone in the candlelight. Two lose straps held it slightly to the right of the midsection of the table. It was ready for use.

She stood. Aleister was back at the end of the table, his pleated pants open. As Robyn barefooted to him she saw his pleasure augment.

"You liked it most on the table," he said. He pressed himself against her. "We had candles, too." He pushed her until the top of her body was lying on the table. The marble was cold but she recoiled more from his touch. He grabbed her legs and lifted them onto the al-

tar. "Let's re-create the conditions and your memory will come back."
He cracked another match and lit a thick candle next to Robyn's head.
Then he approached the match from her face, took a thin strand of
hair, set it ablaze and flicked the dying match on the floor.

In the gold flurry Robyn saw the blackened filaments of her hair
twist. She could try a good kick now. But would that be enough? The
guy was fit. Muscular. She didn't have a chance. Her only option was
to wait for the right time, and the right time was going to come after
some preliminary unpleasantries.

Her hair kept curling in a sickening stench.

Aleister pressed the burning strand between two fingers and the
flame died. He breathed deeply and said, "Love that smell." Rubbed
his fingers against one another. "Where was I? Ah yes. The conditions. We're almost there." He pulled his shirt off, then the rest of
his clothes ended on the floor. Ripped Robyn's thong off. Then he
grabbed the neckline of the tunic and tore the whole thing in two.
Pulled it from beneath her. "How does the altar feel compared to the
dining table?" he said, his eyes up and down Robyn's body.

"Cold and hard," she managed.

"There you go. Cold and hard. Reminds you of anybody?" He
laughed at his own joke. His head was in the halo of the chandelier, and the candle of the altar lit his body, the broad shoulders, the
strong arms, the chest. And the tattoo of a snake.

The rest happened in a haze. His urgent mouth, his groping
hands. She remembered she had moaned in his hotel suite. So she
moaned. Anything to lure him. There was a rattling of chains upstairs and he cursed and shouted to Lebrinski to shut up or he would
end up down the ravine inside the car.

Down the ravine inside the car.

His eyes were wild and his movements erratic. His strength
unbelievable. She shut her eyes briefly when he took her. Then she
forced herself to look at him, to look for the signs. He grabbed her
wrists and pulled her arms apart, hands over her head. She didn't
resist. She accentuated the seeming submission, stretching her arms
apart until her hands dangled from the altar. "Grab it," he said, and
she grabbed the edges of the cold, hard table. Then his eyes went
back to her body and he raised himself slightly and she knew there
was not much time left.

Her left hand let go of the edge of the table and her fingers searched frantically for the knife. His eyes were now almost completely closed, only the whites showing through a thin slit in the eyelids. His body was dripping sweat over hers and she was sweating too, from fear or his heat or both. She couldn't feel the knife. Couldn't find it.

She was groping like mad, hoping he would not feel her movements, when suddenly, her hand almost level with her navel, she felt the knife and closed her hand on it, but on the wrong end. Its blade slit her skin open and dug into her flesh when she slid it out of its straps. She tightened her grip, afraid only to drop the knife. Then the vein on his forefront began to beat. She raised both arms, the left hand holding the knife by its blade. She grabbed the knife's handle in her right hand. Pain shot through her elbows, from her earlier fall, and inside the palm of her left hand. A drop of her own blood fell on her face and mixed with her sweat. His eyes were still closed. Then he stiffened.

Her arms still stretched over her head, she put her left hand over her right. Would the knife make it through the rib cage? Rage took hold of her and with her arms stiffly extended she stabbed him in one quick, powerful blow. She might have screamed, she recalled later. She'd never forget the feeling of the blade going into the flesh, somehow probably making its way in between ribs, how it felt soft and hard at the same time, the unnatural movement, down and toward her, but the relative ease with which the blade entered the body.

Aleister stiffened more, his eyes bulged in surprise, his breathing halted. She struck again, and again, and again. Her wrath unleashed, each blow was easier than the previous.

When a splurge of blood from Aleister's mouth flowed on her own face, she stopped. With her hands and knees she managed to push his heavied, limp body off hers, rolling it to the side. It thumped on the floor. First the legs, then the torso. The head may have bounced once, like a football.

A gurgling, then all was quiet.

No movement from Aleister, save for a flow of blood spreading on the stones from his mouth and his back. A candle knocked off by the body spilled its wax on the floor, the flame dead.

No rattling from Lebrinski.

40

ROBYN WIPED HER face in Aleister's shirt as much as she could. Put her jeans back on and her T-shirt and sneakers too. She spotted her underwear on the floor and stuffed it in her pocket. Her hands shook.

She opened the closet. The inside light went on automatically. She blinked. The triptych was made of clear Plexiglass, and was almost twice the size of the documents it protected. The pages seemed to be floating. They were brighter than anything else in the crypt. Although she'd worked on the whole manuscript, it was almost intimidating to see them showcased the way they were, and to remember how they were worshipped by blood-thirsty cult members.

Each panel of the triptych was made of two sheets of Plexiglass, pressed together by brass winged bolts. Hinges held the panels together. She unscrewed the bolts, enough for the sheets forming the panels to loosen from one another. She tilted the whole thing and shook it slightly. The leaves of the manuscript started to slide down, then fell off. She picked them up. There were more than three. There were two inside each panel, and in between each pair that had formed the outside panels, more leaves were stored. Maybe all the missing pages of the Voynich.

She stuffed them in her back, under her T-shirt and inside her jeans.

Before she left she went through Aleister's clothes and searched for his cell phone. Found two. Stuffed both in her pockets and ran to the staircase.

Her knees were weak. She could hardly breathe. Fear was receding and nausea was taking over, from the exhaustion and the panic and the blood everywhere and the stillness of death that had invaded the crypt. She stumbled over the first step. Caught herself and stopped, forcing herself to breathe steadily, her head dangling down. She pushed her hair back and felt the thickness of blood on her fingers. The nightmare was far from over. She couldn't afford to let go now.

She climbed the steps slowly. A little out of breath would be natural. She banged on the door as hard as she could. A rattling of chains and Lebrinski materialized. He looked at her face and hair. "Cool," he said.

She brushed past him. "Your master wants you." She walked toward the door of the church, one slow confident step after another.

Heard him clunk down the crypt stairs. Two, three, four.

She stopped.

Five, six. His footsteps were fading.

She ran back, bolted the door and secured the chains. Then ran for her life, out in the black night, down the tortuous streets, to the parking lot, to the car.

41

CURLED ON PARKER'S couch, Robyn reached for the bottle of Tequila.

Parker was drinking Margarita from a tall glass, boasting an *I'm with stupid* T-shirt, in her honor, he had insisted. "You proud of yourself?" he asked.

"I am." She started telling him about the monastery.

"Damn Robyn, you got the gold markets closed!" He slapped his lap in a mock laugh. Then his gaze got so intense it almost scared her. "You're trying to get yourself killed, right?" He'd never been that angry before.

"Leave me alone." The stronghold on her chest increased. Two days left, or maybe one. With the jet lag and the sleepless night, she wasn't sure anymore. And she wasn't getting messages.

"Where's Sybil?" he asked.

"Tom took her to the countryside. Somewhere."

He handed her the bottle. "You're better off getting drunk."

"At least have the decency to let me get drunk alone." She took a long draw, her eyes on him, then wiped her mouth with the back of her wrist. "Please."

He backed toward the bathroom, his eyes locked on hers.

She didn't bother figuring out what he was thinking. When he was gone, she put the bottle down and listened to his routine noises. The shower started running. She went to the computer and accessed the internet. Reverse phone number lookup, but with a twist. One of Parker's favorite underground websites, with cell phone numbers, unlisted numbers and internal company directories. She pulled

Aleister's phone out, the one he had used in front of her, and entered the last number. Since she last looked, there were several missed calls from that same number.

A clock ticked on the computer screen. Three seconds. The result popped up.

The Federal Reserve Bank of New York
33, Liberty Street
New York, New York.

She stared at the screen, processing what she saw. There was even a name and title for that particular phone number.

James McIntyre, First Vice-President.

The shower was still running. She scrambled to make some on-line bookings, then logged off and lay on the couch. Maybe she could pull this off, she thought. Maybe she could right all the wrongs.

Parker came out of the bathroom, stopped and looked at her, then went into his bedroom. He started turning pages. She hoped he was reading something boring. Soon enough there was the flicker of a light turned off, then the sound of ruffling and turning in bed. She waited a couple minutes. Tiptoed to the door and heard deep, slow breathing.

With what she knew now, she didn't need to decode the last pages of the Voynich manuscript. She left them on Parker's coffee table and slid out the apartment.

42

FOR THE FIFTH time, Mack punched Barton's number from his desk phone. For the fifth time, the phone rang and rang and no one answered.

He called his workaholic buddy at the New York State Banking Department and told him to roll out the Suspicious Activity Reports on Barton. The workaholic sounded quite happy to oblige. Minutes later he called back saying that wasn't going to work.

Mack tried to hide his frustration. "Why not?"

"His accounts are already frozen. The asshole is dead. Murdered."

Shit. Where was the girl? Who had the documents now?

When his home number came up on the caller id of his phone minutes later, he almost didn't answer. He had enough to deal with right now. But Elaine, his wife, never called the office. He thought accident. He picked up. He got betrayal.

Elaine was sobbing and the story came out in hiccups and sniffing. Mack got the vague idea that Natalie had bragged about getting back at him "big time", but Elaine didn't know why. As to what it was exactly that Natalie had done, all she could say was Natalie repeated Mack and his boss "were just as good as dead". When Mack figured that was all he would get from her, he told her to put Natalie on.

Natalie said, "Wassup?"

He chose to ignore that. "What's your mother all worked up about?"

Silence.

"I don't have time for games. You two work this out by tonight." He'd wait a couple seconds, then he'd hang up.

She said, "I found the diaries, the translations, and the memo."

He stared at his power wall. *The little brat.* "What are you talking about?"

"Retaliation. I emailed the pdfs and the memo to someone who'll know exactly what to do with them."

His skull pounded. "Who?" he yelled.

"Just like you thought you knew what to do about Austin."

"What are you talking about?"

No answer.

"Natalie."

"Honey?" It was Elaine again, with some grip on herself, it seemed.

"Who the hell did she send the stuff to?"

"Some Mike Parker, she says."

He started scribbling the name on the pad, then stopped. *Of all people. The beach blonde's buddy.* "How does she know him?"

"She says from college. It's really no—"

"Anyone else?"

She breathed deeply, as if everything was going to be fine now. "No, I don't think so. Honey, it's just kid stuff, please forgive her..."

He slammed the receiver in its cradle. Looked at the scribble on the pad. *Shit, shit, shit.*

There was another way to look at this. Damage control would be restricted to the same group of people.

Put yourself in the shoes of those two shitheads, he thought. *What would their next move be?* Then he picked up his phone calmly. Dialed the visitors' center and got his answer.

The beach blonde was either ballsy, or brainless. Probably both.

He dialed the extension of Diego, the chief of security with a solid sense of humor.

Two minutes later Diego was informed that one Robyn Gabriel and/or one Michael Parker, both relatively harmless troublemakers, were about to attempt some frat coup within the Fed. That this was all going to be lots of fun when they were shortcut. Mack just needed Diego's help in a couple minor matters, to amp the recreation.

Five minutes later Diego left the office with a pat on the back.

And Mack reached into his drawer, loaded his Smith & Wesson 60-15, straightened his baby blue silk tie, rolled up his shirt sleeves and waited.

43

"**I HAVE NO** idea where your sister is," the man said, "and I sure as hell didn't kidnap her."

Robyn looked into the cold eyes, then down the light blue silk tie and the sweat marks on the white shirt. Skipped the hand and concentrated on the sole of the shoes. Jet black with just a few scrapes in the middle. Sparks under the heels. A thickness that spelled power. Sharp edges, the kind that makes you wonder if leather can cut.

The cold eyes, the sweat marks and the powerful shoes belonged to James McIntyre, who went by Mack.

Her gaze went back up to the hand and the revolver aimed at her. The hand was firm, the gun steady.

They'd been sitting there for a while now and the conversation was not going well.

She hadn't heard from the kidnappers in five days now. Since Beinecke. Two men had been killed there. Maybe that was it. Maybe the deal was over because of the killings, and Sybil's body would be found in a dump somewhere. Or she would go missing forever. The knot in her stomach turned into an acid crater. Bile crept up her throat. Memories flowed again. A picnic in Canada, braiding sweet peas in her long hair. The sweet smell of jam cooking. A rainy afternoon, playing backgammon. Her eyes welled. She shunned the memories. *Not now.*

She'd thought things through at Parker's apartment. She stopped thinking about what she should have done, and made plans. Got on the first flight out of Tampa to JFK.

From the airport, the A train took her right into New York City's financial district. She struggled against the strong smell of urine up the Fulton Street station stairs. Then she became numb to feelings. The closer she got to her goal, the more focused and relaxed she had become. She barely noticed the void that was Ground Zero on her left. Made a right onto Broadway. There was some heavy construction going on, the streets were rugged and the sidewalks uneven. The Wall Street area was unimpressive.

A few short blocks down and she took a narrow, winding street called Maiden Lane lined with vendors and cheap stores and pizza places and even a hooker outfitter that tried to pass as a chic lingerie boutique. Carts were pushed in a rattle and delivery trucks blocked the way. Streets were peopled in all manners of attire and menial occupations. Men clad in Brooks Brothers darted, hunched over their cell phones, unnoticed. They made this district the financial capital of the world but the hustle and bustle of hard-working immigrant America concealed the billions they traded daily. Parker would have said it was a blanket of smoke and that they were probably paid by the tycoons to push the carts and bake the pizzas and in general bring the area to a low profile.

Maiden Lane was short and led directly to the side of the Federal Reserve Bank of New York, a stately rectangle with a first row of large fenced windows ten feet above street level and a back entrance for armored vehicles. The main entrance was at 33, Liberty Street.

A Federal Reserve police car she assumed to be just like the one that chased them through Pennsylvania was parked in front. The door was manned by a Federal Reserve Police Officer in dark blue uniform. She showed the confirmation of a scheduled tour of the vault she had booked online at Parker's and went through security, then was taken to a locker room where she had to store her cell phone.

She joined nine other visitors in a projection room and watched a filmed pre-tour of the Fed. The building's main feature was its vault, harboring hundreds of billions of dollars worth of gold deposited by foreign countries. More than in Fort Knox, where most of the US gold was now stored. The vault was eight stories below street level, five stories below sea level, and eighty feet into the bedrock of Manhattan, which was one of the few places likely to support the weight of the gold and of the vault itself.

Then the group was taken down the eight stories and through a painted cement hallway to the vault. They went through its one and only door, a ten-foot-long steel passageway that shut by revolving one quarter of a circle inside a steel and concrete frame, then settling down a few inches.

The vault itself turned out to be a down-at-the-heels, low-ceiling storage warehouse harboring stacks of bullions behind bars. While people gawked at the gold and listened as the guide explained the different shapes of bullions depending on origin and date, and the necessity for handlers to wear protective shoes because of the extraordinary weight of the precious metal, Robyn stayed in the back of the group and spotted the security cameras. When even the guide was engrossed in her story, pointing to dents made on the cement by dropped bullions, she pulled a note handwritten in thick marker, turned around and held it straight to the camera.

After that things unfolded smoothly. Because she lingered in the back, no one noticed when two strong hands grabbed her. Because she had asked for it, she did not shout or resist.

And now she was facing James "Mack" McIntyre, Aleister's last phone contact, first vice-president of the Federal Reserve Bank of New York.

In other words, senior representative of the Fed system, which was based on twelve American banks, all of which were listed in the Voynich along with the Austrian bank.

Mack had come down to meet her in the vault. After dismissing security, he pulled out a revolver and pushed her away from the vault shown to the group of tourists, down a corridor, inside another vault, large like half a football field. No cameras here.

The place was packed with gold bars on two sides, and wooden pegs on two others, directly on the floor. No extra bars this time. The stuff was within reach. There was a clearing in the center, maybe thirty by twenty feet.

He was now sitting about ten feet from her, against a wall of gold, his legs outstretched on the painted cement floor, his firm hand aiming the gun at her. He had told her to sit cross-legged in the middle of the clearing and she was starting to have pins and needles.

"Someone died here once," Mack said. "Got locked in," he continued. "There's enough air to survive seventy-two hours but he must have been in a hurry." He wiped his brow with his free hand. "So he pulled the fire alarm." He made a face. "Carbon dioxide killed him. By the time they figured out what was going on and who pulled the alarm after closing hours, there was nothing they could do."

Robyn kept her gaze straight on him. "What kind of losers do you hire around here?"

"They are not losers, Robyn. They are far from losers." His eyes hardened. "Matter of fact, we can't lose."

With his left hand he pulled something from his pocket. Her cell phone. She had to leave it in the locker before she could join the group of visitors into the vault. He slid it to her through the ten feet of painted grey concrete that separated them. The phone stopped next to her hip and turned, then settled.

He played with the barrel of the revolver. It clicked and for a while this last little noise hung there like the ultimate argument for her to ponder. "You are going to call your good friend Michael Parker and tell him to get his sweet ass here with the document you illegally came upon."

"Not before we discuss the liberation of my sister."

"That's not going to happen. I don't know where she is. I didn't kidnap her. I might have an idea of who did, and it doesn't look too good."

"Meaning?"

"If it is who I think it is, the guy is dead."

"It was just… one guy?"

He shrugged. Not his problem.

She had a hard time swallowing. What he was saying sounded senseless, that the death of one person would cut the thread back to Sybil, and at the same time it explained the lack of phone messages. The absence of instructions through the final steps.

"Now call Mr. Parker," Mack said.

"Why would I do that?"

"To buy some time."

"You'll kill me anyway."

"There are different ways to die." He shifted the gun from the right hand to the left, then back to the right.

She shrugged. "It's the end that matters, not the means." If Sybil was really lost, she'd rather die. It seemed to her cowardly, then brave, then she didn't care. Empty of feelings, she waited for his next move.

His face didn't twitch and his eyes didn't blink and generally speaking his whole body seemed oblivious to what his right hand was doing. Robyn barely registered the slight movement of the wrist, the straightening of the barrel. The noise was brutal and deafening but before it resonated there was the distinct whistle of the bullet brushing her left ear. She jumped up and put her hand to her ear and checked her hand.

Mack smiled. "Not yet. If you kill the game right away, you can't have the fun." His voice seemed muffled in the aftershock of the detonation. "Sit." He flicked the revolver around his finger, cowboy-fashion, quick and sure.

Robyn sat back cross-legged.

The gun was aimed at her again. "Call your friend. Tell him to bring the document."

"What document?"

"Don't play stupid."

"You were behind this all along, weren't you?'

"The Logonikon is a deadly weapon," he said.

"I can see that. You nearly had my sister killed."

"I had nothing to do with that."

"In France. Before she was kidnapped. You had her nearly killed." Her anger rose as she saw him shake his head in denial. "Then why was Aleister reporting to you?" she shouted.

"Barton is responsible for what he did. I never asked for that. At least not at the beginning. It could have all been taken care of nice and smooth. A search of her hotel room. A bag snatching. But the wacko went out of control. I'm sorry."

"That's it? You're sorry?"

"Why don't you settle this with him?"

"I did."

"You did?" He chuckled. "Who are you? Laura Bullion? Robbing banks and killing people? You took this one step too far." He pointed his chin to her cell phone on the floor. "Call your minion. Maybe we can figure something out for your sister later."

He could be lying about the kidnapper being dead. "The Logonikon is mine," she said. "Not yours."

"This is way bigger than you. Or me." He lifted his gun. The barrel was level with her eyes. "Call him."

She took the phone. Punched in Parker's number and pressed

call. When she brought the phone to her ear she kept her finger pressed on the side command to bring the sound to the lowest level.

The phone rang just once and Parker picked up. She coughed and pretended to be absorbed in the contemplation of some area one foot ahead of her while nothing was happening on the line, when actually Parker was blowing his mind off at her. Then when he stopped to catch his breath she said, "I need Mike. Put Mike on please." And continued looking at the same spot.

"Put the phone on loudspeaker," Mack said.

She looked up and waved the phone away from her a little. "Mike will be on the line."

"Put the damn loudspeaker on and the phone on the floor."

She activated the loudspeaker and set the phone on the floor. "How can you have network eight stories below street level?" she asked matter-of-factly.

The phone was silent, then Parker's voice came out. "Hello." He sounded sleepy.

Maybe I can pull this off, she thought.

"Robyn, is that you?" Parker asked.

Mack shook his gun at her. *Say something.*

"Hey Mike," she finally said.

"What's up?"

"I need the Logonikon."

"So?"

"So you're going to have to bring it to me."

"That's not going to happen."

She glanced at Mack. "I don't think you have a choice," she said toward the phone.

"Sure I do."

She didn't see it coming. The bullet hit the floor right next to the phone, ricocheted and ended somewhere behind Robyn. "Fat chance getting your piece of crap if you kill me, Mack," she said.

"I ain't gonna kill you. Yet."

"Bullet could have ricocheted anywhere."

"Oh no. The way I angled it, it could only go to the right."

"From the back you asshole."

He raised his eyebrows. "Your language, young lady," he said. "No, it would not ricochet off gold. Gold is soft. The bullets cut right into it."

Robyn stared at him. The guy was serious.

"I started shooting since before I could walk. Back in the ranch in Austin." He did the cowboy thing again, the spinning of the gun around the finger. "And I chose to work at the New York Fed because of their firing range. That was way before I knew about the whole thing. At the time of biblical innocence. Now I'm stuck here. But I like it. I have the best of both worlds. The power and the gun. And I ain't gonna lose it because of some empty-headed blonde and her faggot friend."

"What's going on?" Parker's voice was stranded.

Mack looked at the phone. "You have twelve hours to bring the Logonikon to New York City, Mr. Parker," he said.

"I'm in Florida."

"I know that. It's a three-hour flight."

"And if I don't?"

"I think you will."

The screen went dark again.

"Your friend is gone," Mack said. "Friendship is not what it used to be." His gaze wandered and stopped somewhere over her left shoulder. "Used to be, you could count on people, and people could count on you. Take me. I'm stuck here now because of an oath I took thirty years ago." He stayed silent for a long time, his eyes absorbed in the same void, and after a while he took a deep breath and his gaze focused on Robyn and it looked like he wasn't going to say more.

"He's just upset," she said. "He'll call back."

Mack seemed to be assessing how much he could believe her. He toyed with the gun again. A spin around the thumb, left hand, right hand. Finally he rested it on the floor and crossed his arms.

"I made an oath too," Robyn said.

"Did you."

"And that oath brought me here too."

"I'll be damned."

Her cheeks flared. She steadied her hands on her knees. "I'll never forget the shape of my twin's burn." She looked at him silently for what seemed like a long time.

He was smirking, his gaze going from her to her phone on the floor as if he waited for it to ring.

"Like the symbol pi, with loops." She drew it in the air.

He blinked, a fleeting display of discomfort.

"So I'm thinking, you're the missing link."

He said nothing, but the smirk came back.

She said, "I promised myself I would get to the bottom of this."

"Should have been careful what you wished for."

She told him about her sister left to agonize in a dry well, covered in stones. About Aleister's cult, the catacombs and the stabbing of a human body. When she got to the slaughtered nuns, he flinched. She had surprised him, caught him off guard. Struck a chord. For a moment she felt she had the upper hand. He looked dumb-struck enough for her to consider running for it.

Except she was eighty feet below street level, fifty feet below sea level, locked inside an airtight steel vault. Beyond the two doors, the only exit was through a ten-foot-long steel passageway presently angled ninety degrees inside the bedrock of Manhattan.

"The passageway is operated from a distance and lowered three-eighths of an inch to ensure the vault is air- and water-tight," Mack said. He seemed to have recovered from his surprise and been reading her mind. "Story was entertaining," he said, "but you forgot the most important. The mess at Beinecke and Austria." He picked up the gun and began playing with it. "I guess I know that part of it."

"What's at stake, Mack? Can I call you Mack?"

"Our reputation."

"You can't be serious."

"I'm dead serious."

"You'd kill for your reputation?"

"Ours. It's our Nation's reputation. And there should not have been any killing."

She looked at the gun.

"You made this complicated. What happened to your sister was an accident."

An accident. She should be digging her nails in his eyes right now. Instead she said, "Who was the other party to the contract?"

There was some thinking going on across the vault. A tongue clapping, eyes gauging. A glance at the gun followed by a "what-the-hell" movement of the shoulders. Then the answer came, "Longyu, Empress Dowager of China."

44

FALL 1911. WHILE the Chinese Revolution roared outside the walls of the Forbidden City, a lonely and cunning woman, adoptive mother of the six-year old Ming Emperor, was left to negotiate with the revolutionaries. History recorded that she managed to save the life of the imperial family, as well as its ownership of the family's assets.

"Two Jesuit priests organized the shipping abroad of the treasure accumulated by the Ming," Mack explained. "By train and boat, a small portion was shipped to Austria, as you know," he said. "The largest part was invested in the United States. At the time there was little regulation here. We had a huge land but were a small player on the international scene. I suppose the Jesuits saw an opportunity."

So far, Robyn thought, what Mack was saying had a reasonable historical grounding. The Jesuits had a long-time tradition of presence in China, not only as missionaries but as close counsels to the imperial court. Foreign meddling in domestic affairs had been one of the causes of the revolution. Ruling dynasties typically confuse private and public treasure, she thought. The Empress disposed of the Treasure of China. Considered private by the Ming.

"Initially, the investment in Western banks was meant to be temporary," he said. "The Ming just wanted the gold to be out of the reach of the revolutionaries."

"So what happened?"

"One of the priests, Simon, offered to lend gold to the United States when it was facing a crucial monetary crisis, at the Fed's inception."

Just what Parker had said, Robyn thought. The Fed, and the Jesuits. "The Jesuits intervened to save the Fed?"

"You could say that," Mack said.

She thought better than to mention the Titanic, but its sinking by the Jesuits, drowning the only men powerful enough to oppose the Fed, became oddly believable now. "Why didn't the gold make it back to China?"

"First off, a 20% accrued interest rate. It was meant as a deterrent to keep the money too long. If it's too expensive, they won't keep it long, was what Simon, the mastermind, thought. It had the opposite effect. It was so expensive they could not afford to pay it back."

"Why didn't the US try to renegotiate?"

"Maybe they did. We don't know. What's sure is that Longyu, the Empress, had died in 1913. Nutzer, the other priest, disappeared into monastic life around that time. Simon had the good idea to die in 1914."

"There was no reason to worry about it."

Mack nodded. "Except for the Logonikon. Feeling the danger they were in, Simon and Nutzer had drafted the Voynich in 1912, and the Logonikon. We don't know what contingency plan they had in case they both died, but we know that the Voynich recorded all three access codes for each account. The Empress', Simon's, and Nutzer's. They're called keys in banking."

"The system with three keys was a security against unauthorized movement on the accounts?"

"Right, and probably Simon's idea. The Empress, him and Nutzer each had one key to each account. They each had to give their key, which meant their agreement, to any movement on the accounts. This was probably Simon's way to control the Empress. She couldn't do anything without their consent. And he made her believe her consent was necessary too, when in fact he had her keys, at least briefly. He copied each set of keys for the thirteen accounts and recorded them in a cryptic document, the Voynich, which could only be read with the help of the Logonikon.

"After Nutzer's departure, Simon sent the Logonikon overseas," Mack continued. "He died shortly after. For the US, as long as the Logonikon remained hidden, it was business as usual." He stretched his legs and played with his gun. "Been that way almost a century. Until you stepped in."

"How does Vance tie into that?" Robyn asked, to get the conversa-

tion off of her. "And the Asian guy that killed the Skull and Bones guy?"
Mack hesitated.

"Come on, Mack. You can't decently kill me without telling me
the whole story. You must a have a conscience, somewhere."

Mack didn't react. He just continued. "One of the priests, Nutzer,
went back to China. He must have leaked the information to the Triad."

"The Triad?"

"Not your gangster-movie Hong Kong triad. A traditional triad
that was formed to combat the Ming, with a handful of members.
Apparently the founding members knew about the looting, and since
1912 they were looking for the gold, and the rest of the treasure.
Maybe Nutzer got remorseful, I don't know, but anyway he gave the
triad the bank account numbers and his keys to all the accounts.
Told them about the Voynich and the Logonikon. The triad couldn't
do anything with just one key to each account. But they kept tabs
on the bank in France that stored the Logonikon. Somehow Nutzer
knew about that, and he told them.

As far as we know, the triad has always had five members. One
of them was killed at Beinecke."

"Did they kill my parents?"

He seemed to hesitate. "I don't know. Considering you're still
alive, I don't think that was their M.O. They've been watching you
for a long time." He had lowered his gun at some point during his
explanation. Dark circles rimmed his eyes with defeat. His gaze was
lost somewhere behind Robyn.

She was analyzing the whole story, but still could not make sense
of the violence. "So the US owes a tremendous amount of money to
China," she said. "Tell me something new."

With the hand that held the gun he drew an unsteady circle in
the air. "You know where we are?"

"New York Fed vault."

"Are you sure?"

The question wasn't one. "Unload your crap, Mack. Who gives a
shit where we are."

"You will," he said. "We are not underneath the Fed. We crossed
Nassau. We're one block up, toward Broadway. Right beneath the
branch of Taipei National Bank. Taipeh, as in Taiwan, the arch-en-
emies of Communist China. This is more than just about money.

The first Chinese revolutionaries, then the Communists had no idea there had been gold stashed away to begin with. They have no idea of the amount and even less of this 20% accrued interest rate."

"Give me a break. This contract is not worth anything. The parties are dead, it's in no acceptable language."

"Don't play stupid, Robyn. I know about your visit to the Austrian bank. Who do you think got the gold markets closed? I don't want to know how the Mainland Chinese would react and I don't want to know how the clowns in Washington would react. I don't want to know and I won't cause like the saying goes, what happens at the New York Fed stays at the New York Fed."

"Is that how the saying goes?"

"Yes ma'am." He stretched his legs again. "It took a few years for the gold to make it here. When the New York Fed bought this block for their building, they also bought the adjacent buildings, and dug out a second vault there to store the embarrassing portion. Then they had Taiwan install a branch of their National Bank here, and voila! With Taiwan being a democracy, it kind of made sense to let them put the gold to good use. To combat communism."

"You gave it back?"

He shifted to a sideways position. "We made sure it funded the right cause."

"Typical neo-colonial paternalism."

"The mistake, if it is a mistake, happened one hundred years ago. We had to fix it one way or another."

"Does that make it okay?"

"All the players are dead. The good guys, the bad guys. We're left with the mess. We did our best."

Robyn didn't say anything. She looked at her phone.

There was a long silence, then Mack said, "What kind of friend is it that you have here, Ms Gabriel? Did he go to bed or what?"

"The best of friends," she said. "Parker?"

"Hey," Parker's voice came out of the phone.

"Got it all?" She glanced at Mack. He was looking down at the phone, puzzled.

"You bet," Parker said, and then from the phone came Mack's voice. "*What kind of a friend is it that you have here, Ms Gabriel? Did he go to bed or what?*"

When she'd called him Mike, which no one ever did, he understood right away she was in trouble and telling him to start recording. *Activate the mike.*

Around the gun, Mack's knuckles whitened.

"Did you hear that?" Parker asked. "Damn good quality. And how about this here?"

Mack's voice came out of the phone again. "*It's more than just money. The first revolutionaries, then the Communists had no idea there had been gold stashed away to begin with. They have no idea of the amount and even less of this 20% accrued interest rate.*"

"I'm uploading it to youtube right now," Parker said.

"That doesn't prove anything," Mack snapped. "These days you can do anything with a computer. I'll deny it. I'll say it's a montage."

"First off, you can't really get to that sort of seamless quality with a computer," Parker said, "And second, you're forgetting something very important."

Mack clenched his jaws and stared at the phone.

"I have the Voynich and I have the Logonikon and as we speak I am going through an enlightening memo from the First VP of the New York Fed to the President of said bank."

Mack turned ashen, then crimson, aimed the gun at the phone and fired.

Fired again.

Robyn blinked but kept her eyes on Mack. The shattering noise echoed and died.

"Robyn!" Parker's voice.

She glanced at the phone. It was covered in dust. Half an inch right and left of it, two holes in the concrete. She reached over, grabbed the phone and said, "I'll be fine." Then she locked eyes with Mack and speaking into the phone said, "Parker. No youtube." Turned the phone off, took the battery out, and threw both pieces to Mack. "It's only you and me now."

45

"WHY DID YOU do this?" Mack said.

"Cause I don't care anymore," Robyn said. "I got even."

"No. Why did you tell him not to post on youtube?"

"I still care about my country."

He looked at her for a long while. Then he blinked, as if pushing back tears. "Same here." He stood. "Let's go."

"Where?"

"You don't want to die on foreign soil."

With the gun against her ribcage he pushed her to the other vault, through the long corridor, back into the Fed portion of the vault. Motioned her to sit on the floor again. Then walked to the fire alarm, grabbed his gun by the barrel and in one powerful strike of the butt broke the glass and hit the button.

The sound was deafening and fumes rushed down like white fire. Mack motioned her to lie down and crawled toward her. He shouted to cover the noise. "Remember the guy who died in here?"

She nodded.

"They fixed it," he said, looking over his shoulder. "See there?"

She looked where he was pointing, and at first saw only white fumes streaming down.

"After it happened, they fixed the problem."

She noticed a blue light blinking at floor level.

"There's a fire escape that can open only from the inside, when the fire alarm is activated." He pulled on her sleeve, forcing her on her knees. "Hurry up."

She crawled toward the escape, then felt him grab her ankle. Shook him off and crawled faster. The carbon dioxide was replacing the oxygen. The temperature was dropping. In moments she would not be able to breathe. The blue light became clearer. A hatch was under it, with the word PUSH. It was heavy metal and at least five inches thick but when she leaned on it it yielded. Then her ankle hurt. He had grabbed her again, too hard to shake him off. She spun around.

He had his right hand up in the air, fingers open, gun hanging. "Three more things before you go," he shouted. He let go of her ankle and with his left hand reached inside his jacket. "One," he said and pulled a small video tape. "We're kinda old fashion. That's the only proof of your presence here tonight." He put the tape in her hand, and then a cell phone. "Two." He coughed. "That's the cell phone of the guy I killed in Beinecke. Name is Li Mei. He was a member of the triad who was after the Logonikon. You'll find some info on his phone, if it's not too late. Phone numbers and addresses. For your sister." The fumes were becoming unbearable, it was freezing, and she could hardly see him now. "Three. Before the end of the tunnel, there's a trap that leads to the sewer system. Good luck." He turned around and crawled away. She pushed the hatch. It pivoted. Behind it was a tunnel barely high enough to crawl into on all fours. Before the hatch pivoted back and shut with a definite thump, she heard the gunshot.

46

"THANK GOD IT'S summer," Parker said.

They were in a dirty white utility van with no air conditioning, the two only windows rolled down against the stench. Robyn had her sneakers tied outside the window, her jeans rolled up to try to conceal the smell. Crawling out the Federal Reserve Bank, she'd slipped several times in the water lining the bottom of the sewer pipe. Good thing it had been night, and in a business district. No fresh discharge, only the day's leftover to deal with. And a heavy metal bar screen holding three paper cans, a beer bottle and a memorandum to dislodge before she could climb up to the street. Up there, Parker had been waiting on the sidewalk, hands on his hips, still wearing his *I'm with stupid* T-shirt.

"Hey," she had just said, but with relief, and he took her to a van. "Is that where you were all this time?" she asked.

"Got on the first plane," he nodded. "I did all the phone recording in there. Hop in, some people want to see you. And let's get out of here."

Minutes later, one block North on Broadway, she said, "I didn't close the PC? That's how you knew?"

"Nope."

"Then what was it?"

"You didn't look at me when I came out of the shower."

She remembered the tan shoulders, the broad chest, the towel hanging low on the hips, showing the distinct triangle of the abs… She felt herself blush and shook the memory away. "So?"

"It's not like you."

"I don't have time for that."

"Really." He glanced in his rearview mirror.

Robyn looked over her shoulder again. Vance was dozing off on the van's moleskin back seat.

Next to him, Tom said, "Got it," and lifted his gaze from Li's cell phone Robyn had given him. He pushed Vance's head away from his shoulder. "Wake up, kid," he said. "That place ring a bell?" He showed the cell phone's screen to Vance and spelled out an address. Robyn punched it in the portable GPS.

"You have time for other people," Parker said to Robyn, a notch lower.

"I don't like them."

"It's just sex?"

"Yes." *Goddammit Parker. Not now.*

"I wouldn't mind just sex with you."

"Shut up and drive."

Tom placed a call from his own phone and repeated the address. "They'll be there in minutes." Then he handed Li's cell phone to Vance. "Last number. Let's hope that's them."

Vance started speed-talking on the phone, Vietnamese or Mandarin. Parker and Robyn wouldn't have known. When he hung up he said, "It's them, same address."

"Drop me here," Tom said.

Parker pulled over. Tom pushed the gliding door open and before he slid into the night, said to Robyn, "You stay in here."

Parker raised his eyebrows.

"Man, this is simple," Vance said. "I told them my uncle was killed, and they just told me the price."

Robyn pulled César's envelope out of the glove compartment. "How much?"

He said a number. She counted. The envelope thinned. She handed the thick wad to Vance. "You screw this up, I promise, I'll hang you by the balls up the mast and watch your body peel off those nuts, then I'll skin you and tie you sea level and watch the sharks feed off of you."

"I know." He left the van.

"I'm not so sure about the just-sex-thing after all," Parker said.

The GPS indicated a right turn, *Then you will reach your destination.* Parker went straight. They both glanced at the street when they passed it. Scarce lighting, three-story buildings, piles of garbage on the sidewalks. Average Chinatown street. A shadow walking quickly, that could be Vance, or not.

Two blocks up Parker pulled over and turned the engine off. A whiff of garbage, a police car siren in the distance. Parker said, "Let's give him ten minutes." A man came and went, walking his dog.

Parker drummed his fingers on the wheel. "Times like that, I wish I smoked," he said. "I started being suspicious when I saw your phone was missing from the apartment. Then Vance showed up at the boat, and started blabbering about his fake uncle being shot and you being in the Tomb. He kept repeating he was supposed to protect you. Then Tom called in the middle of the night, after you'd come back, talking like crazy about Sybil missing. You were gone. Didn't take long to figure out something wasn't kosher. The computer was the logical place to start."

A police car rolled by and slowed down, then sped away.

Parker said, "Sorry about the jokes earlier. I was just trying to make light. I know this isn't easy. I'm sure she'll be fine. I hope."

"Just shut up," Robyn said. "Please."

"Guy named Toslav came by the boat yesterday. Friend of yours."

"He's alive?"

"Bright as a button."

"That ain't Toslav."

"An antique parchment button."

"Okay." So the mummy wasn't dead. Where had he been all this time?

"He wanted to take a look at our upcoming coin collection."

She frowned.

Parker continued, "He said he witnessed some interesting events in a quaint little Provencal village called Les Baux-de-Provence. Said a whacko got gruesomely killed there just after a stunning American blonde chick he'd met days before came to the place."

"He said chick?"

"It's the general idea. He said the chick had vanished by the time the police got there, and no one mentioned her, even her jailors."

"How does he know?"

"He was held hostage there. In a crypt. Had specific details of the murder. You want to hear them?"

No. "Let's go get Sybil," she said and left the van.

Parker caught up with her and they walked silently two blocks down. When they got to the street, Parker wrapped Robyn tightly inside his arm. She didn't resist. They were pausing as two lovers. They slowed their pace.

She was on the street side, he was on the building side, and looking up toward him she checked the numbers on the buildings. They didn't want to show that they were looking for an address. When they got close, she stopped and kissed him, a light kiss on the lips, then whispered in his ear. Two lovers, getting ready for the night. She chased the idea that she could like this. She was too tense to enjoy the act they were putting. There were a lot of things that could still turn wrong before they got Sybil back.

They walked a little more. She impeded him, the way she was turned toward the buildings. "You all horny?" he said, loud enough. She forced a giggle. He focused on keeping his gaze straight ahead, letting her do the work of finding the place.

When they got to the right building, she teased him into a kiss again, longer this time. He opened his mouth. *Make it look real.*

She pushed herself against him. His open mouth enticing, she let her tongue have a life of its own.

He pulled her inside the door.

She pretended to hit the door bell by accident. The door buzzed open.

They bolted on Vance smack in the middle of a T-shirt warehouse, the place crowded with piles of jerseys toppling like skyscrapers after an earthquake, everything dark except him and a guy sitting at a plastic table counting cash.

The guy lifted his head. Felt inside his jacket. Said, "I don't like that." Went back to counting.

Vance twitched on his chair, then leaned back and crossed one leg on the other, acting relaxed. "It's cool," he said, to no one in particular.

"Where's my sister?" Robyn yelled.

"You late," the guy said.

Parker moved up. Vance raised his hand, pacifying. The guy pulled a gun from inside his jacket and aimed it at Vance. The front door burst open and Tom and three crew-cut packs of muscle crowded the place, pointing guns at the guy. Vance said something in Vietnamese, or maybe it was Mandarin, and Robyn saw the guy's barrel

slow-motion toward her. Two steps, one sideways kick, and the gun
flew over a pile of jerseys. Another kick and she was standing on top
of a mangled mass of limbs trying to protect a bloody face.

Tom shouted something, she told him to shut the fuck up. Parker backed out of the room. The guy underneath her screamed and
Vance stood and said, "It's cool, your sister's right here. I'm gonna get
her." He said something to the guy under Robyn.

The guy answered.

Vance said, "He says he'll never do business with Li again. I
think he's clean. Relax."

Tom shoved the barrel of his gun under Vance's jaw. "*I* say when
we relax. Now go." They went to the back of the warehouse, one
of Tom's guys walking backward in their tow. A door opened with
a squeak. Shuffling, light cries, and Tom came out carrying Sybil.
"Beat it," he said.

Vance ran out first. One of Tom's guys went next, with Tom
and Sybil right behind. Robyn let go of the kidnapper, grabbed the
cash and followed. The two other guys backed out of the room, guns
drawn out. One of them stayed in the hallway until they were all
packed in the van Parker had run to get.

Robyn pushed a strand of hair off Sybil's forehead. Her bruises
had turned yellow. Her clothes looked clean. Her mouth quivered
and she closed her eyes. Robyn pulled her in her arms, said, "I love
you" and let herself start to sob.

Sybil pulled herself away. "Man, Bobby, you smell like shit."

THE END

Robyn Gabriel returned the Voynich manuscript to the Beinecke Rare Book and Manuscript Library. If you ask anyone there, they will, of course, deny the whole story.

She kept the Logonikon.

The Banque des Deux-Rives was closed.

All names were changed in this book so that Lance, Natalie, Elaine, Toslav, Parker, Tom, Sybil and, of course, Robyn can continue leading normal lives, although I doubt Robyn is cut for a normal life.

Please visit www.DianeEcher.com

ACKNOWLEDGMENTS

I'VE RECEIVED TREMENDOUS encouragement and feedback throughout the writing of this novel and truly believe it would not have seen the light of day without the relentless positive energy of so many special people.

For their faith in me, as well as for their honest input, thanks to Kathleen André, Eléonore André, Grégoire André, Annelise André, Marie-Thérèse Burle, Vivian Jacobs and Esther Smoot.

For their support and expert guidance, my extreme gratitude goes to (in order of appearance in my writing life) Barbara Rogan, Les Edgerton, Jonathan Galassi, Nathaniel Rich, Deborah Treisman, John Freeman and Richard Marek.

For their most helpful critique, I thank my fellow writers from The Writers' Institute at the Graduate Center of the City University of New York.

To all, I give full credit for the existence of this book and my growth as a writer. The shortcomings of this work are, of course, my sole responsibility.